the best kept secret

5.39

JUN   2022

the
best
kept
secret

USA TODAY BESTSELLING AUTHOR

TAWNA FENSKE

Entangled Publishing, LLC
10940 S Parker Road
Suite 327
Parker, CO 80134
Visit our website at www.entangledpublishing.com.

Amara is an imprint of Entangled Publishing, LLC.

Edited by Liz Pelletier and Lydia Sharp
Cover design by Elizabeth Turner Stokes
Photo of couple © George Rudy/Shutterstock
Interior design by Toni Kerr

Print ISBN 978-1-64937-030-3
ebook ISBN 978-1-64937-043-3

Manufactured in the United States of America

First Edition March 2022

AMARA

ALSO BY TAWNA FENSKE

WHERE THERE'S SMOKE SERIES

The Two-Date Rule
Just a Little Bet
The Best Kept Secret

FRONT AND CENTER SERIES

Marine for Hire
Fiancée for Hire
Best Man for Hire
Protector for Hire

FIRST IMPRESSIONS SERIES
The Fix Up
The Hang Up
The Hook Up

THE LIST SERIES
The List
The Test
The Last

For the Entangled Publishing team. To say you've elevated my career to a level I couldn't have reached on my own would be an understatement. Thank you for this amazing journey we've navigated together for nearly a decade. What a ride!

At Entangled, we want our readers to be well-informed. If you would like to know if this book contains any elements that might be of concern for you, please check the back of the book for details.

CHAPTER ONE

"Surprise party for Patrice in the physician's lounge at three!"

Nyla Franklin looked up from coding a patient chart. A dark brown curl flopped over one eye, and she blew it off her forehead for a clearer view of Aiko.

Her fellow nurse peered over the cubicle wall like a golden retriever dropping a ball at the feet of a Little League pitcher. "I thought you'd want to know," Aiko continued as Nyla finished typing the code for pertussis. "There's an ice cream cake and one of those old-timey barbershop quartets to sing happy birthday."

Nyla ignored the eager growl in her belly at the thought of that ice cream cake. "I'm leaving at noon," she said. "I'm just here to wrap up the charting from Saturday's volunteer clinic."

Aiko's face fell. "So you won't see Patrice at all?"

Nyla unclipped her name badge from the pocket of her blue scrubs and eyed Aiko with growing curiosity. "Why are you so eager to have me there?"

Aiko glanced around. The halls of the hospital were oddly empty for eleven fifty on a Thursday morning, but Aiko crept catlike around the cubical wall and dropped into the chair across from Nyla.

"Patrice hates surprises," Aiko whispered, leaning forward so far that Nyla had a glimpse of the other nurse's bright pink bra under her scrub top. "And she's *really* not happy about turning—well, it's a milestone birthday. Anyway, we know how you can't keep a secret, so—"

"Hey." Nyla frowned and adjusted her own bra strap, wondering if she could pull off hot pink. Or black. Bold hues looked weird with her pale skin, but maybe light pink. "I can keep secrets."

Aiko waved off Nyla's feeble protest. "No, it's a good thing. Well, sometimes. Some of us thought it would be kinder to let the details of the party slip…*naturally*."

"Naturally." The cogs did a sluggish turn in Nyla's brain. "What does that mean?"

"A Nylagram." Aiko laughed and squeezed Nyla's knee, which cooled the flicker of annoyance she felt at being called out for her flaw.

Aiko did have a point.

"Secrets can be hurtful." Nyla pushed her hair off her forehead again and wished she'd stuffed it in a bun. "It's hard to be sure who knows and who *doesn't* know and who might get hurt if you tell or you *don't* tell, or what if you keep your mouth shut when you shouldn't and then—"

"So you'll do it?" Aiko beamed. "You'll tip Patrice off about the party?"

"Sorry." Nyla pushed back threads of panic that had nothing to do with Patrice's party and popped out of her chair to grab her purse from the locked cabinet. "I have to run. Maybe send an email or something?"

Aiko groaned and stood up. "It won't have the same

personal touch, but fine." She pulled Nyla in for a tight hug that squished the air from her lungs. "Nice job on that clinic. I heard you vaccinated like seventy kids."

"Eighty-five, plus a dozen parents got flu shots." Nyla's chest fizzed with pride, but she commanded herself not to sound boastful. No one liked a braggy nurse. "There's another one next month. I'll send a memo."

Aiko's laugh followed Nyla down the hall. "Like that's ever necessary."

A patient ambled past them, lugging an IV pole, so Nyla refrained from flipping Aiko the bird. Besides, she wasn't really irritated. It was actually kind of sweet when people learned to work with her flaws. Unlike Greg, who used to harp on her for every little slip, needling her about how she talked too much or couldn't manage to—

"Stop it." Nyla looked around, embarrassed she'd said the words out loud. The guy with the IV pole glanced back and she delivered an apologetic wave. "Sorry. Not you. Carry on."

The guy shook his head and Nyla picked up her pace, glancing at her watch as she reached the break room. *Crap.* She yanked the fridge door open and grabbed her big blue Tupperware. She had less than an hour to transport the world's largest batch of potato leek soup to her ex-brother-in-law's place and swap it for her nephew's library book. Seth was constantly forgetting things at his dad's house, but Nyla couldn't blame the kid. It was tough enough being almost-but-not-quite-twelve, never mind the house hopscotch Seth played, bouncing between divorced parents.

Sunlight trickled through a thin net of clouds as Nyla scurried out the door and across the parking lot. The air was thick with the smell of damp grass and cherry blossoms, and she gulped a big mouthful before slinging herself into her little Honda. Aiming the car toward the highway, she hummed along with Stevie Nicks singing about a one-winged dove. Weird, but whatever. Eighties music didn't have to make sense to be awesome.

Cracking the window, she let the blossom-laced breeze ruffle her hair as she pressed the accelerator. Mid-May was always a little wonky in northern Washington, or really anywhere in the Pacific Northwest. Mother Nature would spend the morning hurling raindrops the size of fat caterpillars, but by afternoon, smug little purple lilac buds would sway in puddles of sunlight.

Nyla loved all of it. Even the mud puddles.

She pulled up in front of her ex-brother-in-law's house and scanned for her sister's car. Silly, since Mandi hadn't lived here for six years, but Nyla's brain hadn't quite recalibrated. Leo's big red truck was parked where it always was with the *Sayre Air Tankers* logo emblazoned on the side. Springtime meant fewer forest fires requiring air attack, which was the only reason Leo had agreed to leave the cockpit long enough to have the dental surgery he'd put off for years.

Nyla parked at the curb and got out with the soup container pinned under one arm. Where did Seth say he'd left the library book? If Leo was out cold—which he might be if they'd drugged him for surgery—Nyla would have to go hunting for the book. She hustled up the walkway and rapped twice on the door.

No answer.

She hesitated. Rang the bell.

Silence.

Then the thud of off-kilter footsteps. Nyla crossed her fingers she hadn't woken him. Meds had an odd effect on Leo, which was half the reason she'd stopped by.

The deadbolt clattered, and the door flew open to the echo of Leo's rumbling baritone. "Nyla!"

He swayed on his feet like a drunk pirate as he gripped the edge of the screen door separating them. His espresso-dark hair was overdue for a trim, and a spatter of white paint dotted the shoulder of his faded green T-shirt. "You brought me a human head."

She frowned. "What?"

He nodded at the blue container under her arm. "*'What's in the box?'*" He hooted at the joke, which Nyla vaguely recognized as a movie quote of some kind. It wasn't like Leo to laugh at his own jokes, so her nursing antennae perked up and wiggled.

"It's a head, right?" Swaying again, Leo tapped the edge of the container through the screen door. "You know, the movie *Seven*?"

Nyla studied his face and cursed the damn dentist. They must have given him something that made him extra-loopy. Thank God he'd given himself the whole week off work. Handy to own the company. This was definitely not a man who should be flying planes anytime soon. She watched him closely, noting the sluggishness of his movements. She'd seen plenty of drug sensitivities in her career, but the way Leo Sayre metabolized meds was something else entirely.

"You told them you can't handle Morphine, right?"

"Yep!" Leo smiled proudly. "Codeine, too, since that's a ribbit flib."

"A wha—oh, a derivative?"

"Right." Leo gave her a crooked grin, then turned and walked into the living room.

Nyla hesitated. "I'll just come in, then."

She pushed through the screen door to follow and caught sight of what he was wearing. *Wasn't* wearing.

"Uh, Leo?"

"Yep?" He vanished around the corner to the kitchen, but not before Nyla got an eyeful of his snug blue-and-green striped boxer briefs hugging the muscular curve of his ass.

"What happened to your pants?" she called.

"I took them off," he yelled over the slam of the refrigerator door.

Great.

Ignoring the warmth in her cheeks, Nyla glanced around the living room. "Maybe you could put them back on for just a sec while I check your vitals?" She spotted a pill bottle on the coffee table and picked it up, scanning the label while Leo clattered around in the kitchen.

"No problem," he shouted over the rattle of plates.

"Got it covered."

"I brought you some soup," she called. "I'll uh—set it on the coffee table while you put on some pants."

Nyla studied the pill bottle. *Oxycodone Hydrocloride*. Percocet. Hell, that could make even normal people loopy. She sat down on the gray wing-backed chair before wondering if she should run back out and grab a stethoscope. No, better to start simple.

Footsteps signaled his return, and Nyla looked up to see Leo had ditched the T-shirt and was bare-chested under an apron printed with characters from the Simpsons. Leo's light skin glowed faintly tan, like he'd been working outside without a shirt. Across his broad expanse of chest, Homer Simpson's face tilted at an odd angle as Leo flopped onto the loveseat next to Nyla's chair.

She averted her gaze and tried not to notice the well-toned pec peeking around the edge of the apron. She was here as a professional courtesy. And for Seth. She couldn't forget her nephew's library book.

Leo smiled and dropped an oval-shaped blue melamine platter on the table. "I brought us snacks."

Nyla looked at the assortment. An oblong zucchini, stem still attached. A bowl of dry Cheerios. A carton of raspberry yogurt with the foil peeled halfway back. A red-and-white striped dish dotted with brown pellets Nyla guessed might be cat food.

She looked back at Leo. "They gave you Percocet?"

"What? Oh, yeah—apparently gum grafts can be painful, but I don't think I'll take it again. Makes me feel kinda…*feathery*."

"Feathery?"

Leo held up an arm as though inspecting it for a layer of down, and Nyla did *not* look at his biceps. "Right," she said. "Um, how many Percocet did you take?"

"Only one. Doctor's orders."

Two-point-five milligrams, which was a low enough dose for a guy Leo's size. He was six three, probably one-ninety. Still, the elevator clearly wasn't going all the way to the top floor.

Normal Leo was the dependable guy who owned a multistate air tanker company supplying fire suppression aircraft across the Pacific Northwest. He flew big planes, the ones that swooped low over burning forests to drop retardant with a level of precision that blew Nyla's mind. His smokejumper pals loved to joke how it was amazing Leo could even get airborne, as big as his balls had to be to fly the kinds of missions he did. *That* Leo was valiant, smart, and skilled.

This Leo was a drunk frat boy. A drunk frat boy with an alarmingly chiseled physique, a lopsided grin, and very little clothing.

Also, the room was way too hot.

Nyla cleared her throat and focused on assessing the patient. "Did you drink any beer or wine or—"

"Nope. Nuh-uh, no way." Leo shook his head and reached for the pill bottle, knocking it off the table. He drew his hand back and grabbed a Cheerio instead. "I did just what it said on the label." He looked at the Cheerio a little sadly, then flicked it back into the bowl.

"Can't have solid food, either."

"Right." Nyla studied him, trying to figure out if he looked flushed. Not really, but he did have a certain glow. Or maybe that was her projecting. She should turn on a fan or something.

Howie the Wondercat ambled in, orange-and-white ringed tail swishing like a battle flag. Spotting Nyla, he trotted over and leaped onto her knee. She stroked a hand down his spine, recognizing his move as a ploy for food and not a genuine sign of affection.

"Hey, Howie." She rubbed a knuckle behind his ear, keeping one eye on Leo. "I can't stay long, but you're going to need to keep an eye on this guy, okay?"

Howie gave a grumble-purr and flicked her face with his tail. He seemed to share her suspicion about the contents of the red-and-white striped dish and stretched for it with whiskers twitching.

Nyla turned her attention back to Leo. He was staring at the zucchini and mumbling something about a xylophone.

"Percocet can cause weird side effects, even at a low dose," she said. "Especially for someone with known drug sensitivities."

"I'm a sensitive guy." He looked up and grinned, and Nyla couldn't tell if he was joking. It wasn't untrue, but it also wasn't like Leo to talk about himself like that.

She leaned closer, checking his pupils. They looked normal, two equal-sized black spots swimming in rings of deep maple. "I think the best thing to do right now is get you to bed so you can—"

"I have to tell you something." The earnestness in Leo's eyes was enough to halt Nyla's words.

"What do you have to tell me?"

"I didn't really lose my virginity to Shelby Carmichael my sophomore year." He rested a hand on the zucchini as though swearing an oath. "I know she made this big deal about going around telling people we hooked up after homecoming, right?"

"I—" Nyla stopped herself from pointing out that she'd only been in eighth grade and oblivious to Leo's sex life, fictitious or otherwise. "Okay."

"She wanted to, but she'd had a lot to drink, so I took her home and put her to bed, but I never even kissed her." Leo smiled, revealing the tiny chip in one tooth from the time he caught a metal bat in the mouth while teaching Seth to play baseball. "Hey!"

Nyla jumped as Leo smacked the sofa cushion, sending Howie flying off the couch. The cat glared, but Nyla kept her expression as neutral as possible. "Hey what?"

"I was dusting right before you got here—"

"In your underwear?"

"—and I was wondering why the furniture polish has real lemon in it, but the lemonade mix has artificial flavoring?"

"I have no idea." She also had no idea how a guy who looked like Leo—a guy who owned his own business as well as an apron and apparently a bottle of furniture polish—had managed to remain single for six years. "Did you ever end up going out with that woman who slipped you her number at Seth's ball game?"

"What woman?"

Guess that answered it. "Never mind."

Howie hopped onto Leo's lap, intent on trying his luck elsewhere. The cat curled into a donut shape with his chin on Leo's knee and one eye on the dish of kibble. Leo began to scratch him behind one ear, eliciting a raspy purr so loud Nyla could hear it from her perch on the edge of her chair. "Did you know cats have two-hundred-and-thirty bones in their body?" Leo asked. "I saw that on the Nature Channel."

"No kidding? Humans only have two hundred and six."

"Whoa." Leo leaned back and an apron string slipped off his shoulder. Nyla started to reach out and fix it, then thought better of it. He really ought to put on some clothes.

"There's also the Blue Tits," Leo said as casually as if they were discussing Seth's grades.

"Blue Tits." Nyla was almost afraid to ask. "What are Blue Tits?"

"They're sort of like a chickadee. In these little European villages, Blue Tits would follow the milkmen and poke holes in the foil on top of milk bottles."

"They drank milk?"

"Yep." Leo gave her a mournful look. "But they couldn't really digest it, and sometimes they fell in and drowned."

"That's terrible." She reached over and caught Leo's wrist above the hand that wasn't scratching Howie. She found the steady thrum of his pulse and checked her watch. The seconds ticked past, but Leo didn't pull back. Sixty beats per minute. Pretty normal.

"Blue Tits, huh." She wondered if there really was a bird by that name. She'd have to Google it later. She tried to think of something else to say, something to keep him talking. At least this way she could monitor his vitals, make sure he didn't do anything like cooking naked or drunk-dialing exes. His most notable ex was Nyla's sister, Mandi, and she'd be understanding, but still. It was probably best to watch him a while longer to be sure it was safe to leave him alone.

Birds. Keep him talking about birds.

"I always wondered what the story was behind the one-winged dove Stevie Nicks was singing about," she said.

Leo cocked his head. "One-winged dove?" He gave her an odd look. "You're not talking about 'Edge of Seventeen,' are you?"

Nyla hummed a few bars in her head until she got to the chorus. Yep, that was it. "*Just like a one-winged dove, sings a song sounds like she's singing—*'"

"White-winged." Leo grinned. "You're goddamn adorable the way you hear song lyrics."

A candle-flicker of heat warmed Nyla's cheeks, and she couldn't say if it was embarrassment from a lifetime of singing the wrong words, or the result of his effusive praise. Had Leo ever uttered the word "adorable" before?

"Crap." The song lyrics rearranged themselves in her

brain. "You're right. White-winged makes way more sense."

Leo smiled and picked up the yogurt. There was no spoon, so he held it like a cocktail glass. "Want to know something else weird?"

"If you're going to tell me Jimmy Hendrix isn't really singing 'Excuse me while I kiss this guy,' I already found out."

Leo laughed, but there was a solemnness in his expression that wasn't there a few seconds ago. A tight web of lines crinkled his brow, and his eyes had gone dark. "Did you know Seth's not really mine?"

Nyla stared. "What?" She started to laugh but then stopped abruptly.

He was serious.

Leo shook his head and stroked Howie from neck to tail. "He's mine, obviously. *Obviously.* I'm his father and he's my boy. *My booooooy!*" He cackled at the line Nyla recognized from countless Harry Potter marathons with Seth, but unease pricked at the back of her brain.

"Why would you say something like that?" Her voice snagged in her throat, and she ordered herself not to panic. This was a drug reaction, nothing more.

"It's true," Leo said, and his grave look told her it was. Or at least Leo *believed* it was. "Seth's blood type is O."

Nyla took a steadying breath. "And you are?"

"AB."

"I see." She didn't speak, waiting for Leo to fill in the rest. Her skin was prickly and the big copper clock above the couch made a frantic *tic-tic-tic* sound.

"Mandi's B-negative," Leo said. "I remembered her talking about it back when she did the bone marrow thing with you. I guess it's kinda rare."

"Yes." Nyla slid a hand over her abdomen, not sure what else to say. She'd been the recipient of Mandi's bone marrow, the reason her sister had undergone a painful procedure without batting an eyelash.

This had to be a mistake. Leo was confused, or maybe this was another loopy drug response or— "How long have you thought this?"

Thought, not *known*, but Leo didn't seem to catch the distinction. "Four years." He leaned back against the loveseat and closed his eyes, still gripping the yogurt in one big fist. "When Seth was eight."

Four years? This couldn't be— How could he—

"You're positive about this?"

"One hundred percent." Leo opened one eye and jerked a thumb toward the office, startling Howie. "You can go check the medical records if you want."

"I—maybe in a minute." She swallowed hard, not sure which question to ask first. "Have you said anything to Seth?"

"Of course not." The rough edge to his voice was enough to steer her away from that line of questioning. She watched him peel the foil off the yogurt and lift it to his mouth like a can of beer. His throat moved as he swallowed, and Nyla sat watching, waiting for the rest of the story.

This was a hallucination or something, right?

Questions. She should ask more questions. "What

about Mandi?"

Leo lowered the yogurt container and looked at her. "What about her?"

"Did you talk about it or ask her to explain or—"

"No."

Numbers whirled in Nyla's brain, reminding her of the time Seth stuck his fridge magnets on the merry-go-round and sent dozens of bright plastic digits flipping into the sand. Seth was twelve, and Leo and Mandi split six years ago. So that would mean—

"You think Mandi had an affair," she said. "Is that what you're saying?"

Leo shrugged, but there was a flicker of unease in his eyes. A flash of the real Leo fighting his way up through the fog. "We'd been divorced two years by the time I found out. Best to let sleeping frogs lie, right?"

"I—" Nyla didn't know what to think or say. "This can't be true."

Leo studied her, agitation now clouding his expression. "Sure, maybe not." He cleared his throat. "I think I'm going to go lie down now. I'm really tired."

"But Leo—"

"Seth's library book is on his desk," he said. "Right next to his earbuds. Could you take those to him, too?"

"But—"

"Thanks for the soup." He wedged the yogurt container into the center of an asparagus fern and stood up. "Would you mind locking up when you leave?"

Tic-tic-tic went the clock, while Nyla's heartbeat pounded at the front of her skull. This must be a mistake.

Her senses clouded with the smell of raspberry yogurt and a metallic taste in her mouth.

"Leo," she said again, but he was already halfway down the hall. She stared at his naked back, at the yellow strings of the apron, at the blue-and-green stripes of his boxer briefs.

What the hell just happened?

CHAPTER TWO

The first thing Leo saw when he woke up was a tumbler of water on his nightstand. He sat up and grabbed it, grateful for the cold, sweaty curve of glass against his palm. His tongue felt like shoe leather and his gums ached around the fresh grafts.

He took two big gulps of water before spotting the note.

It was folded in half, creased sharp as though someone had ironed it. He set the glass down as uneasiness rumbled in his gut, or maybe that was regular old nausea. What the hell had that dentist given him yesterday?

No, wait. *Today?* He tapped his phone to confirm, surprised it was still Thursday, just a few minutes before nine. His stomach gurgled, reminding him he'd missed dinner.

Nyla.

She'd brought soup, hadn't she? And something else. A question, or maybe several of them. Memories nipped at the corner of his brain, insistent little puppy teeth trying to drag something out from under a chair leg.

He glanced back at the note, stalling. Something bad was in there.

Howie jumped up on the edge of the bed, and Leo ran a hand down the length of the cat's spine. One stroke, two, stalling, stalling.

What the hell had he said to Nyla? He wouldn't have told her anything about—

No. He would never tell anyone, not even her.

He stared at the note again.

Fuck it. Leo grabbed the folded paper, desperate to fill in the yawing gaps in his memory. Purple ballpoint, and the handwriting was all Nyla, the same slanted script he saw every time she gave him one of the gory medical articles she loved as much as he did.

He took a deep breath and started to read.

Leo,

I hope you're feeling more lucid. Please call when you're up. We need to finish our conversation about blood types. I have many questions.

Nyla

Shit.

A hailstorm of memories pelted him from all sides, stinging his face, his forearms, his brain.

Seth's not really mine.

Holy Christ. He'd said it. He'd really said those words out loud.

He dropped the note in his lap as a cold sweat prickled his flesh. He stared down at the words, noticing the little heart before her name. Standard Nyla fare, maybe a sign things were still normal. Maybe he hadn't just blurted his biggest secret to the one person who couldn't keep one.

Not that Leo blamed her.

She was a fixer, a helper. Nyla lived to aid others, and

she processed everything out loud. A fun combination if you got her tipsy at a party. Not a fun combination if you accidentally told her something you didn't want the world to know.

Leo's hand was shaking as he picked up his phone. Dread curdled his stomach and he stared at the screen without dialing. Maybe this wasn't so bad. Maybe he could convince her he'd been kidding. Maybe—

Quack-quack-quack!

It took him five seconds to shake off the last of his drug-induced haze and decide there was no family of ducks in his bed. Nyla's ringtone, a hat-tip to Mandi's nickname for her. *Duckie.* Leo had never called her that, but the ringtone fit.

Quack-quack-quack!

"Hello?" he answered cautiously, keeping his tone even.

"Leo." She sounded relieved. "How are you feeling?"

"Good. Fine." He swung his legs out of bed and tugged on a pair of jeans. It felt weird talking to her without pants on, and another ripple of unease moved through him.

"I just woke up, but I'm feeling much better."

"Any pain or nausea?"

"Nope. All good."

He moved toward the kitchen, reminding himself to keep breathing. Everything was normal. Everything was fine.

What had the dentist said about eating after a gum graft? Liquids, maybe, and no straws. He spotted a card taped to the fridge and recognized Nyla's handwriting.

Soup's in the blue Tupperware. Dentist's instructions are on the table. Please call when you're up.

Leo put a hand on the fridge but didn't open the door. "I was just getting ready to forage for food." His voice sounded calm, normal. He could do this.

"I made potato leek. Your favorite." A pause, then Nyla took a shaky breath. "Do you remember me stopping by? What you told me?"

Leo gripped the fridge handle tighter. "I told you about birds, I think," he said. "I was watching this special on the Nature Channel about—"

"Leo, you told me about Seth." Her voice was shaky but determined. "About how you think he's not biologically yours."

Leo closed his eyes and stared at the pink blur of his inner eyelids. The stainless-steel handle felt solid and cool under his palm, and the kitchen smelled comforting, like toast.

Nyla said nothing for a long time. So long, he thought maybe she'd disconnected.

"Leo—"

"You can't say anything."

Another long pause.

"I'm coming over," she said. "I'd like to look at that lab work. There must a mistake. Maybe you read it wrong."

"Okay." He clicked off, dread pooling thick and syrupy in his gut.

He hadn't read it wrong. He knew that much.

He remembered that awful day in the hospital, the day he had looked down at his son with tubes snaking out of Seth's small hands and a goofy grin on the boy's freckled face.

"Did you see me make that jump, Dad?"

"Yeah." He'd tousled Seth's hair. "I sure did."

The doctor had spoken in hushed tones outside Seth's hospital room. "We want to keep him overnight for observation." She'd glanced down at her clipboard. "Looks like he's O-negative. You should consider donating blood if you're O. Even if he doesn't end up needing it, we can always use more O here."

"Absolutely. Of course."

So Leo had rushed down to the lab, the first time in his whole life he'd had a needle in his arm. He'd gone woozy at first but gripped the blue squishy ball and reminded himself this was for Seth.

The lab tech had frowned when she pulled up the results. "Hmmm, sorry." She'd shot Leo a strange look he couldn't quite read. "You're AB. Not a match. Maybe get his mom in here?"

But Mandi had been in Baltimore for work, and Leo had felt a niggling sense of unease. When they'd gotten home the next day—Seth was fine, no surgery needed— Leo got his boy settled with a cherry Popsicle and a big stack of comics.

Then he'd turned to Dr. Google.

And then he'd called Dr. Parker.

"You are correct," Seth's pediatrician had said after

Leo spit out his long, rambling string of questions that probably weren't questions at all. More like incoherent babbling.

The doctor had continued in the same calm, clinical tone Leo recognized as the one Nyla called her Bad News Nurse Voice. "Assuming the information you've just provided is accurate, Seth is not biologically related to you." Another pause from Dr. Parker while Leo's lungs ached like someone stood on his chest. "I take it this is a surprise to you?"

"Yes." A surprise. Like his son's paternity was a birthday cake or an unexpected Amazon delivery instead of the biggest fucking shock of his life.

He still remembered that feeling, the sense that he was watching someone else have this conversation. Someone else was breathing in and out with lungs burning in acid, someone else was tasting sour brine on the back of his tongue.

The doorbell chimed, jolting Leo back to the present. *Nyla.*

Christ. What was he going to do?

Spotting his favorite green T-shirt on the kitchen floor, he yanked it on. "Be right there!"

He ran his hands through his hair, wondering if she'd just let herself in. She had a key, though she rarely used it. Only when she needed to grab things for Seth—a forgotten book, a worksheet for school—and Leo never thought twice about her walking freely through the house. The records were well-hidden, and it never occurred to him that his stupid secret would leak right out of his own mouth.

"Coming," he called as he jogged down the hall toward the front door. He flung it open to find her standing in the pale-yellow glow of the porch light.

"Leo."

She'd said his name a thousand times before, greeting him at Seth's games or asking him to pass the pepper at family dinners. But there was something heavy in it now. Something that made his breath leaden in his lungs.

Curls the color of dark maple syrup were pulled up in a topknot, and she'd scrubbed off all her makeup. She looked young, pale, and very worried. "How are you feeling?"

"Good." Leo dragged a hand through his hair, wishing he'd had time for a haircut. Wishing a lot of things that had nothing to do with hair. "My gums don't hurt at all. Got a call from the air base. Looks like the new MD-87 Air Tanker is getting here a week early, so I'm making it the new lead air attack plane for the contract with the Forest Service. Should time out well for me to fly it over to Hart Valley myself."

He was rambling ridiculously and doing himself no favors if his goal was to convince Nyla everything was normal. His palms leaked sweat as her pool-blue eyes studied him with a look that was more than clinical. It was something else. Something unsure. Her hands were fisted in the pockets of a pale pink hoodie, and Leo wished like hell he could rewind the last twenty-four hours.

"Come in," he said, stepping aside and moving toward the kitchen. "Is it weird to offer you some of your own soup?"

"I ate a few hours ago. Besides, I made it for you. Pureed so you don't have to chew. You should be able to handle solids in just a few days. That's the upside of using donor tissue for grafts."

"Thank you." His throat tightened, and he felt like a jackass for taking her kindness for granted. "Let me at least grab you a drink."

"Thanks."

She seated herself stiffly at his butcher block table, a piece he'd built with Seth helping to sand and varnish the gnarled surface. "Hard cider okay?"

Nyla was the whole reason he kept his fridge stocked with bottles of Angry Orchard, but she shook her head. "Just water would be great."

That seemed like a bad sign.

Leo took his time filling a bowl with soup, stabbing the buttons on the microwave, getting out a spoon and napkin and a glass of water for each of them. He knew he was stalling, but he had no idea how to open this conversation.

"So, start at the beginning." Her voice was achingly calm, and he turned to see her folding her hands on the table. Healing hands. Elegant hands. "You said you found out four years ago?"

Leo didn't say anything right away. Just got himself settled at the table with a steaming puddle of soup in a bowl and a fist-sized lump in his throat. He chugged half his water in hopes of washing it away. When he set down the glass, Nyla was still watching him.

He took a deep breath and dove in. "Remember when Seth flew over the handlebars on his bike?"

Nyla's eyes flashed and she nodded. "Spleen laceration. They admitted him for observation. Serial hemoglobin, hematocrit checks, the whole nine yards."

"Right. They suggested I donate blood in case he needed it. For surgery or whatever. That's—that's when I found out."

"They told you?"

He shook his head, wondering how common this was. How often did men end up raising kids they hadn't actually fathered while doctors whispered behind their clipboards about mommy's little secret?

"No," he said. "But something seemed off when they gave me the results, so I went home and did some research. Pulled out Seth's birth records, just to be sure."

"That would have Seth's blood type," she said. "Mandi's, too."

"Yep." Leo cleared his throat. "If I didn't watch so many damn science shows, or read all those freaky medical articles you give me—"

"Show me."

"What?"

"I need to see it for myself. Please, Leo."

Her eyes glittered with an emotion he couldn't identify. He wasn't sure if his legs worked at the moment. His knees felt gummy and weak, and he didn't know if he could handle looking at that paperwork again. "Okay," he said. "Can you grab it?"

"Where?"

"The file cabinet in my office," he said. "Top drawer, in the folder that says, 'data backup.'"

"Data backup?"

Leo swirled his spoon around in the soup, feeling foolish and out-of-sorts. "It was the most boring thing I could think of. Seth wouldn't bother looking in a folder like that."

"The lab work's in there?"

"No. But there's a key that goes to the trunk in my bedroom. You'll find everything in a big yellow envelope."

Nyla seemed to hesitate. Then she stood and retreated toward the back of the house. Leo's head was pounding, and he wondered if he should take another pain pill. No. He needed to be clear-headed for this. He spooned up some soup and listened to Nyla's footsteps padding softly through his house.

When she returned, she took her seat and set the envelope on the table. Leo's gut did a painful twist as her eyes met his. "You're sure you're okay with me looking at this? They're your private medical records."

This was his out. His chance to say he'd been kidding, that it was all a joke.

But she'd never believe that now. He took a deep breath. "You're a nurse. This is how it will make sense to you."

Like this could possibly make sense to any of them.

She nodded and turned her attention to the contents of the envelope. Not sure what to do with his hands, Leo focused on the soup. It was warm and creamy and perfect, just the way she always made it.

But he hardly tasted a thing. As he scraped the bottom of the bowl, Nyla looked up. He tried to read her expression, to figure out what was happening behind those pool-blue eyes.

Confusion.

Uncertainty.

Resignation.

"So, you've known for four years."

"Yes." He cleared his throat. "Since Seth was eight."

"And you haven't said anything to Mandi."

He shook his head, conscious of the fact that he needed to tread carefully. Nyla was his friend, but she was Mandi's sister first. He knew that better than anyone.

"At first, I thought maybe there was a mix-up at the hospital," he said. "Like maybe the babies got switched or something."

Nyla frowned "Not with all the protocols in place. Microchip bracelets for mom and baby, the color-coded room tags."

"Right." Leo's throat clogged again as he remembered that day in the delivery room. He hadn't taken his eyes off Seth from the moment the boy emerged red-faced and squalling with his little fist in the air like a prize fighter. Besides, Seth had Mandi's cupid-bow mouth and an identical chin dimple.

So there must have been an affair.

"Things were weird for us the year before Seth was born," Leo said slowly. "We weren't fighting or anything, but—"

"You think she was seeing someone else?" Nyla's blue eyes flickered. Leo watched her face, gauging her response. Defensiveness? Surprise? He honestly couldn't tell.

"She was traveling a lot back then," he said carefully. "We'd started drifting apart even before that. She must have said something to you?"

"About an affair?" Nyla shook her head. "No. Never."

"I meant the drifting apart," he said. "We made all these plans in high school, stuff about how we wanted to travel together after she got her degree."

Nyla's expression softened, and she looked down at her hands. "Not a lot of guys could do diaper duty and run a business while putting someone else through school."

Pride bloomed in the center of Leo's chest, but he held his tongue. It hadn't been easy, not by a long shot, but he'd been damn glad to do it. Mandi had big dreams, and Leo was happy to help her chase them. Yeah, he'd started out fighting wildfires on ground crews, eventually busting ass to be a smokejumper. But when his dad died and left the air tanker company to Leo, it just made sense to shift to the air attack side of the business. Better schedule for raising a kid, plus it gave him the means to help his wife, to be the kind of dad he'd always wanted to be.

He could do it all. He'd *wanted* to do it all.

How the hell was he supposed to know dreams could change so much between eighteen and twenty-eight?

"We'd started growing apart even before Seth was

born," Leo said slowly. "But things got better for a while after that." He shrugged. Nyla knew the rest of the story. "And then they weren't. You know how it went down."

Nyla nodded, her expression still shell-shocked. He wasn't telling her anything she didn't know, right? He braced for more questions about Mandi, maybe a theory to cancel out the one about the affair. Her next words caught him off guard.

"You didn't feel Seth had a right to know?"

"He's twelve." Leo's words were clipped, and he wished for more soup. For something to do with his hands. "He's barely accepted the fact that Santa isn't real."

"Fair enough." Nyla of all people knew that. She'd been the one to pick him up at school the day Kellan Keith told him only babies believed in a red-suited fat man who squeezed himself down the chimney.

Nyla took a shaky breath. "What about Mandi?"

"What about her?"

"Don't you think she should know? To have a chance to explain herself?"

Leo snorted. He couldn't help it, the sound just came out. "Like she was forthcoming with the fact that she fucked someone else?"

Nyla flinched. "Maybe there's another explanation."

He stared at her. "You have a bachelor's degree in nursing and you read medical articles like they're romance novels. You want to tell me what other explanation you could possibly come up with?"

"I'm trying, Leo!" She whacked the table with her

palm, and he realized he'd only seen her riled up a handful of times. Fury turned her eyes into pools of turquoise glitter. He started to reach for her hand, then stopped himself. Reached for his soup spoon instead, before remembering the bowl was empty.

"I'm sorry," he said softly.

"You've had four years to process this," she said. "I've had four hours. This is all a little raw, okay?"

"Sorry," he said again. Taking a deep breath, he thought about what else he could offer her. "Look, Seth is my son. He'd be my son whether we shared DNA or not. Plenty of adopted kids never know their biology."

"I'm not arguing whether he's your son," she said. "Don't you want to get to the bottom of what happened?"

"Honestly, I'd rather remove my tonsils with a claw hammer."

She shook her head, not smiling at the joke. "When Mandi got pregnant with Seth—"

"That's when she was spending time in upstate New York," he said. "She had that internship, remember? She was back and forth between here and there all the time, plus there was that trip to Uganda—"

"You think she was seeing someone overseas?" Nyla frowned.

"I've tried not to think about it at all."

"But—"

"Look, I might have given a shit if I found out about this when we were still married, but we'd been divorced for two years by then." Leo raked his fingers through his hair, willing her to understand. "I don't care who Mandi was fucking."

"Please stop saying it like that." Nyla's voice was pleading, and she pressed her palms flat against the table like she thought it might fly away. "I just—Mandi's not that kind of person."

Leo said nothing, not wanting to go any deeper. He knew firsthand about the loyalty between the two sisters. He'd only been married to Mandi a year when she came home and announced she was donating bone marrow to Nyla. Just like that, no hesitation at all, no concern for her own health and safety.

But the sisters' connection went way deeper than medical stuff. His split with Mandi had been fast and amicable, but he'd gone from seeing Nyla three or four times a week to once a month. Family barbecues, casual coffee dates, a drop-in to borrow a tool—it all dried up, and it took a year for them to ease into a new version of family. The version that didn't have a sharp line drawn between "Mandi's side" and "Leo's side."

Part of it came down to this weird belief his ex-in-laws had that he and Mandi would get back together. No way in hell, they both agreed, but it didn't stop Ted and Laurel from pushing them together any chance they got.

Leo took a deep breath as the silence stretched out and Nyla took a drink of water. He watched her throat move, noticing the tiny scar on her middle knuckle. He'd been the one to drive her to Urgent Care, the one to promise her she wasn't a fool for slicing her hand when she smashed a framed photo of Greg against the wall. Afterward, he'd built her a dartboard with the asshole's picture in the center, and he taught her to throw until her arm ached more than her heart.

They had that in common, he and Nyla. Life-changing breakups, the kind that knocked your knees right out from under you. They'd both licked their wounds and eventually learned there was life on the other side.

"I need to ask you not to say anything about this," he said slowly. "Not to Mandi, or to Seth—"

"Leo." Nyla set her water down and shook her head. "There are legitimate medical reasons Seth needs to know about his paternity. Genetic stuff. Questions he might eventually have about who he is and where he comes from."

Leo felt his jaw clenching and ordered himself to speak slowly. "Seth's fine," Leo said. "He's healthy and happy and he knows who he is."

"But later he might want to know—"

"Then I'll tell him later."

Nyla frowned. "What about Mandi?"

Fizzy bubbles of anger rose up his throat, and he swallowed them back. "Right now, she has even less of a need than Seth to know about it." He reached across the table and put his hand over hers, like he could somehow keep the secret between them with the shield of his palm. "Please, Nyla. I'm asking you not to say anything."

She looked at him for a long, long time. Then she shifted her eyes away, directing her gaze toward the wall.

No, not the wall. The photo beside the door, the one of him with Seth. They gripped a fat, slippery trout, grinning with their arms slung around each other.

My boy. My son.

Nyla turned back to him like she'd heard the words out loud. Her swimming-pool eyes held his. Then she nodded. "Okay."

"Okay?" His chest filled with gratitude, and he realized he was still touching her hand. "Thank you. That's all I can ask for."

"I know it's ridiculous." She gave a hollow little laugh. "How hard it is for me to keep a secret? I'm a nurse, for crying out loud. I protect patient information all the time."

"That's the law," he said. "It's different with family."

"It's not on purpose." Nyla's cheeks flooded with color as a bright ribbon of hair fell over her eye. She tucked it back, using her left hand, while her right stayed curved under Leo's. "I tell myself I'm not going to say anything. I'll sit there reminding myself over and over and over not to say whatever it is I'm not supposed to say, but then I start thinking about who knows and who *doesn't* know and who might be hurt by all the lying and hiding and keeping secrets. Just the thought of causing someone else pain makes me physically sick."

"It's part of what makes you a good nurse." Also a good person, though Leo sometimes wondered what else caused her compulsion. Was there a deeper reason behind Nyla's agony over secret keeping?

He usually saw it as an endearing quirk. It was funny

the time she blurted over Thanksgiving dinner that they could all stop searching for the water pitcher because Aunt Trish had broken it and hid the pieces under her mom's prized redleaf roses, and what if someone cut their hand weeding the flower bed?

But this kind of secret was different. This kind of secret was life changing. Not that he thought Mandi would try to keep Seth from him, but—

"Just do your best not to say anything," he said. "Please."

"I'll try," she repeated. "I promise."

"I'll help you."

She shook her head, looking torn. "I already feel like I'm betraying my sister. My nephew. What if he does one of those at-home genetic tests and finds out on his own? Or what if—"

"We'll deal with that if it happens."

She sighed and fiddled with her ring. It was a fat, round opal, a gift Mandi brought back from Australia. "I'm sorry," she said softly, not meeting his eyes. "It must have been hard for you to find out. I wish I could have been there for you."

Leo nodded, grateful she wasn't looking at him. That she couldn't see the flood of emotion in his eyes. He tipped his head back, getting control of himself. "I'm okay," he said. "I've had time to get used to it. I hardly even think about it anymore."

Not until he blurted it out like a fool. Why the hell had he done that? Must be some kind of switch on his subconscious that got flipped by the Percocet.

Silence stretched out between them. The refrigerator hummed like an oboe in an action flick right before the shark takes a bite out of a surfer. Leo was conscious of Nyla's hand under his, conscious of the strong ridge of her knuckles. He should pull his hand back and stop touching her, but he didn't want to. Something about this connection felt right. Necessary.

He'd been carrying this secret alone for so long. Was it wrong to feel grateful he had someone to share the burden? Someone like Nyla, someone sweet and kind and generous and beautiful and—

No, not beautiful. Well, yes, she was technically beautiful, but he'd never looked at her that way before. His sister-in-law, for crying out loud.

Ex-sister-in-law…

At last, Nyla sighed. "I'm meeting Mandi on Monday for brunch," she said. "We were going to talk about the menu for Mom and Dad's barbecue this weekend."

"Cancel."

She frowned. "But—"

"Nyla, you know she'll take one look at you and start dragging out secrets like she's snaking a hairball from the drain."

"Gross."

He managed a small smile. "You're the one who prints weird medical articles about degloving accidents and that woman who inhaled the earring."

That got a smile out of her. See? They could do this. They could be just like normal, like the cat was still stuffed safely in the bag.

Howie chose that moment to walk in, to headbutt Nyla's shin. She reached down to scratch his soft orange ears as she took a deep breath. "Fine. I guess Mandi and I could plan the menu on the phone or something."

"Text is better," he said. "Or email."

She shot him a look of exasperation. "I can't do this forever, Leo," she said. "You know Mandi and I don't keep secrets from each other."

He lifted an eyebrow, waiting for her to get there herself. He didn't want to be the one to say the words out loud.

Her face dropped into a frown. "Right." She sighed. "The affair. Seth's sperm donor."

He loved that she didn't say *father*. The other guy— whoever the hell he was—didn't deserve the title. Leo was Seth's dad. He'd always be Seth's dad, no matter what.

"Family secrets are nothing new," he said. "I'm just asking you to help keep one of them."

"For now," she said, and he heard the concession in her voice.

"For now," he repeated, aware of the dread in his own.

CHAPTER THREE

"What do you think about build-your-own pulled pork sandwiches?"

Before Nyla could open her mouth to answer, Mandi gave a gasp of dismay. "Ugh. Dick soap. No."

And this was the reason Nyla had been willing to risk seeing her sister in person.

A novelty soap company had donated fifty-two crates of soap bars to relief efforts in Haiti, where Mandi was traveling in a few weeks to oversee a massive water sanitation project and a series of hygiene classes.

Sorting the cutesy soap flowers and kitty cats from the risqué shapes required Mandi's full attention, which meant less focus on Nyla.

Or the fact that Nyla was biting back her big secret. *Leo's* big secret.

"I'll take those." Nyla grabbed the box of penis soap and set it under the worktable in Mandi's garage. She let her hair fall over her face, hoping Mandi didn't look too closely. That her sister wouldn't pick up on anything suspicious.

Nyla stood up in time to see Mandi lift an eyebrow. "What on earth are you going to do with forty soap dicks?"

"I volunteered to teach a safe sex course at the college next month. These can be prizes."

"Love it!" Mandy grabbed another box and began tearing open the flaps. "Anyway, I was just thinking that would be a nice change of pace from weenies."

Nyla was still hung up on the penis soap, so it took her a second to remember what they'd been talking about. "Pulled pork sandwiches instead of hot dogs," she said. "You know Dad's still going to want bratwurst."

"Yeah, I know. But at least the pulled pork will give us some variety." Mandi braced an arm against the wall and stretched, easing the tension in her hip. She'd been one of the rare bone marrow donors to have complications from the procedure, developing stiffness in the muscle around the draw site. It never quite went away, but Mandi never complained. She usually went to great lengths to keep Nyla from noticing any pain, so it must be especially bad today.

"I'm fine, quit looking at me like that." Mandi stopped stretching and smiled. "Must've strained it in yoga or something."

"Sure, okay." Nyla knew that wasn't it, and guilt pinched the edges of her heart. Not just for her sister's pain, but for keeping secrets. Hiding something big from the one person who'd given her so much.

She kept secrets from you…

"Bratwurst and pulled pork should be perfect." Nyla ordered herself to sound normal, wondering if Mandi could hear the worry in her voice. If she knew how hard Nyla was working to speak normally, to look normal. Her gut balled tight as she thought about who might get hurt if she kept her mouth shut. Or if she *didn't*. Or…

see, this was the problem with secrets. Just thinking about her family's pain, remembering that other pain she caused so long ago when she kept her mouth shut and shouldn't have. Nyla's throat pinched tight, her chest compressing until she couldn't breathe, couldn't think, couldn't—

"I can make that pineapple cabbage slaw." She forced out the words past the surging panic attack. "The one I made last Christmas."

"Oooh, that would be awesome!" Mandi finished prying open the box and tossed her elbow-length hair over one shoulder. She'd worn it like this for as long as Nyla could remember, a mahogany waterfall that Nyla used to brush and braid and envy from time to time. Her hair made the perfect contrast to Mandi's porcelain complexion, versus Nyla's too-pale flesh prone to furious flushing. "Maybe Mom can do her homemade potato rolls?"

"Yum." There. Single-syllable words were good. Less risk of Mandi hearing something in her voice, picking out the questions that screamed through Nyla's brain.

What happened?

How did Seth get someone else's DNA?

Why didn't you tell me?

"Golf ball soap." Mandi held up one of the dimpled white spheres and shrugged. "Sort of weird to take to a third-world village without running water, but I guess it's not offensive."

"Nope."

Mandi looked up from the golf ball and cocked her

head to the side. "You okay?"

"Sure, of course. Why?"

"Just wondering. You seem sort of quiet."

"Just tired." That was true. Not the same as admitting she'd slept restlessly the last few nights because she was worried about Leo's secret. Or was it Seth's secret, or Mandi's? See, this was the problem with secrets. How the hell did you know who owned them? And how did you know when someone might get hurt—hurt badly, *so badly*—if you didn't share what you knew?

Think about Seth. Think about how crushed he'd be if he found out.

Yes, that was key. She needed to focus on her nephew's welfare. On Seth's happiness. But what about the study she'd read showing it was better for a child's mental health to learn young if they'd been adopted or conceived via donor sperm or—

"Stop."

Mandi cocked her head. "Stop what?"

Crap. Nyla hadn't meant to say that out loud. "Headache." She pressed her fingers to her temples, relieved to be telling the truth. "My head's been pounding all day. I just want it to stop."

"I've got you." Mandi smiled and unscrewed the little pill locket she wore around her neck. "Extra-strength Tylenol for migraine emergencies."

She handed it over, and Nyla gulped back fresh waves of guilt. She swallowed the pill dry, half wishing she'd choke on it. At least then she'd be physically forced to keep her trap shut.

"Thank you," Nyla managed.

"No problem."

Mandi was still staring at her, and Nyla knew she needed to fill the silence. "So, we just need a salad or something," Nyla said. "I've got one of those big packs of romaine if you wanted to do Caesar."

"Nah, let's let Leo do salad." Mandi turned and reached for the next box, which was a stroke of luck for Nyla. It kept her sister from seeing the color drain from her face. "You know how Dad loves that kale thing Leo makes."

"Leo's coming?" Nyla swallowed and ordered her voice not to wobble. "I didn't know that."

Thank God, Mandi was elbow deep in a box of soaps shaped like dentures. Bright white teeth nestled in a row of bubblegum pink flesh, and Nyla couldn't help thinking about Leo and his gum graft. How was he doing?

"We changed up the schedule again," Mandi was saying as she repacked the box of soap dentures and set them in the keeper pile. "We're switching on Fridays now, right after school."

"So Seth's with his dad on Saturday for the barbecue." Nyla felt her voice wobble on the word *dad*, and she prayed Mandi didn't notice.

Mandi was busy tearing into the next box. "I hadn't realized the conflict until I looked at the calendar," Mandi continued. "I figured Leo would want to trade for a different day, but Mom and Dad begged him to come to the barbecue, so—" Mandi shrugged. "You know how it is."

Nyla did know how it was. In the past year, her parents had stepped up their game in pushing Mandi and Leo back together. Bizarre, since they'd seemed fine when Mandi divorced him. Maybe they'd gotten sentimental seeing their eldest daughter stay single, or maybe they'd come to realize what a catch Leo was.

Not that Nyla thought about that. Ever.

"Is it weird having to see Leo like that?"

Mandi looked up and frowned. "Why would it be?"

Nyla held her breath and tried to think of the right thing to say. "I don't know. Having your ex-husband come to family functions?"

Her sister looked thoughtful for a second, then shrugged. "It's better for Seth when we do the whole harmonious co-parent thing. We both know we're not getting back together, so he just ignores Mom and Dad's silliness."

"Good. That's good."

Leo often turned down the invites so he didn't have to deal with Ted and Laurel's not-so-subtle hints about getting back together with Mandi. Was he coming this time to make sure Nyla kept her trap shut? Not that she minded. Honestly, it would be nice to see him again. Nice to know she wasn't the only one sitting on this great big goose egg of a secret. Nice to see his warm brown eyes or those broad shoulders or—

No. Stop thinking about him like that. Just because you saw him pantsless and shirtless is no excuse to have illicit thoughts about your ex-brother-in-law.

She grabbed a box off the stack and slit it open,

needing to do something with her hands.

"Anyway," Mandi continued, oblivious to Nyla's distress. "I'll text Leo and ask him to bring the kale. Anything else you want him to bring?"

A folder full of lab work.

A plan for discussing Seth's paternity with you.

A report from a private investigator explaining how your son came to have different DNA from the guy we all think is his father.

The words took absurd forms in Nyla's brain, but she swallowed them all back. "Nope," she said. "You think this box of s'mores soap would be a good prank for Dad?"

Mandi peered into the box Nyla was holding and laughed. "Wow, those are good. Who the hell buys s'mores soap?"

"No one, apparently. Maybe it's why they're going out of business?"

"Good point." Mandi took the box from Nyla and set it on the keeper pile. She turned back to grab another box, then frowned. "You sure you're okay?"

"Positive," she said. "One hundred percent."

Mandi kept staring. Suddenly, her eyes flew wide. "Oh! I know what it is."

"What *what* is?"

"May twenty-first," she said. "Wasn't this your anniversary with Greg?"

A trickle of ice slithered down Nyla's spine. Relief, mostly, but it sucked having to lie to her own sister.

She lied, too. She never said a word to anyone about Seth.

"You're right," Nyla fibbed, hating the taste of the words on her tongue. "I guess that has been on my mind a little."

"Come here, Duckie." Mandi didn't wait for a response. She just pulled Nyla into a tight, soap-scented hug. "Breakups are annoying like that. You think you're totally fine with everything, totally over the guy—"

"I am," Nyla said into her sister's hair, wanting to make sure Mandi didn't think she was pining away over Greg. "Completely over him."

"I get it." Mandi drew back and looked deep into Nyla's eyes. Nyla held her breath, worried what her sister would see there. "You spent nine years thinking he was the one," Mandi said. "Even if he turned out to be an asshole, even if you're better off without him, you don't just flip a switch and stop expecting to see his toothbrush in the bathroom every morning. It takes time."

"Time," Nyla repeated, back on safe, monosyllabic ground. "Is that how it was for you and Leo?"

This. This was Mandi's cue to tell her something. To open up about the divorce or the affair or whatever the hell she was hiding. "Kind of." Mandi shrugged, her blue eyes skittering away like she was already mentally unpacking the next box of soap. "We were just kids when we got together. Best friends, you know?"

"Right."

"But we were young and dumb and had no idea what it meant to plan a life around someone else," she said. "Marriage is so much tougher than they tell you it will be.

So much harder than Mom and Dad make it look."

Nyla nodded, not trusting herself to speak. Is that what happened? Did marriage get too hard, too lonely for her smart, compassionate, independent sister?

Why didn't you tell me you were hurting?

Why didn't you say something so I could help?

Her throat burned, her skin prickled where Mandi's hands gripped her shoulders. "It'll be okay," Mandi said. "It gets easier, I promise."

Nyla gave another nod, pretending her sister already knew the truth. That they were talking about Leo and Seth instead of Nyla's ex-boyfriend she hadn't spoken to in almost a year. "I know it will," she said. "Everything will be fine eventually."

The fib had a salty, bitter taste, unexpected and unfamiliar.

She wondered how long it would take to get used to it.

• • •

A few days later, Nyla sat on a barstool at her mother's kitchen counter, shoving carrot sticks in her mouth to keep from blurting anything she shouldn't.

Lucky for her, Laurel Franklin was a master at filling silence.

"So, then I said to Georgia, 'Georgie, honey—that color isn't right for your skin tone. I'm sorry, I know you love violet, but it makes you look like a big blueberry."

Nyla nodded and chewed harder, grinding the carroty

flesh until her teeth squeaked together. Her mom glanced up from dicing onions.

"Oh, don't give me that look," she said.

Nyla froze, hand over the veggie tray. "What look?"

"The look that says you think I was too blunt." Laurel kept chopping, missing Nyla's shoulder-sag of relief. "Sometimes the kindest thing you can do is tell someone the truth. Even if it stings, even if it's not what they want to hear, it's what they *need* to hear."

Nyla swallowed hard, forcing down bits of half-chewed carrot and a building surge of panic. It didn't take a genealogist to figure out where she'd picked up the habit of running her mouth. All right, Nyla had reasons besides being a busybody. Something beyond basic impulse control, something so much worse. She knew better than most people how hiding secrets could hurt someone, hurt them badly. She'd give anything to go back in time and scream from the rooftops. To tell her mother or father or some other grownup what she knew.

But that was a long time ago. A different secret. Besides, she was doing okay. She'd managed to keep her trap shut for ten days now, and wasn't that a sign of progress?

"Aunt Nyla!"

She spun her barstool in time to catch her torpedo of a nephew in a bone-crushing hug. Someday Seth would be a surly teen too preoccupied with texting his friends to hug his aunt. Today was not that day.

"Hey, dude." She squeezed hard and let go, conscious of Leo hovering behind him. She deliberately didn't meet his eyes. "How was your math test yesterday?"

"Good! I got a hundred percent, plus two extra-credit questions."

"He must have gotten that from you, Leo," Laurel said from the other side of the counter. "Mandi used to hate math."

Nyla breathed deeply, wishing she had another carrot. She turned to fix that, snatching a handful of them from the bowl beside her. Shoving one in her mouth, she chewed and swallowed, belatedly realizing she should have spent more time on the chewing part. Half a carrot lodged in her throat and Nyla's eyes bugged.

"Hurgh. *Hurgh.*"

She tried to get air, but that made it worse. Eyes watering, she jumped off the barstool and spun it around so the back nudged her diaphragm. Her lungs burned as she ran the mental checklist for self-administered Heimlich, then leaned forward just as two hands gripped her from behind.

"Hold still." Leo's voice was low in her ear, his body warm and solid against her back.

If she weren't dying, it might feel good.

He looped his arms around her torso, hands pressed into her ribs. His fist grazed her breast and a tiny burst of electricity shot through her.

Air. I need air.

And that hand to brush my boob again.

It was an absurd thought, but her head whirled with plenty of them. Then Leo squeezed and her brain short-circuited as he pushed hard against her diaphragm.

"Urg," said Nyla as she choked up the carrot. The nub went flying across the counter, bouncing to land next to her mother's cutting board.

"Whoa." Seth gaped at her. "Are you okay?"

Nyla nodded, eyes streaming, as Leo unhanded her and took a step back. Her chest hummed where he'd touched her, and she wondered if she'd have bruises. An imprint of his hand right below her breastbone.

The thought made her shiver, or maybe that was the near-death experience.

"Oh my God." Laurel gasped and grabbed a glass out of the cupboard. "Here." She filled it with water, sloshing the liquid over the sides. "Drink this. Honey, are you all right?"

Nyla nodded and chugged the water, sputtering a little but managing to keep it down. She turned to Leo, hardly trusting herself to speak. "Thank you." The words were a croak.

"No problem." Leo's brown eyes stayed glued to her. "You sure you're okay?"

She nodded and drank more water. "Fine. Just embarrassed."

"Don't be. Things happen." His eyes didn't leave hers, and something dark and secretive passed between them. Nyla looked away first.

"I can get that, Laurel." Leo rounded the corner and stretched up to lift the big wooden serving platter out of the cupboard over the fridge. His T-shirt rode up above the waist of his jeans, showing a muscular patch of tawny abdomen that sent heat flowing to Nyla's cheeks.

What the hell was wrong with her? Since when did she ogle her sister's husband?

He hasn't been Mandi's husband for six years.

She reached for another carrot, then thought better of it and grabbed a radish instead. Maybe the spicy zing would render her speechless again.

Seth scooted up beside her and boosted himself onto the second barstool. He gave her a cautious smile. "You're sure you're okay?"

"Positive." She took a tentative nibble of the radish as she surveyed her nephew. "You're growing so fast." She ruffled his hair, the same dark shade as Leo's. Or not. She commanded herself not to think about that. "By this time next year, you'll be taller than me."

"I've grown a quarter of an inch since January," Seth boasted. "Dad measured me last night."

"That's great." Nyla folded her hands in her lap while Leo busied himself piling potato rolls onto the serving platter on the other side of the counter. "You're probably due for another growth spurt, huh?"

"I hope so." Seth stole a glance at Leo as something wistful passed over his face. "I hope I'm like my dad and not my mom. I want to be tall. I'm still shorter than most of the girls in my class."

Nyla swallowed hard and forced herself to keep a neutral expression. "That's totally normal. Girls go through puberty earlier, but boys catch up pretty quick. You'll get there."

Laurel went back to chopping onions, while Leo continued arranging the buns. If Nyla didn't know better, she'd think he was just really, really picky about the presentation of potato rolls.

"When did you hit your full height, Leo?" Nyla's mom asked.

He shrugged and kept his eyes on the buns, not looking up. Nyla was grateful. Maybe they could just avoid each other all night. "Fourteen, maybe fifteen?" Leo said. "I grew six inches between my freshman and sophomore year. My mom said she started worrying I'd eat the furniture if she ran out of food."

"There you go." Laurel smiled at Seth. "You've got plenty of time to catch up to your daddy."

Nyla breathed in and out, not trusting herself to look at anyone. Not even Seth. *Especially* not Seth. Protecting her nephew had to be her focus, which meant keeping the secret. She could do this.

Maybe she should go outside and keep her father company at the barbecue. At least he wasn't likely to pepper her with questions. Ted Franklin was a good man, a good dad, but not the most...*observant* guy on the planet.

"Hellooooo!" Mandi's familiar singsong voice rang out from the foyer, and Nyla planted her butt back onto the barstool. Then she stood up again, pretty sure Normal Nyla would greet her sister standing up.

Jesus, she was never going to pull this off.

"Hey, Duckie." Mandi tossed her sleek, dark ponytail over one shoulder and pulled her into a one-armed hug. With the other arm she balanced a lidded crockpot that smelled like smoky meat and heaven. "You look kinda red in the face. Are you coming down with something?"

"She almost choked to death." Seth's exuberance suggested it was way cooler than anything he'd seen on TV that week. "Dad saved her life."

"No kidding?" Mandi looked from her to Leo and back again. "I guess those Red Cross classes finally came in handy."

"Guess so." Leo wasn't looking at her, and Nyla wondered if he remembered the class had been a present from her. A baby shower gift, actually.

"Every parent should know basic First Aid and CPR," Nyla had told them as she handed the gift certificate to Mandi just a month before Seth made his appearance in the world. Mandi had worn a bright orange maternity dress and an exhausted, glowing smile. Leo had hovered protectively beside his wife, one hand on the small of her back.

Had Mandi known then that Seth might be someone else's?

She stole a look at her sister, hoping to God Mandi couldn't read her mind. Luckily, Mandi was focused on setting up her crockpot. "Sorry I'm late," she was saying. "We got this amazing donation from Home Depot for all these power tools for clearing the roads so we can access the water supply, but getting all that stuff over to Haiti is going to be a logistical nightmare."

Seth grabbed a carrot stick, picking up Nyla's slack. "My social studies teacher was telling me some stuff in Creole that I can use when we go there," he said. "He said he'll talk to my teacher next year about giving me extra credit if I come back and teach the sixth graders about our trip."

"Awesome," Mandi said. "You're doing it, right?"

"Totally." Seth grinned. "I always do the extra credit."

"That's my boy." Mandi stretched her hand across the counter, and mother and son exchanged the complicated high five they'd been executing since Seth was just out of diapers. "Did you tell him we got approval so you can help drill the wells?"

"Yeah. He said to make sure I drink lots of water but not the kind from the sink."

"That's what we're trying to fix," Mandi said. "Everyone should get to have clean water that's easily accessible."

Laurel smiled and nudged Mandi with her hip. "I think it's great what you're doing. Managing water systems in the U.S. is one thing, but saving the world—"

"It's not that heroic, Mom." Mandi rolled her eyes at Nyla, their private exchange. Laurel loved to boast that her babies grew up to save the planet, though it seemed truer in Mandi's case. Nyla's volunteer clinics helped seventy, eighty, maybe even a hundred people.

Mandi worked on water systems that helped thousands.

"How about you, Leo?"

"What's that?" He didn't look up from the rolls.

"Your summer plans," she asked. "Obviously, you'll fly a lot for fire season, but are you helping your mom with her remodel while Mandi and Seth are traveling?"

Leo shook his head and rearranged two of the rolls.

"Nah, it should be done by then. I'm trying to get the bike finished so it's ready once fire season's done."

"That's right, the motorcycle." Laurel looked delighted, but Mandi gave Nyla a knowing look. The inside joke was almost as old as Seth.

Leo ignored them all, intent on arranging buns. "I'm doing a three-week solo trip along the Pacific Coast Highway. Testing things out."

Mandi rolled her eyes, but there was a fondness in it. A familiarity that made Nyla's throat ache. "Test driving the Selfish Dream?" Mandi teased.

"Shellfish dream." Seth grinned at his contribution to the family joke.

"Leo's Selfish Dream, trademark, patent pending." Nyla infused her lines with as much enthusiasm as she could, slipping into her familiar role. She could do this.

"I think it's great," their mother said. "You've always been a hard worker, Leo. You've earned your me-time." She smiled at her ex-son-in-law with the same affection she'd shown the day Mandi brought him home as her date to junior prom. Even after the divorce, Laurel had been adamant that the father of her grandson was still family.

Nyla nibbled a carrot and fretted. Would that change if everyone knew? Would her mother be more or less likely to nudge Mandi to get back together with her ex?

Leo's eyes lifted to hers and held for a moment, like he heard the question and had an answer at the ready: *They can't know. No one can know.*

A knot tightened in her chest, and Nyla had a sudden

need for air. Tearing her eyes from Leo's, she stood up.

Too fast, and her barstool nearly toppled.

"Jeez, Aunt Nyla."

"Sorry." She stepped back, skirting around Leo as Mandi shot her a *what's your deal?* look. "I'm going to see if Dad needs any help with the grill."

The thought of Ted Franklin needing grilling aid— especially from her—was laughable, but no one snickered as she made a beeline for the door.

No laughter, but she could swear she felt Leo's eyes boring into her, willing her to be careful.

CHAPTER FOUR

Leo did his best to keep his eyes off Nyla throughout dinner.

It wasn't easy, and maybe it wasn't even smart. Would someone notice things were off between them? Hell, maybe they'd suspect a clandestine affair.

He started to laugh at the idea, then stopped. What was up with that flash of attraction bolting through him when he'd wrapped his arms around her? Choking was pretty much the unsexiest thing ever, and what kind of creep got turned on by administering the Heimlich?

But he had. Like things weren't awkward enough without him lusting over his ex-wife's sister.

Nyla's more than that. She's always been more than that.

"Dinner was great, guys." Mandi smiled across the patio table and set her napkin aside. Late-afternoon sun glinted off her dark waterfall of hair, and Leo remembered a time that would have stirred something inside him.

These days he felt—nothing. Not for Mandi, anyway.

"Loved the new potato salad, Mom." Nyla smiled at her mother, and something warm squeezed in Leo's chest.

A faint breeze kicked up and sent a paper napkin tumbling off the edge of the table. Nyla scrambled after it, and Leo ordered himself to stop looking at her. To quit noticing the curve of her hips in those blue cotton shorts, or the way her dark maple curls slid around her shoulders like a soft curtain.

"Whose turn is it to do the dishes?" His voice sounded weird and gruff.

"Seth's," Mandi put in, earning a groan of protest from the kid.

"No grumbling," Leo said. "Everyone else contributed to the meal. What did you do?"

His son gave him an impishly hopeful look. "Sat here looking adorable?"

"Nice try." He pointed to the kitchen. "Get to it."

"And don't just shove filthy plates into the dishwasher," Mandi added. "Rinse first."

"I *know*." Seth stood up and began gathering plates, one on top of the other, silverware separate, just like Leo had taught him. The kid was getting strong, and so damn smart it made Leo's chest sting with pride.

So what if his DNA wasn't in the mix? He was still making a difference, raising his boy to be a good man. That counted for more than fucking biology.

Why the hell was he thinking about this, anyway? It's not like he'd spent the past four years obsessing over his son's parentage.

But something about Nyla knowing brought it all to the surface. Made him wonder if he was doing the right thing keeping Seth in the dark.

Leo smiled at his son as he handed Seth his plate. Seth smiled back and moved on to Nyla.

"Don't tell anyone I didn't finish my broccoli," Nyla stage-whispered with a wink as she returned to the table and handed her plate to Seth. "Grandma won't let me have dessert."

Seth laughed and kept moving around the table. "Your secret's safe with me, Aunt Nyla."

Secrets. Leo fought the urge to grimace. Was that the fucking theme of the day?

"Thank you, sweetheart." Laurel beamed at her grandson as she handed him her plate and an empty wineglass. "I think I might have some of those coconut lime cookies in the freezer that you can take home with you. Remind me, okay?"

"Thanks, Grandma." Seth headed for the kitchen, his blue flip-flops smacking the floor.

Mandi reached across the table to grab the half-empty water pitcher. She tipped it into her glass as another breeze ruffled the daisies in a blue vase at the center of the table. "We went clothes shopping yesterday," she said, and it took Leo a second to realize she was talking to him. "He needed summer stuff, and he'd outgrown last year's sandals."

He nodded and took a sip of his water. "Shoot me the receipt and I'll add it to the check."

"Don't worry about it," she said. "You got the snow boots last winter."

Across the table, Leo caught a flicker of something from Nyla. What was that about? It had never been a secret that he paid child support. Sure, they split custody fifty-fifty, but Mandi handled things like sports fees and school clothes and Seth's phone bill, and it only seemed fair to Leo that he should kick in a little more.

Or maybe it wasn't that at all. Maybe Nyla was remembering just how *not* fair her split with Greg had been, right down to the part where the bastard stuck her with a pile of credit card debt. That split had been ugly, much uglier than the breakup between him and Mandi.

Would things have gone differently if Leo had known about the affair?

"I love that shirt he's wearing." Laurel was still chattering about Seth's new summer wardrobe, and Leo ordered himself to pay attention. "The color brings out those pretty hazel flecks in his eyes."

"Right?" Mandi raised her arms overhead, stretching like a housecat. "He picked that out himself."

"What size shoe is he wearing now?" Nyla asked.

"Nine, and still growing." Mandi sipped her wine and looked at her sister. "Isn't that usually a sign he's going to have another growth spurt?"

"It can be." Nyla leaned back in her chair a bit, and Leo tried to read the print across her T-shirt. *This nurse needs a shot.* He started to smile, then realized he should probably stop staring at the front of her shirt.

Nyla wasn't the only one having a hard time acting normal.

"…driven by an increase in testosterone," she was saying, and panic flashed through Leo as he wondered if she'd read his thoughts. But no, she was still talking about Seth and puberty. "You'll start noticing things like increased appetite, a need for more sleep, lengthening bones that make his joints stick out a little awkwardly."

"Ugh, puberty." Mandi made a face. "That means pimples and stinky socks and more Mr. Grumpypants."

"And adorable things like crushes on girls," Laurel supplied with grandmotherly optimism. "Or peach fuzz on his face or his voice changing."

Across the table, Mandi and Nyla's dad looked thoughtful. "We never went through that stuff with you two. That's the thing with girls." Ted chuckled good-naturedly as Nyla and Mandi exchanged a look that said, *"here goes Dad again."*

"I remember when my voice started cracking," Ted continued. "Thought I had throat cancer or something. Tried to convince my mom to let me stay home my whole last semester of seventh grade."

Laurel dabbed her mouth with a napkin and looked at Leo. "How old were you when your voice changed?"

Leo fixed his face in the nonchalant mask he'd perfected over the last four years. "Twelve or thirteen," he said, avoiding Nyla's eyes. "My mom got all choked up the first time my voice cracked. She insisted on recording me saying, 'I'm the man of the house.'"

The whole table laughed, but Leo felt a sharp stab in his gut. He didn't like talking about this stuff. They'd known then about his dad's cancer, but they all thought he'd beat it. He had on that round. The next time, Leo's father hadn't been as lucky.

"This water is really great," he said, picking up his glass. "What did you put in it?"

If Laurel noticed the abrupt subject change, she

didn't show it. "Mint, cucumber, and lemon," she said. "I saw it in Martha Stewart *Living*."

"It's terrific," he said, draining his glass. "Really refreshing."

"So how about pimples?" Mandi looked at him, and Leo felt a twinge of anger pinch his chest. "Nyla and I both had crappy skin in middle school. I don't remember you having zits."

For fuck's sake. Were they still having this conversation? His brain screamed out the same questions that had been bouncing around in there for four years, the questions he'd gotten good at ignoring before he blabbed everything to Nyla.

Who was the guy?

Did you know right away Seth wasn't mine?

Were you ever planning to tell me?

Leo swallowed them all back and focused on Mandi's question. "My skin was pretty bad in seventh grade," he said. "Then my mom introduced me to Clearasil and all was right with the world."

"How *is* your mom?"

God bless Laurel Franklin. Her pale blue eyes watched him with something like sympathy, and he wondered if she knew how much he hated this conversation. Why had he come today?

Nyla.

He caught her eye across the table and remembered all over again. Tearing his gaze off her, he focused back on Laurel. "My mom's good," he said. "I've almost got her kitchen done, and I'll start on the master bath next week."

"You're such a good son." Laurel smiled and refilled her water from the blue-and-white pitcher, her elegant hands so much like Nyla's. "You must have saved her a bundle doing all those renovations."

Leo shrugged and downed the rest of his water. "Bob's not much of a handyman, so I'm happy to help." His mother's second husband had many great qualities, but building things wasn't one of them.

He could see Nyla squirming in her chair across the table, but he didn't look at her. Maybe that was the trick. A lack of eye contact could minimize the risk of her exploding like a shaken bottle of soda, spewing secrets like foamy cola.

"Nyla, sweetheart, did you try that dating app I told you about?" Laurel looked hopefully at her younger daughter. "Betsy's daughter met her husband there."

"I don't think Tinder is really my thing, Mom."

"Well you're not getting any younger," she said. "If you want babies someday—"

"I think I'll go help Seth." Nyla stood and grabbed her glass, draining it in a few gulps before turning to hustle back inside. "Thanks for dinner, everyone."

A wave of murmured acknowledgments trailed after her as she vanished through the sliding door and into the dining room, making her way to the kitchen.

The second she was out of earshot, Mandi started whispering. "Did anyone else think she was acting kinda weird?"

Ted took a sip from his wife's glass, then slid an arm around her shoulders. "You know she hates it when you bring up the whole ticking clock."

"I don't think that's it." Laurel frowned. "Maybe it's the near-death experience." She smiled at Leo. "You really were a hero."

"Hardly." He could feel his ex-wife looking at him. Back in his smokejumper days, Mandi hated when people called him a hero. She wasn't a fan of the erratic schedule, the danger smokejumpers faced each time they suited up.

He hadn't quit for her, not really. Flying air tankers meant he still got to fight fires while keeping his dad's legacy alive, and yeah, he still got to be part of air attack missions. But smokejumping was something he'd willingly abandoned when marriage and fatherhood took a front seat in his life.

He ordered himself to pay attention, since the family was still chattering about Nyla.

"I don't think it's the choking upsetting her," Mandi was saying. "She's acting like she used to when she and Greg would get into a fight. She hasn't heard from him lately, has she?"

Laurel leaned in with a conspiratorial glint in her eye. "I'm not sure, but you know what Susan Miller told me last week?"

His former mother-in-law loved this stuff as much as Mandi did, and it always annoyed Leo just a little. Couldn't people mind their own business?

But Mandi leaned in, too, hanging on her mother's words. "Susan always gets the good gossip."

"She heard they're expecting," Laurel whispered.

"That Greg and Wendy were at Target two weeks ago with one of those baby registry things. The price gun doohickey?"

"People still do that?" Mandi made a face. "I figured everyone did registries online now."

"Maybe they *wanted* people to see them." Laurel's smile was knowing, and Leo felt queasy. "It would be just like Greg to go and make a big production out of—"

"Maybe I'll go see if they need help with the dishes." Leo stood up and grabbed his glass. Even awkward silence with Nyla was better than this gossipy stuff. In all these years, Leo had never gotten used to it. "Dinner was great."

He jerked open the sliding door and moved through the bright yellow dining room, past the family portrait on the wall. Nyla and Mandi as gangly teenagers, Ted and Laurel standing behind them with matching smiles. That's what Leo had hoped to have for himself. A family that stayed together no matter what. A long-lived marriage and happy home life.

How the hell could he know it was harder than it looked?

He strode into the white-tiled kitchen, breathing deeply for the first time in an hour. He was so busy moving oxygen through his lungs that it took him a second to register Seth was alone at the sink.

"Where's Nyla?"

Seth didn't answer. Leo spotted the earbuds crammed into his ears and gave one a tap.

His son looked up, then smiled and pulled out one

earbud. "Yo."

"Where'd your aunt go?"

Seth shrugged and stuffed a half-washed plate in the dishwasher. "I told her I had it covered, so she left. I think she went to pee or something."

He shouldn't go after her. Especially not if she was in the bathroom, though Leo could see she wasn't. The door was ajar, and the room was dark inside.

But the guestroom door at the end of the hall was shut tight. Had she gone in there?

He looked back at Seth. "Great job with the dishes."

"Thanks. Nyla did the cast iron pans, but I got everything else by myself."

"You even hand-washed the wineglass." He squeezed Seth's shoulder, earning himself another crooked smile from his kid. "Nice work."

"Thanks." Seth fiddled with his earbud. "Can I put this back in? Lil Pump has a new album and I was kinda in the zone."

"Sure, no prob." He glanced back down the hall at the closed bedroom door.

Stay away. Don't go there.

But his feet were already moving that direction. "I should check on her," Leo mumbled, even though Seth couldn't hear him. "Make sure she's okay after the whole choking thing."

It was a lame excuse, but Seth couldn't hear it, so what did it matter? He shuffled down the hall, telling himself he just needed to be sure she was okay, that he owed it to her to say thanks for hanging in there through dinner, through the awkward questions and prying glances.

Voices echoed from behind the closed door and Leo froze.

No, *one* voice. Nyla's. Was she on the phone?

He edged closer to the room. Her voice sounded frantic and muffled, and wasn't that a reason to worry? He only meant to lean close and listen. Just two seconds, then back out to the patio with no one else the wiser.

But his shoulder banged the door, knocking it open because apparently the damn thing wasn't latched. *Crap.* Sunlight burst at him bright and sudden, and it took him a moment to register what he was seeing.

"Nyla?"

She took two steps back and lowered the pillow from her mouth. "What are you doing?"

"What are *you* doing?" He took another step into the room, keeping his voice low in case someone came inside and needed the bathroom.

Her hair was wild and curled around her ears, and her pool-blue eyes glittered with a feverish quality. She clutched an orange-and-blue throw pillow with both hands like a drowning victim gripping a life ring. Her body radiated a nervous energy he could feel pulsing off her like heat waves.

"I'm talking into a pillow." She said it like it was the most natural thing in the world, and maybe it was for Nyla.

"This is your solution for keeping your word," he said. "Biting a bolster?"

"It's not a bolster, it's a neck roll."

"What the hell is the difference?"

"A neck roll is smaller than a bolster and why on earth are we talking about accent pillows?"

Leo nudged the door shut behind him and leaned against it, making sure no one would come barging in the way he had. "You seemed like you needed to get some words out," he said. "Pillows were a safer topic than the obvious."

Nyla looked at him, and he caught himself staring at her mouth. Had she always had such bee-stung, kiss-stung lips, or was it from smashing her face into a silk-covered hunk of foam?

Leo took a deep breath and grabbed for the leash latched to the elephant in the room. "Look, I know it's weird out there." He kept his voice low, even though he could hear Mandi and her parents chattering loudly on the back patio. "You're doing a good job."

Nyla looked uncertain. "We don't usually spend this much time talking about puberty and genetics, do we?"

"We're approaching Seth's twelfth birthday. It's normal they'd gab about that stuff."

"You don't think it's because I've given it away some-how?" Her eyes flashed electric blue, and she didn't seem to notice when the pillow fell from her grip and bounced at their feet. "Because I feel like they can see it all over my face. Mandi, my mom—hell, even my dad. I swear it's like they're reading me."

"They're not reading you," he said. "We just need to act normal."

Nyla shook her head and took a step closer, closing

the gap between them. "There is no normal now," she hiss-whispered. "Not knowing what I know, worrying about Seth. Wondering if keeping this secret could mess him up somehow."

Something about how she said it made the back of Leo's neck tingle. Or maybe that was Nyla, the way he felt her body heat, standing inches from him.

He cleared his throat and forced himself to stop thinking like that. "Is there a reason you're such a secret spiller? Something besides having Laurel for a mom?"

She flinched. Just a little, but he caught a flash of panic in her eyes. "What?" he asked. "What is it?"

"I—no one's ever asked me that before."

So there *was* a story. "Do you want to talk about it?"

She hesitated, blue eyes searching his. He watched her fingers brush her throat, her body trembling, like she couldn't figure out how to get air.

Was this what a panic attack looked like?

Leo touched her hand and felt her flinch. "Nyla? Whatever it is, you can tell me."

She dragged in a ragged breath. "When I was six, I had a sleepover with my best friend. We were putting on our pajamas when I saw bruises."

Oh, Jesus.

He took his time replying. "Someone was hitting her?"

Nyla nodded, tears glittering in her eyes. "Her father. She begged me not to tell and I didn't and *oh God, Leo*—she ended up in the ER. That was a year later. *A year.* Can you imagine the hell she went through? All because I kept a secret I shouldn't have."

"That's different, Nyla."

It was different, wasn't it? Seth wasn't in danger.

Or hell, maybe the danger just came in a different form. If Seth found out on his own, if he learned they'd hidden something this huge—

"You were six, Nyla," he said, focusing on her more immediate pain. "You can't blame yourself."

She shook her head, clearly not believing him. "I just don't want to see Seth hurt."

The urge to touch her overwhelmed him. To hold her against his chest, to stroke her hair and lend her some comfort.

Or maybe he was just a horndog. How had he never noticed how beautiful she was, how her mouth looked lush and kissable?

She licked her lips and half the blood left his brain. "How can you stand it, Leo?" she asked. "How can you sit there knowing what you know and not want to ask a million questions?"

He hesitated. "Maybe I don't want to know the answers."

He'd never voiced anything like that out loud. He couldn't believe he'd said it at all.

Nyla looked at him, assessing. "I guess I can understand that." A shock of hair fell over her eye, and Leo had the inexplicable urge to tuck it behind her ear. He shoved his hands into his pockets to keep himself from reaching for her.

She bit her lip, snapping Leo's attention to her mouth

again. For fuck's sake.

"I can see why you might feel better not knowing the who or the why," she said. "But don't you at least want the *how*?"

Leo frowned. "What, like sex positions or something?" He shook his head. "No. No way."

"That's not what I meant." Her voice had gotten louder, and she glanced at the door behind him and lowered it again. "I'm talking about the logistics. Did she know about it when she was pregnant, or figure it out after? Or maybe she doesn't know at all, but if she does, is she planning to tell you someday? Like what if Seth develops some form of Myelofibrosis like I had? It can run in families, you know, and if Seth needed a transplant or—"

"You have to quit thinking of worst-case scenarios." He stepped closer, conscious of the heat of her body. He ordered himself to stop creeping on her as he lowered his voice. "Look, there's plenty of time for us to have the tough conversations when Seth gets older. For now, can't he just enjoy his puberty?"

Nyla laughed, but the sound was brittle and a little wild. "That's just it, Leo. Twelve is the age where he'll start asking questions. He's trying to figure out where he fits. You heard him out there—'am I going to be tall like my dad, or short like my mom?'" She kept going, voice quivering on the edge of hysteria now, and Leo was starting to wonder who could hear them. "'Will I be a math geek like my father, or am I going to struggle?' What about musical talent or personality traits or his sense of place in the world? A kid this age, a sensitive kid like Seth, and what if he finds out on his own somehow, like if he does one of those tests for—"

He lunged for her mouth. Not in a surge of passion, though that changed the second their lips touched. He'd only meant to stifle her words, to get her to shut up for just a second.

Or maybe he was kidding himself, because the instant they connected, his plans screeched to a halt. Her lips parted, and the kiss shifted from a chaste press of mouths to something carnal, something hungry. His tongue grazed hers, and Nyla gave a soft moan. She arched her body against his, and Leo found himself threading his fingers into her hair, tilting her head to deepen the kiss.

She didn't fight him. She was kissing him back, kissing him like they'd done it a thousand times and still couldn't get enough.

His brain screamed a warning. *Nyla. This is Nyla!*

But the rest of him didn't listen.

How long did the kiss go on? Five seconds, or maybe five minutes. He was so dizzy that he lost track of time, lost track of anything but the heat of her body curved against his, the softness of her mouth, the sweet strawberry taste of her.

When he broke away, it felt like ripping off his arm. He drew back and peered into her eyes. Nyla stared back, her chest rising and falling like she'd sprinted laps around the neighborhood. She was looking at him as though she'd never seen him before. Maybe she hadn't.

Not like this.

He'd never seen this Nyla before, not the one standing in front of him with desire in her eyes and a fistful of his shirt in her hand.

"What the hell was that?"

Leo had no answer. "I was trying to calm you down."

Her pulse fluttered in the spot where her throat met her chin, and Leo could hear his own heart pounding in his skull. Nyla's tongue darted out to touch the edge of her lip, the spot where his lips had been just seconds before. "That's your idea of calm?"

"I may have missed the mark."

"You think?"

Leo clenched his fists and took a step back. Or tried to, anyway. His back was already against the door, and Nyla was still holding his shirt, so he slid sideways instead. "I'm sorry," he said. "I didn't mean—"

"That was—" She shook her head, looking dazed and more frantic than ever. She dropped her hand from his chest, bumping his hip with her fingers on the way down. "Wow. I don't even know what to say."

"Which I guess was the point?" He forced a hopeful smile, willing her to see this as something innocent. Something that wouldn't change things, that wouldn't alter their friendship any more than last week's bombshell had done.

Too late, screamed his brain.

Nyla touched her fingers to her lips like she was still trying to wrap her head around it all. "You *kissed* me."

"Yes."

She stared at him. "I kissed you back." Her voice was somewhere in the ballpark between bewilderment and scandal, with maybe a little *what the fuck* mixed in.

Leo just nodded. "Yeah."

Hearing it spelled out like that made it real. Leo held his breath, not sure of his next move. Nyla continued to stare. Her throat moved as she swallowed.

"I—I should go." She stepped forward, and her feet tangled in the throw pillow. She started to topple, but Leo caught her.

Her body moved against him as his hands cupped her shoulders. One second she was moving away, and the next she arched against him with a spine made of candle wax. Heat bloomed in his body as she pressed closer, an energy like nothing he'd felt before. Not with Nyla—hell, not with anyone.

She looked up with her pool-blue eyes flashing and he knew she felt it, too. She didn't step back. Just leaned into him like her body was glued against his. Her lips parted and he wasn't sure if she was going to kiss him again or tell him to go to hell.

"We can't do this," she whispered.

Leo nodded and let go of her shoulders. "Of course."

He moved aside, letting her grab hold of the knob and fling the door open like she was fleeing a house fire. There was an apt description. Everything inside him was flaming as though she'd doused it in kerosene and lit a match. Lungs burning, chest throbbing, brain flickering with little electric crackles.

He'd kissed Nyla.

Nyla, for fuck's sake.

It was wrong, the last thing they needed right now.

But as her footsteps faded down the hall, the only thing Leo could think of was doing it again.

CHAPTER FIVE

He'd kissed her.

Leo Sayre had kissed her.

The fact that her brain filled in "Leo" instead of "ex-brother-in-law" told her plenty, but not as much as the fact that she couldn't stop touching her lips. Not for hours. Days, even. She couldn't stop replaying that kiss in her brain, knowing it was silly, but urgently wanting to do it again.

Hell.

It couldn't happen again. Not with everything still up in the air with Seth and Mandi, but still. She'd never had a kiss that left her feeling like someone filled her knee joints with warm vanilla pudding.

By midway through the week, she was jumping out of her skin. When Seth texted around three on Wednesday, begging her to swing by the air base on her way home from work to grab the pill case he'd left in his dad's truck, she texted "sure!" without thinking.

Not true, she was thinking a lot. About seeing Leo again, about the way her heart thudded faster the closer she got to the airfield.

As she eased into the space beside Leo's truck, she spotted him out on the tarmac beside a big red-and-white plane with bright blue numbers on the side. He was talking with two guys she recognized as smokejumpers out of the Hart Valley base in Oregon. One of them waved as she strode toward them on shaky legs.

"Hey, Nyla." Tony pulled her in and gave her a tight squeeze. "I was hoping I'd see you. Kayla says hi."

"Tell her hi back." Nyla pushed her hair off her forehead, avoiding Leo's eyes. "How are the wedding plans?"

Tony flashed a sheepish look. "Does it make me an asshole if I say I'm not totally sure?"

The tall guy beside him—Grady?—snorted and slugged his teammate in the arm. "It makes you smart." Grady grinned. "A wise man stays out of the way unless he's needed. You're still an asshole, but not for that."

The two guys cracked up as Leo met her eyes and nodded toward his truck. "You're here for Seth's pills?"

"Yeah, sorry." Why did her face feel hot? It never had before with Leo, not like this. Maybe she was coming down with something. "I can grab them myself if you give me the key."

"I'll come with you." He nodded at the other two guys. "I was just showing off the new plane, but we're done here."

"Pretty sweet plane." Tony patted the aircraft's big white belly. "You should get him to take you for a ride sometime."

Nyla's cheeks flamed, and she dropped her car keys on the ground. Scrambling to scoop them up, she noticed her hands trembling. Even Leo looked uncomfortable as he led her over to his truck.

"I swear that wasn't a dirty joke," he murmured once

they were out of earshot. "The 'take her for a ride' thing? I didn't breathe a word about—"

"I know." She chewed her lip as he unlocked the truck door and rummaged on the passenger seat for Seth's little blue pill case. "And it's not like they can tell by looking at us that we made out like teenagers."

Wild, irresponsible, lust-drunk teenagers who might both be wishing we could do it again.

Leo glanced at her like he'd read her thoughts. "You want to talk about it?"

Of course she didn't want to talk about it. But like always, the words came bubbling out of her throat. "Look, I appreciate what you were doing, trying to keep me from flipping out," she whispered frantically, even though they were well out of earshot of the other guys. "It was an act of mercy and I'm really grateful, and just because I kissed you back doesn't mean anything, and I really don't think we should make a big deal out of this or go trying to analyze it or lie awake night after night thinking about it or anything ridiculous like that."

She clamped her mouth shut, willing herself to be quiet. For God's sake, she was making this worse.

A slow, easy grin spread over Leo's face. "You done?"

She nodded, pressing her lips together so she couldn't say anything else.

"Good." Leo took a deep breath. "I just want to state for the record that it wasn't a pity kiss. I wanted to kiss you. Hell, I want to kiss you now, if we're being honest."

A flood of heat moved through her, though Nyla fought to ignore it. All right, she wanted it, too. *Badly.*

Just looking at his mouth made her ache to taste him again.

But no, that wasn't an option. "We shouldn't do that."

Leo grinned. "I wasn't going to. It was just a figure of speech."

"Right." Nyla bit her lip. "Okay, so we'll just pretend it never happened."

"Not sure about that." Leo shrugged. "I probably can't forget about it, but I won't bring it up again."

"Fair enough."

He placed the pill container in her hand and closed her fingers around it, shooting sparks all the way to her elbow. "Thank you for doing this," he said. "He's having a harder time lately remembering things. Might have to step up the consequences."

"Go easy on the kid," she said. "It's tough bouncing back and forth between two homes."

"Yeah, I imagine." A flicker of sadness lit his eyes, and Nyla felt guilty for bringing it up at all.

And for what she knew she needed to say, even if she didn't want to. "Look, I think we should tell Mandi."

Leo's brow furrowed. "About the kiss?"

"No. No! Of course not. Definitely not." *Good God.* "About Seth's paternity. It's only going to be a bigger issue as he gets older, and don't you think we should get all the information from Mandi and make a plan now before it becomes an even bigger, hairier secret? I mean, imagine her finding out or Seth finding out some other way, and how painful it would be for him if he knew you'd kept it from him and you weren't prepared to—"

"Okay."

Nyla blinked. "Okay?" She must have heard wrong. "Wait, you're agreeing?"

He sighed and dragged a hand through his hair. "Not completely, but I see your point. And I also know you're going to explode if we don't get this out in the open, so yeah...let's tell Mandi."

She took a shaky breath, recalibrating her thoughts. "I was sure you'd say no."

He smiled. "And yet you still asked?"

"Well, yeah. It seemed like the right thing to do."

"And we're all about doing the right thing." His voice held no trace of bitterness, but Nyla couldn't help the way her gut shifted with unease.

That was true of Leo's whole life. Giving up his smokejumper career for family. Getting his pilot's license because he still needed to do his part fighting wildfires and saving lives. Taking over his father's air tanker company a few years after the old man died to keep his father's legacy alive.

All that before Nyla even knew he was raising a child who wasn't biologically his. How much could one man sacrifice for family, for strangers, for the greater good?

A lump lodged in her throat and she had to swallow it back before she could speak again. "You're sure?" she asked. "About telling Mandi. I don't want to force your hand."

"I've been thinking about it." He sighed and leaned back against the truck. "I guess I can't keep burying my head in the sand. There's no way around it. It's going to come up eventually, and it'll be better if I have all the facts."

"Wow, that's…that's great, Leo." She swallowed hard, trying to look anywhere but his mouth. "You're so brave."

"Hardly." He snorted and kicked a pebble with the toe of his boot. It went skittering off toward the hangar, bouncing when it hit the side of the building. "She's gonna freak out."

Nyla opened her mouth, ready to defend her sister. Then she closed it again because yeah, he was probably right. "Do you want me to be there?"

Leo's brows lifted. "What, you mean when I tell her?"

"Yeah. Maybe it would make things easier for both of you."

His brow furrowed as he thought it over. "Maybe."

Her gaze snagged on his mouth, and dammit, she was thinking about that kiss again.

She tore her eyes away, determined to be an adult for this conversation. "It's going to be awkward enough to bring it up," she said. "If I'm there, at least you can use me as the catalyst. Talk about how you found out and then how *I* found out and how it's just going to keep getting bigger. I can explain about the medical side of things, in case she denies it."

She couldn't deny it, not really. Not based on the medical evidence Nyla had seen. There was no possible way Seth was Leo's biological kid. It was as simple as that. And Mandi would have the answers about how that came to be.

"That makes sense." Leo shoved his hands in his pockets. "Bringing it up with you there should go a little smoother. She'll be less likely to lash out or play it off as some big misunderstanding."

Again, Nyla ached to defend her sister. To insist Mandi was calm and cool and rational.

But yeah, being backed into a corner never brought out Mandi's best side. She reacted like a trapped animal, feral and defensive. Her sister's passion was one of the things Nyla loved best about Mandi, but it was also the thing that made her a bit...unpredictable.

Leo was staring off into the distance, his brown eyes troubled. Nyla hesitated, then reached out and touched his arm.

A mistake. Her whole body lit up, buzzing with an unfortunate mix of lust and electrified nerve endings. She drew her hand back and stuffed it in her back pocket.

"Hey," she said. "It'll be okay, I promise."

He sighed. "I'm sure you're right."

He didn't sound sure. Was it the prospect of confronting his ex-wife, or the fear of what he might learn?

Or that he'd kissed his ex-wife's sister. God, how awkward.

His gaze swung back to hers. "I almost forgot. I ran into Greg yesterday."

Nyla flinched. "Speaking of awkward encounters with exes?"

"Yeah, sorry. He asked me to say hi."

"Hi." Nyla gave a goofy little wave to prove how

totally-cool-and-not-weird-at-all this was. The trembling fingers gave her away, so she shoved her hand back in her pocket. "How's he doing?"

"Good." Leo seemed to hesitate. "He had Wendy with him."

There was something he wasn't saying. Something about her ex-boyfriend's new wife, which Nyla was absolutely, totally cool with. One hundred percent.

All right, she was still a little bitter it took him nine years to cut her loose. Nine years of waiting for a proposal, being certain they were almost there. She didn't regret giving him the ultimatum.

She only regretted it took so long for her to open her eyes.

Greg, on the other hand…well, he'd taken a lot less time to recover from the breakup. He'd moved in with Wendy just four months after his split with Nyla.

"I guess when you know, you know," she said now to Leo, trying to play it cool. "I hope they're very happy together."

"Yeah." Leo still had that *sick to his stomach* look. It was the same one he'd worn the day he had to tell Seth his hamster, Helga, had gone missing while Seth was at summer camp. They'd found her later, curled up sleeping at the bottom of the hamper, but the five days before that had been hell. Delivering bad news ripped Leo's guts out, and Nyla could see he had something bad on his mind.

"What?" she asked. "What is it?"

He met her eyes and took a deep breath. "She's

pregnant. Wendy's pregnant."

Nyla let the words wash over her, gauging her own reaction. She waited for the sting, for the deep ache of regret.

She only felt...numb.

"I'd heard rumors," Leo continued, looking guilty. "But this was the first time seeing with my own eyes. You okay?"

"Yeah. Yes, of course." Nyla curled her nails into her palms. Tried to, anyway. Since her hands were shoved in her pockets, she only managed to grab her own butt.

"It's fine," she said, extracting her hands from her jeans. "I'm happy for them. I really am."

"Yeah?" Leo looked dubious. "If karma exists, the kid will get Greg's nose and Wendy's weird forehead."

Nyla laughed and pushed her hair back behind her ears. "That's Botox, I think," she said. "Wendy's forehead. Greg's nose is just genetics, so odds are good that'll get passed on."

And now they were back to discussing DNA. Had conversations always circled that direction and she'd just never noticed? Or maybe it was her doing, her guilty conscience colliding with her habit of running her mouth.

"I'm glad you're telling Mandi," she said softly. "It's the right thing to do."

"*We're* telling Mandi." Leo gave a funny smile and pushed off the side of the truck. "When should we do it?"

"How about Friday? Seth's going straight to that

ballgame when you drop him at Mandi's, and wasn't he staying the night with your mom?"

"That could work." Leo scratched his chin. "My mom and Bob are taking him to a car show in Lupineville, so there's no risk he'll come home at some awkward moment."

"So Friday works."

He nodded. "And you'll already be at Mandi's for your clothing swap."

"Exactly." Funny how they knew each other's schedules, from Seth's weekend plans to which night she and Mandi had their seasonal clothing exchange. She'd never realized just how tangled up their lives were.

Which was one more reason she should absolutely not tangle tongues with Leo again. Not ever.

She stepped back and yanked open her car door. Sliding into the driver's seat, she set her nephew's pill case on the passenger seat and jammed the key into the ignition.

Leo caught the car door with one hand and smiled down at her. "Thanks for agreeing to do it with me."

He must have registered Nyla's quick flicker of surprise, because he added, "Telling Mandi. It'll definitely go better with you there."

"No worries." She turned the key and felt the engine purr to life. So did her stereo, blasting the cheerful chorus notes from Olly Murs's song "Kiss Me."

Nyla smacked the power button, silencing it. She could feel Leo's eyes on her, feel her cheeks flushing with heat.

"So anyway," she began, not sure what she meant to say next.

"Great song." Leo patted the car door and stepped back. "Drive safely."

"You, too." She cleared her throat. "Fly safely, I mean. Are you taking the new plane out?"

"Soon."

"Okay. I hope it goes well."

She dared to meet his eyes and wished she hadn't. There was heat there, simmering just under the surface. She recognized it because she felt it, too.

Leo took another step back. "See you Friday," he said. "Thanks again, Nyla."

She nodded, not trusting her voice as she pulled the car door shut and peeled out of the parking lot. She kept her eyes on the road, not daring a glance in her rearview mirror.

That's where Leo belonged, in the past. Mandi's past, not Nyla's future. That's all they could be to each other.

She took a deep breath and hit the gas.

• • •

"Ohh, I've wanted this top since you bought it." Mandi stripped off her pale blue concert tee and tossed it onto the bed, snatching the cute white ruffled top Nyla had pulled from the back of her closet that morning. "What's wrong with it?" Mandi asked with her head wrenched halfway between hem and neckline.

"It always looked weird with my arms." Nyla reached

over to help her sister tug the top down, then adjusted the ruffles at Mandi's shoulders. "These floofy bits just looked like wings springing out of my biceps."

"I see what you mean." Mandi turned to study her reflection in the mirror. "I might like it anyway."

"It looks good on you." Nyla turned to paw through the colorful heap on the bed, determined to find something good in her sister's pile of castoffs.

Bike shorts, no. Jeans that hugged Mandi's butt perfectly but would make Nyla look like a sausage squished from its casing? Definite nope. Something lacy and sexy and…no way.

She tossed the nightie like it had cooties, eyes averted in case Mandi looked at her. Her sister could always read her, and right now, Nyla had to keep the book cover shut tight.

"This is pretty." She picked up a flowery dress she'd admired since the day Mandi wore it home from her first volunteer trip to Haiti. The pink and orange flowers rioted against a backdrop of teal, and it was so not Nyla's style.

"That would look great on you." Mandi pawed through her pile and came up with a pair of ballet flats. "Try these."

Nyla tugged her shirt off but kept her jeans on. Leo would be here any minute with Seth, so she'd rather keep this quick. Pulling the dress on over her head, she tugged it into place and turned to the mirror.

"Oooh, I love it." Mandi adjusted the sash at Nyla's waist, turning the bright band of fabric so it tied at the hip. "I always wore it like this."

Nyla turned sideways, admiring the flow of the fabric and the cheerfulness of the pattern. "I like it better in back." She spun the sash around, then turned the other way.

"Suit yourself." Mandi plucked another top out of the pile as Nyla peeled off the dress and folded it neatly into her "maybe" stack. Her stomach gurgled with nerves, or maybe hunger. She hadn't been able to eat all afternoon, worried about how this conversation would unfold with Mandi.

Would her sister deny it? Get upset?

Or maybe there'd be some relief in finally having the cat out of the bag.

Voices at the other end of the house jerked Nyla out of her thoughts. Spinning around, she kicked Mandi's bedroom door shut and scrambled for a top.

Mandi laughed and took her time locating her T-shirt. "Guess they're early." She pulled the top over her lacy white bra, comfortable in her own skin. "Want to say hi before Seth takes off again?"

"I'll be right out." Nyla didn't meet her sister's eyes as she pulled her own shirt into place. Her hands were shaking, which was ridiculous. This wasn't even her secret.

Or maybe it was the thought of seeing Leo again, wondering if her sister would be able to see right through her. Through him. Was she more worried about the paternity issue, or that kiss?

Voices echoed from the living room, Leo's firm

baritone mixing with Seth's cheerful banter. As Nyla glanced at the door, she heard her sister's voice join the fray.

"Hey, sweetie. Got a kiss for your mom before you race out of here like the house is on fire?"

"Mom, I've gotta go." An obedient smack told Nyla that Seth had indulged his mom's request. "Brandon's gonna be here in two minutes and I need to find my green shirt."

"I just folded it," Mandi called. "It's in the pile on your dresser."

Nyla took a deep breath and grabbed the doorknob. As she pulled it open, Seth rushed past.

"Hey, buddy," she called.

Seth turned and flashed a broad grin. "Hey, Aunt Nyla." He squeezed her in a tight hug that took her breath away. "I didn't know you were here."

"Just hanging out with your mom."

And getting ready to have a conversation about your DNA.

She took a deep breath, willing herself to keep the words locked up tight. As she extricated herself from the hug, she prayed he couldn't see it on her face. "You heading out already?"

"Yeah, Brandon's mom's taking us to Poppy's Pizza for dinner before the game." He darted into his room, then popped out seconds later with a wad of green fabric in his fist. "Gotta go."

"I love you, kiddo."

She moved into the living room as Seth sprinted past.

"Love you, too."

And then he was out the door.

She turned in time to see Mandi regarding Leo with a friendly but perplexed look. "Did you need something, Leo?"

Leo nodded once, looking like he'd rather be anywhere but in his ex-wife's living room. Nyla glanced away, not daring to make eye contact. She could feel herself itching to defuse the tension, to exhale all her secrets in a long, slow squeal like air leaking from a balloon.

"Oh!" Mandi clapped her hands, jolting Nyla's gaze back to the pair of them. "Actually, could I borrow you both for a second? It'll be quick, I promise."

Leo shoved his hands in his pockets. "What's up?"

Mandi rushed past him, hands flying as she cleared knickknacks off her sofa table. "I need to move the couch. My new one gets delivered tomorrow, and this thing weighs a ton."

Nyla dared a glance at Leo and wished she hadn't. His broad chest stretched the front of his shirt, a glorious billboard for the words "Hart Valley Smokejumpers." That was the crew out of Oregon, not even Leo's base, but everyone in the smokejumper world knew everyone else.

Stop staring, Nyla.

She yanked her gaze from his chest to his face, eyes locking with his. Half the blood in her body rushed from her brain to parts she'd never previously been aware of in the presence of her ex-brother-in-law.

But she was aware of them now. Aware of so many things that had flown right past her for years.

Leo cocked his head like he'd read her mind. He offered a small smile, then glanced at Mandi. Her back was still turned as she bustled around her living room, moving plants and books and her little tabletop water fountain.

"Sure," Leo said slowly. As his gaze swung back to Nyla's, he gave a resigned shrug. "Let's do this."

CHAPTER SIX

Leo picked up one end of the couch as Nyla grabbed the other. He tried to catch her eye as a curl fell over her forehead, but she blew it back and glanced away quickly.

All right, it was probably best if they didn't look at each other. He could see that.

"Sorry it's so heavy." Mandi bustled into the space between them, doing her best to lift the sofa from the middle. "I just need to get it into the office to make room for the new couch."

"No prob." Leo grunted and shifted his grip. Damn, the thing weighed a ton. "I'll go backward, 'kay?"

He turned to the side, stepping around the coffee table as he backed his way toward the hall. Nyla gritted her teeth and followed, while Mandi kept chattering between them. "It's a sofa bed, that's why it's so heavy. Oh! Hang on, it's coming unfolded."

Leo paused and braced his shoulder against the wall. He caught Nyla watching him and saw the strained look on her face. He'd made a point to bear most of the weight himself, so it must be the tension getting to her. The heaviness on her shoulders, the burden of holding back his secret.

Hell. Maybe he should get this over with.

"Uh, Mandi." He adjusted his grip again, taking more

of the bulk as his ex-wife fussed with the latch on the hide-a-bed. "There's something I wanted to ask you about. It's funny, actually—"

"Damn it, I can't get this thing hooked." Mandi spit a hunk of hair out of her mouth. "Sorry, you can put that down."

"Right." Leo started to set the sofa at his feet, Nyla bending in sync with him. He glimpsed away from the lush view down the front of her shirt, her breasts warm and round and—

"Wait, no, hang on!" Mandi waved a hand. "I can't reach it when it's on the floor like that. Could you lift it again?"

With a grimace, he heaved the sofa up and glanced at Nyla. "You doing okay?"

She nodded, though the look on her face was less certain. "I'm fine. I think you've got most of the weight."

He braced himself against the wall as Mandi pushed hard against the middle of the sofa. "Dammit," she muttered, shoving again. "Maybe if we turn it sideways? Nyla, set your end down and move over there with Leo so he's not stuck holding the whole thing."

Nyla looked like she'd rather pour hot soup in her ear, but she didn't argue. Just set down her end of the couch and moved to where Leo stood wedged against the wall. Slipping into place between him and Mandi, she offered an awkward smile and grabbed the edge of the couch.

"Hey, Mandi." She didn't wait for her sister to look up. Just forged ahead as she got a solid grip on the leg of the sofa. "Did I tell you I went to Leo's house that day he had surgery? He had a pretty bad drug reaction and—"

"There! Got it." Mandi flipped a shock of mahogany hair off her forehead and offered an apologetic smile. "I love that you're looking after Leo." She dusted her hands on her jeans and reached for the center of the sofa again. "Every family needs a nurse who makes house calls."

Okay, so she was listening. Mandi had always been good at multitasking, so maybe this could work. Just slip it into conversation casually, keeping it low-key. He could do this.

Nyla shot him a *now what?* look, so Leo took the lead again.

He cleared his throat. "Remember when Seth was in the hospital?"

"God, what a nightmare." Mandi moved around to the other end of the sofa and hefted it up, throwing Leo off balance. Nyla, too, since she toppled sideways. He couldn't catch her with both hands still on the sofa, so he angled sideways to let her fall softly against him. Her body crashed against his bicep, which was hopefully better than his elbow.

"Oof." Nyla put a hand on his chest, lingering there a little longer than necessary. "Sorry."

"S'okay," he managed, forgetting for a moment what he'd been talking about.

Seth in the hospital, right. "So when the doctors thought he might need surgery, they suggested I donate blood," Leo continued. "I guess that's standard procedure."

"God, I hated seeing him like that." Mandi shook her head and started walking the sofa forward. Leo pushed off the wall and moved backward, following his ex-wife's lead.

"Those awful tubes snaking out of him," Mandi continued as they trudged toward the stairs. "I hated how it happened when I was traveling for—"

"Yeah, that sucked." Probably a dick move to gloss over her maternal pain, but come on already. This segue wasn't going the way he'd hoped.

Leo kept moving backward, glancing over his shoulder to see where the stairs were. "So anyway—"

"Sorry, hold up," Nyla squeaked. "I'm getting pinched off here."

Sure enough, she was slowly being squished between the wall and the bottom of the sofa. He started to pull back, but Nyla dropped to her knees in front of him.

"Um, Nyla…"

"Hang on."

Dear God, what was she—oh, right. She ducked under the couch and slid between his feet. Some part of her body brushed his thigh, and he ordered himself not to look down. Not to think about the awkward pelvic thrust he was currently performing for the sake of balancing the load.

"Nyla?"

"There!" She popped up on the other side of the sofa and grabbed the edge of it. "I'm good, keep going."

Mandi frowned. "You okay, Duckie?" Her forehead creased as she studied her sister. "You look a little flushed."

"I'm fine, I'm good, I'm great!" Nyla's smile wobbled, so Leo tore his eyes off her, needing to focus.

He also needed to turn the sofa so they could make it up the first four stairs to the landing. "We've gotta flip it on its side, okay?"

Both women nodded, so Leo braced his weight against the wall and adjusted his grip. "Ready? One, two, three..."

He gave a quick heave and turned the sofa. One leg caught on the banister and he grunted as he tried to free it. "Hang on."

Nyla staggered beside him. "What if I move over here?"

She edged closer, and Leo ignored the soft brush of hair on his forearm. "Yeah, that's better." He rested one sofa leg on the banister, turning the couch the rest of the way on its back.

Too quick, since a cushion flew off and bounced against Nyla's chest.

He grabbed for it. "Shit." His hand grazed her breast and he jerked back like he'd been burned. "Sorry."

Nyla's blue eyes flashed as she gave a sharp intake of breath. "No problem," she squeaked.

Dammit. This was never going to work if they kept getting distracted by each other's proximity. By the heat of one another's bodies.

Or maybe that was just him. Leo shoved the cushion back into place, his gaze skittering away from her.

Fuck. Where was he?

"So, the hospital." He cleared his throat and picked up the sofa again. One step backward, then two, he moved slowly up the stairs. The heel of his boot caught the edge of a tread, and he strained to keep his balance as he overcorrected. "The doctor started talking about blood types and—"

"Whoa, whoa, hold on a sec." Mandi gasped, and for an instant, Leo thought his job was done. She'd guessed what he'd been driving at and she could take it from here with an explanation.

"I'm losing my grip." Mandi winced as her knees started to buckle. "Hang on, let me adjust."

"I'll get under it again." Nyla ducked back down, bracing the sofa from underneath. "Mandi, you've got more of the weight being down at the bottom. I'll support it from here."

Hell, Leo should have thought of that. He'd figured he was taking the brunt of it going backward, but he'd forgotten how weight shifted at an angle like this. "Want to switch spots?" he called to Mandi.

"I'm fine," she said, though her voice was a little weak.

"I've got it, I've got it." Nyla's voice echoed from crotch level, and Leo glanced down to see her face-to-face with his...not face.

Fuck.

She grinned up at him and his goddamn heart melted. Dragging his eyes off her, he gripped the sofa harder as he met Mandi's gaze again. "You good?"

His ex-wife flashed a crooked smile. "Sorry this is

such a pain. I really appreciate the help."

"No problem." Maybe he should shut his trap for now. They'd be at the top of the stairs soon, and the office was right around the corner. This conversation might go better once they stopped moving.

He took another step backward, taking it slow as Mandi held her end and Nyla crawled along beneath it, sofa balanced on her spine. Leo kept moving, kept rehearsing the words in his head.

"I was wondering how our kid came to have someone else's DNA?"

"What were you up to that autumn nine months before Seth came along?"

"I couldn't help noticing that—"

"So, anyway," Nyla continued, voice echoing from somewhere near his feet. "Like I was saying earlier, Leo had this really bad drug reaction."

"Oh yeah." Mandi flashed him a concerned look. "Are you okay?"

"Fine." He stepped backward again, glancing behind him to see where the landing was. Fuck, six more steps.

Nyla kept going, crawling up the stairs at his feet as she balanced the sofa on her back like some kind of weird turtle. A weird turtle with tousled curls and blue eyes and a shirt gaping open in front.

She flashed him another grin, this one a little shaky, and kept going. "Percocet." She shifted the weight on her back and something clattered to the floor. Probably a picture off the wall or an old remote falling out of the couch cushions. Nyla ignored it and kept going. "It does crazy things to some people, and you know how you see those YouTube videos sometimes of people getting loopy and weird when they're on pain meds? It was like that, only…well…"

Only what? As she trailed off, Leo stumbled on the next step. Was he supposed to fill in the blank?

He glanced down, ready to take his cue from her. Nyla was staring at something on the stair tread in front of her. Something purple and oblong and—

"Uh, Mandi?" She glanced over her shoulder toward her sister. "Do you have a purple vibrator?"

Mandi gasped. "Oh my God, are you serious?"

She let go of the sofa, diving for the object tumbling down the steps toward her. Leo staggered, bracing himself against the handrail to keep his balance. The sofa tilted, falling heavier on Nyla's back.

"Ooof." She grunted and pushed back against the added weight. As she moved, her hair snagged on his wristwatch. "Ow."

"Shit, sorry." Leo hefted the sofa in time to see Mandi snag the purple vibrator off a lower step.

"Sorry, sorry." Mandi shoved it in her back pocket, one hand still gripping the bottom of the sofa. She gave him a pained look. "Can we pretend that didn't happen?"

"Yeah, sure." He'd prefer to pretend this whole thing wasn't happening. What was he thinking, trying to have this conversation while moving a goddamn couch?

From somewhere below, Nyla shouted words of encouragement. "Just two more stairs."

Leo shifted his weight, arms flexing as he took another step back. He could almost drag the whole thing himself at this point. Maybe that would be better, just get this over with and finish the conversation later.

Another step back. As his heel hit the top of the landing, he breathed a sigh of relief.

"Oh shit." Mandi yelped, eyes flying wide as the sofa started to slip. "Nyla, get out!"

Nyla gave a startled squeak as the sofa lurched. Good God, she'd be squished like a bug.

He didn't think. Just gave a mighty heave, dragging the whole thing off her like the goddamn Hulk as Mandi gave a flailing shove from below. "Nyla, move!"

"Oh God." She scrambled toward him, crawling like a frantic animal.

But there was nowhere to go. No space between him and the wall, and he couldn't move back without crushing her.

"Mandi, you got it?" he wheezed, struggling to drag the couch upward.

"I'm trying, I can't get a grip."

Nyla scrambled toward him with panicked eyes. Another squeak as she charged ahead on all fours. In a split second, he realized their only option. As he widened his stance, Nyla burst through the space between his legs.

"OhGodohGodohGod."

Leo swayed, determined not to drop the couch, not to lose his balance, not to land on Nyla's back in the world's most awkward game of horsey.

"Go, go, go," Mandi urged, and Leo wasn't sure if she meant him or Nyla.

He heaved up his end of the sofa and lumbered back. Too fast, he toppled backward. He couldn't tell where Nyla was, if she'd cleared the space behind him. He made a split-second decision to roll sideways so he wouldn't land on her.

Too late, he realized his mistake.

In slow motion, the couch came down. It teetered in midair for the briefest second, then toppled with one leg aimed straight for his crotch.

"Fuuuuuck." Leo howled as the weight came down hard on his nuts. He crumpled in on himself, couch forgotten as it went sliding back down the stairs.

"Oh my God, Leo!" Mandi ducked, flattening herself against the wall. She called out to Nyla. "Duckie, are you hurt?"

"I'm fine." Nyla scrambled toward him, concern etched on her brow as she peered down at him. "Leo, say something."

"Fuck!" Stars flickered behind his eyes as he tried to catch his breath. Good Lord, why did getting nailed *there* have to hurt this much?

"Let me see." Nyla reached for him as Leo struggled to sit up. He'd rather curl into a fetal position, but he had to make sure the couch couldn't fall on anyone else.

Mandi came charging up the stairs, eyes sweeping between them. "Are you o—*oh!*"

She pitched forward, toe catching the tangled pile of limbs at the top of the stairs. Down she came, landing on her sister. Nyla winced and threw her body over Leo, shielding him from the brunt of it.

His nuts throbbed and he wondered if he might black out.

"Leo, say something," Nyla ordered. "Can you talk?"

"Christ, my nuts."

Mandi made a choking sound as Nyla slid under him so his head was in her lap. His blood *whooshed* in his ears, and oddly enough, the pain ebbed a little. For the moment, all he could see was her. Nyla with her soft hair, peering down at him, Nyla with the undersides of her breasts straining against her T-shirt.

Concern filled her blue eyes. "You're too pale, Leo."

He tried to grin, but it felt more like a grimace. "You'd be pale, too, if a hide-a-bed crushed your junk."

"I'm so sorry," Mandi panted. "It's not serious, is it?" She gave a strained little laugh. "I mean, it's not like he's never been hit in the nuts before, but—"

"Stop it!" Nyla put a hand on his brow and glared at her sister. "Testicular trauma can lead to scar tissue that hinders sperm production or even result in the loss of testes and cause infertility and *ohmygod* Leo—say something! Are you okay?"

Crap, she must've seen something in his eyes. The strain of struggling not to pass out or throw up or kiss her again like he'd been dying to for days. The dizziness was getting to him, and it might have nothing to do with getting nailed in the nuts.

He licked his lips, figuring he needed to answer. "Yeah."

It came out an unconvincing croak, and Nyla's brow creased. "I'm serious, Leo. An injury like this isn't something to laugh about."

What had she said about infertility? He'd gotten lost in the words, or maybe that was Nyla's eyes. Had he ever seen this exact shade of blue? Maybe once, flying over the Cascade Mountains. God, his crotch hurt, but looking up into Nyla's sweet, lovely face with her palm on his cheek—

"'S'okay," he managed to wheeze, forcing a small smile so she'd know he wasn't dying. "Pretty sure my junk still works."

Because of course he felt twinges *down there*, and not just the painful kind. The kind that said, "hello, pretty lady with your hand dangerously close to my cock." He was a red-blooded man with his head in the lap of a beautiful woman. If he was dying, this would be one helluva way to go.

Nyla frowned. "We should get you to the hospital. If there's damage, you could lose any chance of ever fathering a child someday."

Mandi made a soft sound. "Well, there's Seth…"

She trailed off as they both stared at her. Mandi's brow furrowed as her gaze darted from him to Nyla and back again. "What?" Her voice sounded strained. "What just happened here?"

Leo groaned. "That didn't go like I planned."

He closed his eyes as he willed himself to pass out.

CHAPTER SEVEN

Mandi sat frozen beside her on the sofa, face cupped in her hand. Nyla held her sister's other hand, too stunned to offer much more.

On Nyla's other side, Leo clutched a bag of frozen peas to his groin. His clenched jaw, the rigid posture, told Nyla plenty about how he was handling this.

"Explain the last part again." Nyla shifted on the couch, making it teeter. They hadn't moved it from its landing spot at the bottom of the steps, and she was pretty sure a leg had come off. "Say it slowly this time," she said. "I couldn't understand when you were crying."

Mandi took a shaky breath. "Which part?" She spoke the words into her lap, face still smashed against her palm. "The part where I was a cheating whore, or the part where I screwed up my marriage?"

"Quit it." Nyla squeezed her sister's hand, then reached over to adjust the ice pack on Leo's groin.

She stopped herself just in time, grimacing as she avoided his gaze. For God's sake, this wasn't the hospital, and he definitely wasn't her patient.

She drew her hand back as Leo gave her a pained look.

With heated cheeks, Nyla turned back to her sister. "How could you not know who fathered your own child?"

"I didn't know, okay?" Mandi sniffed and lifted her head to meet Nyla's eyes. "I swear I didn't know. I mean, I had an idea it was possible, but—"

"But you didn't think to mention that to me?" Leo frowned and Nyla fought the urge to run for a fresh ice pack. He'd refused medical help and insisted there was no real damage. With that reassurance, his testes were the least of their concerns.

"You could have told me," Leo said with gravel in his voice. "Given me some inkling there was even a question about it."

"I was so ashamed." Mandi gave a hiccupping sob and drew her hand back to wipe her eyes with her sleeve.

Nyla wanted to reach for her again, to comfort her sister if she could. But that didn't feel right. Not with Leo in pain beside her, reeling from blows both physical and emotional.

She assumed so, anyway. He hadn't said a whole lot. Shock, probably, so it was up to her to ask questions. To get to the bottom of Mandi's story, however long it took.

"Explain how it happened," Nyla said. "In detail this time."

Mandi took a deep breath and closed her eyes. "I met Johan on that medical mission to Uganda." Her voice shook a little, but she kept going. "That two-week trip in September. You remember that one where all the flights got screwed up and—"

"Get to the part about screwing some other guy." Leo gritted his teeth and adjusted the ice pack.

Mandi flinched. She looked ten years older than she

had at the start of this conversation, and Nyla felt torn between sympathy and anger.

She dared a glance at Leo, and another thread of emotion wrapped itself snug around her heart. This had to be hard to hear. Harder still with his testicles throbbing. Should she insist on going to the hospital? Get him another pack of peas?

He met her eyes and shook his head, reading her thoughts.

Nyla folded her hands in her lap as Mandi spoke again.

"Things had been rough between us for a while, Leo," she said softly. "You remember that. We'd been growing apart, and you were still smokejumping and gone for weeks at a time and I was so lonely. *So lonely*, and I know that's no excuse, but when I met Johan on the flight over, I just felt…well, it happened."

"It happened." Leo snorted. "What, the flight attendant bumped you with the beverage cart and knocked you onto his dick?"

Mandi flinched again. "It wasn't on the plane. It was—well, it doesn't matter. It was only one time. Once, and I never saw him again."

Nyla took a few breaths, pushing back the urge to ask more questions. This was Leo's life. Leo's concern. She should shut up and be here for moral support.

She stole another glance at him. Leo stared straight ahead, gaze fixed on the framed photo hanging crookedly at the bottom of the stairs. A family photo, one of several Mandi had left up after the divorce. Seth sat wide-eyed and grinning, small hands gripping a plate that held a lopsided birthday cake. The six candles, the gap of missing front teeth, they all seemed like relics of a past life.

Nyla took a steadying breath and resisted the urge to put a hand on Leo's knee. To pull his head into her lap the way she had at the top of the stairs. God, it felt good to comfort him. To feel needed and helpful and close to the man she'd known nearly half her life.

Stop thinking about that.

She cleared her throat. "So this encounter, it was unprotected?" She flinched a little at her own words, but someone had to ask, and it may as well be a nurse. "What about STDs? Could you have passed anything along to Leo?"

Leo tensed beside her as Mandi shook her head. "We used a condom." She winced. "It was in his wallet, and I know you teach all your sex-ed kids how that's not the best place to store them. I guess that's how it happened."

"Fucking great," Leo muttered.

Mandi's eyes filled with tears again. "I got tested right away, after I found out I was pregnant, I mean. Everything came up clean. I thought—well, I thought it might not be helpful to worry Leo unnecessarily."

"Unnecessarily?" He turned slowly to look at her. "It didn't seem necessary to clue me in that someone else might have knocked up my *wife*?"

The harsh language, the steel in his voice, caught Nyla by surprise.

So did the sharp prick of jealousy, the sting from the

possessiveness in Leo's words.

"I'm sorry," Mandi whispered, and Nyla turned back to her sister. "So sorry."

Nyla wasn't sure what to say. Leo sure as hell wasn't jumping to accept any apologies, and she didn't blame him. And it wasn't Nyla's place to reassure Mandi, so she sat silent for a moment, combing her brain for more questions she could ask. More ways to be useful.

"When did you learn you were pregnant?" she asked. "How long after Uganda?"

"Three months after I got back." Mandi glanced at Leo, then closed her eyes like she couldn't bear looking at him. "You and I hadn't slept together for weeks before the mission. Just that one time the night before I left, but once I got back...well, you remember. Or maybe you don't. We were all over each other. Like horny teenagers again, we couldn't get enough of each other."

Nyla took a few steadying breaths. She felt claustrophobic with Leo on one side of her and Mandi on the other. Maybe she shouldn't be here for this. Maybe she should leave them to have this conversation alone. She started to get up, but Mandi put a hand on her knee and mouthed a plea.

"Stay?"

So Nyla stayed, glancing once at Leo. He was staring at the photo again.

"Yeah, I remember," he muttered. He stared ahead for several more seconds, then shook his head. "You must have known. Had some inkling—"

"I didn't." Mandi blinked back tears again. "We were getting along so well and when the test came up positive, I thought...I thought..." She gave a hiccupping little sob. "I thought it was our second chance. You were so excited to be a dad, and I wanted to believe that's what happened."

Leo said nothing. Nyla couldn't tell if it was helping or hurting to learn details. Maybe she should shut up and let Leo ask the questions.

But he wasn't saying anything, and maybe she should help. At least help gather more clinical facts, the things a nurse would think to ask.

"What did he look like?" Nyla asked. "This Johan guy—were there any physical traits that made you think Seth resembled him and not Leo?"

Mandi shook her head, darting a quick glance at her ex-husband. "Brown hair. Caucasian. Brown eyes. Tall, more than six feet."

In other words, like Leo.

The fact wasn't lost on him. He shook his head slowly, one hand clutching the bag of frozen peas to his groin. "Does he know? This—this—other guy—does he know about Seth?"

Mandi looked down at her lap. "He's dead."

Nyla blinked. "What?"

"I never saw him again after that night," Mandi said slowly. "We were stationed at different field offices, so we didn't work together. After that night, he went off to Namibia and I was stationed in Masindi the whole two weeks. It wasn't until Christmas I got the newsletter from the relief group. His picture was there, something about 'lives lost.' There was an accident of some kind, something to do with elephants. I never asked. I just took it as a sign."

Leo looked at her. "A sign of what?"

"That the door had closed," she whispered. "That my future—our future with Seth—was all that mattered."

"I see." Leo's voice was clipped and brittle. "I think we're done here."

He stood up quickly, peas clattering to the floor. Nyla stooped to grab the bag, but so did Leo. Their fingers touched, and Nyla jerked back like he'd bitten her.

"Sorry," she murmured.

He looked at her a moment, brown eyes holding hers as he straightened with the bag in his hand. "So am I."

Turning away, he gripped the peas as Mandi stood up. "Wait," she said. "Leo, I'm so sorry. You have to believe—"

"I don't have to do anything." He whirled to face her, dark eyes blazing. "You stopped having the right to tell me what to do the day we signed the divorce papers."

"I know, you're right, I'm sorry." Mandi's throat moved as she swallowed. "Can we...talk more about this?"

"No." Leo turned around again, striding toward the door. "I'm done for the day. I'll pick Seth up at the usual time."

Nyla felt awkward sitting lumplike on the couch, so she stood. Her knees quivered as she started after Leo. She wasn't sure what she planned to say or do. All she

knew was that she wanted to comfort him, to let him
know he wasn't alone. She made one step toward him
when Mandi put a hand on her arm.

"Nyla?" Her sister's voice trembled. "Are you leaving?"

She turned back to Mandi and the ache in her sister's
eyes froze Nyla on the spot. As Leo's footsteps faded
toward the door, she felt something tear apart inside her.

"I'll stay," Nyla murmured as the door slammed shut
behind her. "I'm here for you."

· · ·

Two hours later, Nyla stood on Leo's front porch with
her heart in her hands. She also gripped two pints of
Ben and Jerry's, which were hopefully a better offering.

She rang the bell and waited. Howie the Wondercat
hopped up onto the windowsill and studied her with
disdain, then flicked his tail and looked away.

"Same to you, Howie," she muttered. "See if I bring
you any of that good catnip next time."

Howie ignored her and began to clean a paw. Still no
sign of Leo, which could mean he'd been called out on
an early-season fire.

Or it could mean he was avoiding her. She couldn't
blame him. She'd been the one to push for telling Mandi,
which meant she was mostly to blame for any pain Leo
was feeling. Both the testicular variety and the other.

She glanced at Howie again. "One more try, okay?"

This time when she pressed the bell, she heard Leo's

lumbering footsteps. A few seconds later, he swung the door open.

"Oh." She took a step back, startled to see him wearing nothing but boxers and a frown. "I can…um…come back later."

"You might as well come in." He turned and stalked away from the door, leaving Nyla staring after his muscled back, sculped arms, toned backside, and—

"Okay." She stepped inside, getting her bearings. As a nurse, she was well-acquainted with the human form. No big deal, nothing to see here.

But Leo wasn't her patient. When he turned at the end of the hall, facing her with a look she couldn't read, she took a shaky breath.

"Okay," she said again. "So this is how you answer the door now." She was trying for gentle teasing, but her voice came out weird. "Last time it was a T-shirt and boxer briefs, and now it's just boxers?"

He folded his arms over his chest, making muscles ripple in places she'd never noticed muscles. "You'll have to pardon me if I don't feel much like snug underwear."

Nyla swallowed and fought back the urge to glance down. "Is everything…uh…okay?"

"I was checking things out when you rang."

Oh. Heat crept into her cheeks, which was absurd. She examined male bodies all the time. Plenty of them, in all states of undress, though not often did they look like Leo. Hauling firefighting gear and piloting planes must be good exercise.

She kept her gaze to his face and cleared her throat. "Do you want me to take a look?"

One corner of his mouth twitched as he looked at her. "Yes, Nyla. That's definitely what I need to cap off this exceptional day. My ex-sister-in-law—a woman I kissed in her childhood home with my son in the very next room—inspecting my junk like it's a car engine."

The heat in her cheeks was a full-on flame now. "For the record, I know a lot more about human parts than car engines," she said. "And I could at least tell you whether you need to see a doctor."

"I don't need to see a doctor." He turned and stalked away, giving her another glimpse of those perfect glutes. Was she supposed to follow? She glanced at Howie, who squinted his eyes and ignored her.

"Some help you are," she muttered.

Ten seconds later, Leo ambled back into the living room, wearing sweatpants and a worn T-shirt. He looked tired and rumpled, and the urge to throw her arms around him was almost overwhelming.

"Want a beer?" he called as he moved past her into the kitchen.

"Ice cream!" She'd almost forgotten she had Cherry Garcia and Brownie Batter Core.

"I don't have any ice cream," he called from the depths of his freezer. "How about an Otter Pop that may have been in here since Seth's eighth birthday?"

"No, I mean I have ice cream." She trailed him into the kitchen and set the pints on the counter. "I thought it might help."

He quirked an eyebrow at her. "For eating or icing my junk?"

"Whichever would be more helpful?"

He laughed and picked up the Brownie Batter Core. "I'm fine. Everything's in tip-top shape, for the record."

"You're sure? No bruising or swelling or difficulty with—"

"I'm gonna need you to stop right there." He peeled the top off the ice cream and held it up. "Okay to dig right in?"

"Of course." Nyla swallowed, getting her bearings again. "I got that for you. Mine's the—"

"Cherry Garcia." He dug two spoons out of the drawer and headed back into the living room. "Come on. If we have to talk about stuff like affairs and exes and the condition of my junk, we can at least be comfortable."

Nyla glanced out the window at her car. She had two whole bags of Mandi's castoff clothes in there, everything from jeans to a sequined bustier she'd grabbed for its costume party potential. No sweatpants to speak of, but maybe she had an extra pair of scrubs?

"Want some sweats?" Leo called, reading her mind again.

"I'm fine." She peeled the top off her pint and headed into the living room, kicking her shoes off by the doormat.

She hesitated, glancing at the loveseat, the easy chair, the sofa where Leo sat spooning ice cream into his mouth. His eyes lifted to hers and her heart flipped over.

"You coming?"

"Yes." She took a breath and folded herself into the space beside him. He handed her a spoon and Nyla took it, conscious of her hands shaking. "I don't know where to start," she said. "Asking you how you think it went seems woefully inadequate."

He shrugged and spooned ice cream into his mouth. "Honestly? It went about like I expected. Minus the nut crushing, though I probably could have predicted that."

Nyla winced and took a bite of ice cream. It was cool and creamy with chunks of chocolate and tangy cherry. She took her time savoring, choosing her words carefully. "She's pretty torn up about it. Mandi, I mean. She's sorry for what she did. I know that's not much, but it's better than nothing."

"Better than nothing." He looked down at his pint and sighed. "How about we not talk about this for a bit?"

"Okay." God knows the man deserved a break. To enjoy his ice cream in peace. "Want me to tell you awkward medical stories?"

He laughed and took a bite of ice cream. "Yes, please."

She settled back on the couch, spooning up another from her own pint. "Years ago, I accompanied this patient down to X-ray. She'd had trouble breathing, and we suspected pneumonia."

"Is this the drunk lady who demonstrated her BJ skills on the scope?"

Nyla laughed, surprised he remembered, and that she'd been comfortable enough to tell blowjob stories to her brother-in-law. Right now, she couldn't look at him without blushing. How the hell had everything changed so fast?

She swallowed back the awkwardness with more ice cream. "Different patient," she said. "This one was really nervous about the X-rays for some reason, so I went in with her while the tech got things set up."

"Nice of you."

"It's my job." Swallowing another bite, she continued. "Anyway, the tech calls out to her 'on the count of three, I want you to hold your breath.' And the patient looks at me for a minute and says 'I'm really glad you're here. This is embarrassing.'"

Leo cocked his head. "Huh?"

"That's what I was wondering." Nyla set her ice cream down and dabbed at a speck of it on the knee of her jeans. "So, the tech counts down and the woman reaches up and grabs her breasts. Real dramatic, like this."

Leo's mouth fell open. Nyla glanced down, realizing what she'd done. Shit, she'd just grabbed her boobs in front of Leo. Was still grabbing them, which she really ought to stop.

Cheeks flushing, she dropped her hands and picked up the ice cream. "The patient heard 'breasts,' not 'breath.' I guess she thought she needed to move them out of the way or something."

"Oh, man." Leo laughed, licking ice cream off the back of his spoon. "Was she mortified?"

"We just rolled with it," she said. "Told her she'd done a great job and that we needed to do another one. The next time we told her to rest her hands on her lap and the tech was really careful to enunciate his instructions."

Still laughing, Leo shook his head. "You're making me feel a lot better about the couch incident," he said. "Tell me another."

"There are so many." She scrolled through her mental file cabinet, shoving aside anything that might violate patient confidentiality. "You remember when I worked in private practice? That little clinic over on the south end of town?"

"Barely," he said. "Not long after Seth was born, right?"

She nodded, watching for a dark cloud to pass over his face. For memories to come flooding back.

It didn't happen. He kept on scraping his spoon around the inside of the ice cream container.

"This one time I asked a patient to fill a specimen cup," she said. "Sent him into the restroom after showing him which line to fill it to."

Leo made a face. "I'm not sure I like where this is going."

"The clinic was old school," she continued. "No screw-top lids or little doors to discretely pass the specimen cup."

"I *definitely* don't like this story." Leo grinned. "Continue."

"There was this rug in the hallway," she said. "They'd tacked it down so no one would trip on it, but I guess they missed an edge, and when the patient came out with the cup in his hand—"

"No, stop." He groaned and scraped the bottom of the cup with his spoon. "Okay, don't stop. He doused you, didn't he?"

"Almost." She grinned and tapped her spoon on the edge of her container. "I've got quick reflexes. He did water the potted fern for us, though. It never really grew right after that."

Leo laughed some more, clattering his spoon around the bottom of the ice cream container to get every last drop. Nyla glanced down, surprised to see she'd barely made a dent in hers. "Want more?" she offered.

"Weird medical stories? Definitely." He grinned. "You keep your ice cream. I'll make us some dinner later if you want."

"If only Seth could see you ruining your appetite like this."

"I'd lose major dad points for sure." Something flickered in his eyes but vanished quickly. She wanted to reassure him, to insist he was a father no matter what Seth's blood type said.

But Leo already knew that, didn't he? It's why he'd never wavered in raising Seth, feeding him, coaching him, loving him. Seth was Leo's son, and Leo was his father, DNA be damned.

"So, you know how I kept checking your pupils after you…after your injury today?" she asked.

Leo held her gaze as he toyed with the fringe edging the quilt that draped the back of the couch. "I thought you were just gazing deep into my eyes."

"Funny." He was teasing, obviously. But there was a

little thread of truth in that. A part of her that loved looking into Leo's deep brown irises, getting lost in the golden flecks around the pupil. "Anyway, we once had a guy take a foul ball to the groin."

"Poor guy." Leo shook his head, grimacing a little. "Maybe we need a support group."

"Yeah, well this guy blacked out."

"No kidding? Must have been a hard hit."

"It gets worse. He lost consciousness and hit his head. Whacked it on one of those concrete barriers at the ballpark. He came to at the hospital, but he was really out of it. Started confessing all these crazy things."

Leo's brows lifted. "Like what?"

"At first it was believable stuff," she said. "Like that he'd ghostwritten a famous memoir for Hugh Heffner, or that he cheated in a pie-eating contest."

"That's a thing?"

Nyla shrugged. "No clue, but it seemed reasonable enough. But then he kept going, telling wild stories about swimming with piranhas or hang gliding into North Korea or making a secret porn tape with six famous actresses."

"Did he name them?"

"Yeah." She laughed. "Right between Jennifer Lawrence and Betty White, his wife walked in. She just looked at him and shook her head and said, 'he does this when he hits his head.'"

Leo laughed. "It happened regularly enough to be predictable?"

"Guess so." Nyla spooned up more ice cream. "All

right, I need real dinner. What do you have that we can make?"

Plucking the ice cream container from her hand, he stood up and headed toward the kitchen. "I've got this," he said. "You relax. You've done your part by shaking me out of my funk."

Nyla stood up, too, not willing to be waited on by the guy whose life she'd helped unravel in an afternoon. "I'm not just going to sit around and let you wait on me."

"Why not?" He shoved the ice cream in the freezer and rummaged around, pulling out a bag of raviolis. "This okay with some tomato sauce and salad?"

"I can make the salad if you'll just—"

"Sit." He pointed to a chair and Nyla sat, feeling less like a German Shepherd and more like a woman being tended to by a large, attractive male who was definitely not her boyfriend. She needed to remember that.

"Can I at least set the table?"

"You can drink the cider I'm about to pour for you and keep me company while I throw dinner together."

She nibbled her lip, still feeling guilty. "Thanks, Leo."

He shook his head as he poured her cider into a glass and handed it to her. "I used to get so pissed at Greg."

She blinked at him, trying to follow the conversational shift. "What do you mean?"

"How he'd just sit on his ass while you bustled around taking care of him. Grabbing him a beer, making whatever he wanted for dinner, letting him change the channel when you were already watching something."

"I—" Nyla stopped herself, not sure what to say.

"That's part of being in a relationship. Looking out for the other person, wanting to take care of them."

"And it only works if both people are doing it." He twisted the top off a jar of Trader Joe's marinara and set it aside, then filled a pot with water from the Insta-Hot beside his sink. "I want you to know, I don't take it for granted."

"Take what for granted?"

"The way you look out for me and Seth. The way you're always swinging by with soup or picking up Seth's books or pills or whatever he's forgotten. The way you tell weird medical stories to make me laugh. I appreciate it, Nyla."

"It's nothing." Something warm began to bubble in the center of her chest. "You're the one who's always taking care of people. Fixing your mom's house. Rescuing Mandi when she locks her keys in the car. Taking care of your friend Tony's mom before she left that abusive jerk she married. You deserve someone taking care of *you*, Leo."

He didn't say anything right away. Just stirred the sauce into a pan, then added the raviolis to the pot of boiling water. On the counter, he'd already chopped up a head of romaine, and she watched as he piled it into a big mixing bowl and drizzled it with bottled Caesar dressing. He reached into the cupboard and pulled out the cornbread croutons he knew she liked, even though he wasn't a crouton fan at all.

Her heart squeezed as she thought about how many times he'd done this for Seth. For Mandi. For everyone but himself.

We're more alike than I realized.

As Leo turned, his eyes locked with hers and he smiled. She felt it all the way to her toes, to her elbows, to a few spots in between that she'd rather not think about. She also felt a wash of dread, but it ebbed away fast, rinsed clean by those other feelings.

What the hell was happening? To her, to Leo, to them as a pair.

And why didn't she want it to stop?

CHAPTER EIGHT

"How did it get so late?"

Leo glanced at his watch as Nyla yawned and stretched on the sofa beside him.

"Because you made us watch an entire season of *Sons of Anarchy*." She stretched some more, and Leo ordered himself to keep his eyes off the space where her breasts pressed soft and round at the front of her T-shirt. "Not that I mind," she added. "Charlie Hunan's pretty easy on the eyes."

It wasn't the first time she'd made a comment like that. They'd watched three seasons before this, and each time she remarked on the actor's physique.

But it was the first time Leo felt a miniscule pinch of jealousy in the center of his chest.

Nyla yawned again. "How's your bike coming, by the way?"

"Good." He flicked the remote so the TV turned off and went black. "I got the catalytic converter on last weekend."

"Yeah? Getting closer to 'Leo's Selfish Dream'?" She made the trademark symbol with her fingers, grinning at the shared joke.

Only he must not have grinned back, because Nyla's smile fell. "You know that's just a joke, right? Irony? Because you're pretty much the least selfish guy on the planet and you deserve to have something all to yourself after a lifetime of giving things up for other people."

Something pinched in his chest again as he nodded. "It's fine. Just feels weird, you know? Seth was just a baby when I found the picture of my dad with that old Triumph Bonneville. Even after I started rebuilding my own, it seemed like such a long way off before I'd have it done."

"And set off into the sunset on your own with no responsibilities, no stress, no demands on your time." She smiled again, eyes searching his in a way that made him worry she saw straight into his soul. "You've earned it, Leo. Truly, you have."

"Okay." He took a swig of his beer, which had gone flat and tepid in the last hour. "I just can't believe Seth's growing up so fast. That in six years, he'll be out of the house."

Years ago, drowning in diapers and daycare and loving 99 percent of it—truly, he had—he'd hatched his plan in the one percent of the time he'd been exhausted and stressed. He'd been a full-time father, a full-time husband, a full-time pilot and business owner.

But he'd never just been Leo. What would that even be like?

"You okay?" Nyla's voice held nearly as much worry as the lines in her forehead.

As his eyes locked with hers, some of the tension melted from his shoulders. "I'm great."

She bit her lip. "You want to talk about anything?"

"Anything?" Like the fullness of her bottom lip, soft and lush and perfect for kissing.

"About things with Mandi. How it went tonight."

"Oh." Not at all what he'd been thinking. But oddly enough, he did want to talk about it. "I keep waiting to feel jealous or enraged or hurt or whatever. And yeah, there are twinges of that. But mostly, I'm just…relieved."

The word surprised him, and judging by Nyla's face, it surprised her, too. "Really?"

He shrugged. "I've had four years to speculate about this. I mean, mostly I tried *not* to think about it, but—"

"You're human," she said, totally getting it. "You were bound to wonder."

"Sometimes," he admitted. "To be honest, it wasn't as bad as I thought."

Nyla chewed her lip again, thoughtful. "I see what you mean. I guess I haven't fully wrapped my head around my sister cheating. Until you guys divorced, I didn't even know you had problems."

"Every relationship has problems."

Nyla snorted. "Tell me about it."

He stretched his arm over the back of the couch, fingertips grazing the ends of her hair. He told himself it was an accident but knew in his gut that wasn't true.

She glanced at his hand, seeming to fixate on it for a long time.

"You still have this scar." She reached over, picking up his hand. Leo sucked in a breath as heat shot straight to his groin. "This is from that time Seth dropped that motorcycle part on you?"

"Six stitches." He turned his hand to the side, praying to God and anyone else who'd listen that she wouldn't stop touching him. "Bled like a son of a bitch."

"I remember." Nyla pressed two fingertips to her lips and kissed them. Shifting her gaze to his, she smiled as she touched the thin white line of the scar. "There. All better."

He smiled back, even though the fire in his core was fast becoming an inferno. "Is that how you treat all your patients?"

"Most of the time," she said. "Gets pretty awkward with pelvic injuries."

He burst out laughing, squeezing her fingers before she could draw them back. "I'll bet."

She bit her lower lip again, and Leo couldn't stop himself from staring at her mouth. From wondering if she tasted as sweet as he remembered.

"Want me to kiss anything else better?"

His gaze snapped to hers as he drew in a breath. "What?"

She held his gaze, not blinking, not backing down. "You sustained a pretty serious injury today," she said slowly. "I was wondering if you'd let me kiss it better."

All the breath left his lungs. This had to be a joke. Some wicked, unbelievable joke he'd never before imagined but now couldn't stop thinking about.

"Nyla—"

"I want to, Leo." She slid closer to him on the sofa, the heat of her body drawing him to her like a magnet. "Let me make you feel good. Let me make it all about you for a change."

He wanted it so badly. More than Leo's Selfish Dream or anything else he'd wanted in his life. His breath stalled in his lungs, and he knew he wouldn't be able to form words even if he tried.

She started to move, one hand reaching for his fly as she edged closer and—

"Wait." He caught her wrist, hesitating. It would be so easy to say yes. To give in to the pleasure, damn the consequences.

But he wasn't that guy. He'd never been that guy. "We can't."

Nyla's throat moved as she swallowed. "Okay. I'm sorry."

"Jesus, don't be sorry." He barked out a strained laugh. "You have no idea how much I want that. I just—I don't think I could live with myself in the morning."

His dick throbbed in protest as his brain screamed *"what the fuck are you doing?"* against the drum of his own heartbeat.

But he couldn't let himself go there. Not yet, not like this. "Kiss me, Nyla."

A slow smile spread over her face. She licked her lips. "Okay."

His heart sped up as she slid closer on the couch and touched her lips to his. She was soft at first, tentative like he might break.

As his brain screamed for more, he slid his hands to her waist and pulled her onto his lap. She came willingly, knees falling to the sides of his hips as her warm center pressed against the hardness between his thighs. His parts that were very definitely still working.

She kissed him deeper then, hips moving as she rubbed herself against him. His hands found their way under her shirt, memorizing her skin, relishing the heat of her. Arching her back, she pressed against his fly. Leo groaned.

Her eyes flashed wide as she broke the kiss. "Did I hurt you? Oh God, I'm sorry, I forgot about your—"

"No." He said the word against her mouth, silencing her. He moved his hips, grinding into her, leaving no doubt that everything was in fine working order. God, he wanted her. Wanted to bury himself inside her and make her cry out beneath him.

It was too fast, too risky, way too complicated, but he couldn't stop thinking about it. Couldn't stop kissing her as Nyla moaned and pushed her breasts against his chest.

He slid his hands up her shirt again, toying with the clasp on her bra. Temptation, white hot and dizzying ripped through him as he thought about unhooking it. About how good it would feel to have her breasts spill into his hands, to feel her soft and warm and bared to him. Had he forgotten how good this could feel, these first dizzying moments with someone new?

He hadn't forgotten. He'd just never known before. Never felt anything like it, this wild, hungry, desperate urge to connect with someone he already knew inside and out.

Maybe not inside.

He broke the kiss, fingertips poised at her bra clasp. "Nyla," he breathed. "I've got about six working brain cells right now. Three of them are telling me to tear off your clothes, carry you into the bedroom, and spend the rest of the night making love to you."

Her throat moved as she swallowed, pupils dilating as she searched his eyes. "And the other three?"

A faint fog of sanity swirled in his mind, muffling the buzz of lust and heat and desire making him dizzy. "The other three say we should cool our jets. This thing between us—whatever it is—we shouldn't rush."

She nodded, though he could feel her hips twitching. Feel her rocking to press her core against him, even as the rest of her drew back. "You're right. Of course, you're right. We need to slow down."

Leo took a breath, annoyed with himself for being right. For his desperate urge to make good decisions, set a good example of how a man should behave. His son wasn't here—thank God for that—but he'd want Seth to grow up and be the sort of man who'd follow his conscience and not his dick.

But God, the way Nyla was moving against him—

"Okay," she said, and slid off his lap. She smoothed her hair back, cheeks flushed as she tugged at her T-shirt. "We should give this some time. Get past the adrenaline rush of what happened earlier tonight and come at this clearheaded in a few days."

He nodded, wanting to agree with her, wanting to believe he'd done the right thing by shutting this down.

But at the moment, all he wanted was her.

• • •

Leo knocked on his mother's front door, then walked in without waiting for a response. She'd be out back in her garden anyway, and she always urged him to just come right in.

The kitchen smelled just the way it had when he'd grown up here. Gingerbread and Lemon Pledge, with a hint of coffee from the pot in the corner. Her stainless-steel sink gleamed, a new addition Leo had put in four years ago. He moved through the living room, reminding himself to find time this week to work on the addition. A powder room off the parlor, and new windows in that space behind the couch.

His heart squeezed with the memory of growing up here. Of the Christmas tree in the corner and his father laughing as he guided the model train around the track that ringed the trunk.

"All aboard!" Leo's dad would shout as he plunked the blue conductor's hat on Leo's head. "Think you're ready to drive this year?"

Leo shook off the memory as he made his way out the back door. His mom was in the garden, as expected, stooped over the row of raspberries, with Seth beside her holding a silver bowl. His son looked up as Leo walked out and his face broke into a grin.

"Dad!" He jogged across the grass, bowl clutched to his chest like a trophy. "Check it out—we're making raspberry crumble. And Bob set up the ice cream maker."

"Sounds great." He pulled his son in for a hug, grateful the boy hadn't outgrown his love of baking with his grandmother. Or hugging, for that matter. He smiled at his mom over the top of Seth's head, watching as she peeled off her gardening gloves and tucked them in her back pocket.

"I wasn't sure you'd make it for dinner," she said. "I heard on the scanner about that fire down south."

"I've got Mike flying today," he said. "We changed up the schedule so I wouldn't miss Seth's game later this week."

"Such a good dad." The misty look in his mother's eye told him she remembered all the times his own father had done the same thing. Joe might have had his hands full building the air tanker business and setting up contracts with everyone from the Forest Service to the U.S. military, but he'd always made time for Leo. Always worked to be the kind of dad Leo himself aimed to be.

His heart squeezed again, and he let go of Seth to hug his mother. "Was Bob able to get that sink fixed?"

His mom rolled her eyes. "You know how he is. Thinks he's Mr. Fix-It, but he's really more like Mr. Bean."

She'd said it with enough fondness to wipe out any weirdness Leo still felt about his mother remarrying. He liked Bob well enough, and God knew his mom spent way too many lonely nights before meeting Bob and marrying again.

But still, it felt weird sometimes knowing his dad never got to be a grandpa. That his mother lost the love of her life, the father of her child. Or maybe some folks got more than one true love.

Nyla's face floated in the back of Leo's brain, and he pushed it aside in case his mother could still read his mind the way she had when he was a kid up to no good.

"I've got my toolbox in the truck," he said. "I'll take a look at the sink before I go."

Seth clamped a hand around Leo's arm. "Dad, can I go get my skateboard out of the back?" he asked. "I want to show Grandpa Bob this sick new trick I learned."

His mom ruffled Seth's hair as Leo nodded permission. "'Sick' means 'good,'" she reported. "I just learned that." As Seth scampered off, she watched after him with adoring eyes before turning back to Leo. "He reminds me so much of you at that age. Same zest for life. I don't know many kids his age who'd follow their grandmother around the garden pulling weeds. Such a good boy."

"I think I'll keep him." The old joke caught in his throat as he forced a smile. Now that the secret of Seth's DNA was bubbling out, how would his mom feel? Would she look at Seth differently knowing there was no biological link between them?

He didn't think so, but he also never thought his wife would have an affair and get pregnant by someone else. If there's one thing he'd learned, it's that life rarely went the way he thought it would.

Nyla.

That was certainly unexpected. The way she'd felt in

his arms, pressed against him with her—

"Is everything all right?"

He blinked himself back to the backyard with his mother. "Yeah, why?"

"You had a funny look on your face," she said. "You're recovering okay from the gum graft?"

He'd almost forgotten about that. "Everything's great," he said. "The dentist says it's healing just fine."

"Wonderful." She reached up and smoothed the hair back from his face. "Work's okay? You're not flying too many hours or staying too late at the base, tinkering with planes?"

He snorted. "Tinkering with planes keeps food on the table. Gotta do it sometimes."

"Yes, but you know how I worry. I'd like you to find someone. After the way Mandi left you high and dry—"

"It was a mutual decision," he reminded her. "And I'm fine on my own."

He needed to tread carefully. His mom had always been cordial to Mandi, but Leo could read the cues. Deep down, his mother blamed Mandi for the divorce. She'd never said as much, which he appreciated. Leo might not be Mandi's biggest fan right now, but she was still the mother of his child.

"I still don't think it's healthy for you to spend so much time with that family," his mom continued like he hadn't spoken at all. "It's holding you back, Leo. The way the parents never respected your boundaries, and how Mandi was so clingy with her sister. I know they're close, but honestly—"

"Mom." He gritted his teeth, feeling some of his happy glow fading. "They're still family."

"Not *your* family." She patted his arm and pasted on a bright smile. "Shall we go check the ice cream? And after that, I'll show you where the faucet's leaking."

He stifled a sigh and followed her into the house. "After you, Mother Dearest."

CHAPTER NINE

"Dinner was great, Mom." Mandi pushed back from the table and gave Nyla a look.

The look said dinner was not, in fact, great, and she'd be sneaking out to the Dairy Queen down the road the first chance she got.

Nyla fought back a smile, relishing the familiar joy of having secrets with her sister. Way better than having secrets *from* her sister, which was what she'd felt since the moment she'd kissed Leo.

Both times.

But they hadn't slept together, and didn't that count for something? Not that she hadn't thought about it. A lot. All the time, really.

She glanced at her parents as guilt settled in her gut. Could they tell she'd spent the whole dinner thinking about sex?

Sex with Mandi's ex-husband, with Seth's *father*, which was so much worse.

Her own father flashed a look of concern as he folded his napkin on the table. "Something on your mind, kiddo?"

"Nothing." She grabbed her water and chugged it down, desperate to keep herself from blurting anything. About Mandi's affair or Seth's biology or the things she'd been thinking—*been doing*—with Leo.

Hell.

"Your father's right, you look very flushed." Her mother stood up and put a hand to her forehead. "You're a little warm. You sure you're not coming down with something?"

Mandi shot out of her chair like she'd been electrocuted. "I know what would help." She grabbed Nyla's arm and yanked her to her feet. "Ice cream."

"Ice cream?" Nyla stumbled obediently after her sister as Seth stood to clear the table. "But we need to help with the dishes."

"I've got it, Aunt Nyla." Seth flashed his trademark grin. "Bring me a Butterfinger Blizzard, okay?"

"Okay." Since when did Seth not beg to come with them?

"He's grounded," Mandi whispered as they pushed through the front door and stepped out onto their parents' tidy brick walkway.

Nyla breathed in the scent of spring blossoms and her mother's favorite boxwood hedge, pushing back pangs of childhood nostalgia. "Why is he grounded?"

"I caught him making plans to TP a house with some friends." Mandi led the way to the sidewalk, kicking a stray dirt clod back into a flowerbed. "Kid stuff, but I don't want him getting in trouble."

With a snort, Nyla pointed at the tall blue house at the end of the block. "You mean like the time we TP'd the Johnsons because Pippa asked Brandon Peters to homecoming when she knew you wanted him to ask you?"

"Exactly." Mandi laughed and nudged her with her shoulder. "Thanks for not saying anything."

"What do you mean?" She sensed they weren't talking about toilet paper anymore.

"About Seth. About what I did." Mandi lowered her voice, even though there were no neighbors out watering lawns or barbecuing on the quiet spring evening. "I know it's hard for you to keep a secret. I could tell that day with the couch that you were about to burst. You looked like that all through dinner tonight, so I figured…I don't know. I'm sorry it sucks to hide things from Mom and Dad."

Nyla swallowed hard, hating how lousy it felt to hide things from all of them. How would Mandi react if she knew what she and Leo had been up to on his couch the other night?

She shivered, feeling his hands on her again. Glancing at her sister, she wondered if Mandi could tell.

Mandi gazed out over the Whitakers' vegetable garden, seemingly fixated on carrot shoots. "On a scale of one to ten," she said slowly, jarring Nyla from her thoughts, "how pissed do you think Leo was when I told him?"

Nyla blinked, regrouping. "Um—"

"I shouldn't say pissed," Mandi clarified, stooping to pick up a discarded foil gum wrapper. "He deserves his anger. I guess I'm more worried about him being hurt."

Nyla took a few breaths, stalling for time. "I don't know." There, that was a safe answer. Maybe Mandi would change the subject.

"Come on, Duckie." Mandi nudged her with an elbow. "You've been around him half your life. Probably more than me lately. You must have some sense of what he's feeling?"

She bit down hard on her tongue, afraid she'd blurt some asinine comment about feeling Leo. Feeling his lips, his arms, and his chest and—

"He seemed pretty hurt," Nyla managed. "But maybe not surprised."

Mandi kicked a rock as they turned a corner. "That sucks. I hate that I hurt him." Another pebble went skittering down the sidewalk as Mandi dropped the gum wrapper in a trash can at the fringe of Pioneer Park. "Sometimes I wonder if guilt about the affair was why I pushed him away. Like—would we still be married if I hadn't screwed things up?"

The breath stalled in Nyla's chest. It took her a few beats to form a response. "Are you saying you want him back?"

Mandi didn't answer right away. "No," she said slowly. "I don't think so anyway. But seeing him hurt like that—I mean, I spent a decade of my life with him. I don't like seeing him in pain. Knowing I'm the one who caused it makes it worse. I don't know, maybe I still feel protective."

Nyla didn't say anything. She couldn't, afraid she'd start spewing secrets and never stop. "What's it like when he's dated other women?"

God, why had she asked that? She gritted her teeth, certain Mandi could see right through her.

But Mandi kept walking, blessedly oblivious to Nyla's turmoil. "I hate it," she murmured, choking on a self-deprecating little laugh. "Don't ever tell him I said that. I know I have no right to say anything about his life or who he dates or any of it. But yeah...it stings, you know?"

Nyla nodded, hating that she did know. Deep down, didn't it still feel like fingernails on a chalkboard to hear about Greg? To know he'd moved on with someone else, someone prettier and younger and more fun than Nyla.

"I'm sorry." Her voice quivered from the weight of guilt and from genuine sympathy for her sister. "I know it sucks."

"It's fine, *it's fine*." Mandi forced a hearty laugh that sounded a little off. "I'm just feeling shitty for hurting someone I love."

Love. Not loved, *love*.

An accidental slip, or was she talking about the sort of platonic love someone has for the father of her son? She didn't dare ask, didn't dare give anything away.

God, it sucked keeping secrets from Mandi.

Mandi kept a pretty big one from you.

She breathed deeply and kept walking, praying they'd reach Dairy Queen before she exploded.

"Remember that time we knocked over the outhouse right there?" Mandi pointed to a corner that no longer held an outhouse, but Nyla recalled it like the whole thing happened yesterday.

"I was sure we'd get caught," Nyla admitted. "That someone had seen us or maybe we'd left fingerprints."

Mandi laughed and bumped Nyla with her hip. "I could have killed you when you told Mom and Dad."

"It seemed like it was only a matter of time until they figured it out," she said. "I thought we'd get in less trouble if we confessed."

"Oh, Duckie." Mandi gave a fond little laugh. "I love that about you. I mean, not then, obviously. But I admire that you want to do the right thing. Not keep secrets or whatever."

Nyla hesitated. She'd wanted to move on, to steer the subject away from anything close to Leo.

But there was still something nagging at her. Something she hadn't found a way to ask in the days since she'd spewed secrets over the couch.

Screw it, she couldn't keep holding it in. "Is that why you never told me about the guy in Uganda?" she blurted. "We tell each other everything, even though you know I'm a blabbermouth, but you never mentioned that once. Never even hinted you were having trouble."

Mandi was quiet a long time. So long, Nyla thought she might not answer.

"I didn't tell you because I wanted to pretend it hadn't happened," she said softly. "I was embarrassed and ashamed and just wanted to push the whole thing into the back of my mind and forget all about it."

"Oh," she said, feeling a weird sense of relief. "Only Seth made that impossible."

Mandi grabbed her hand and pulled her back from the big puddle of spilled milkshake she'd nearly stepped in. "He didn't, though. When you told me the other day that Leo wasn't his father—"

"Leo's still his father," Nyla snapped.

Mandi glanced at her, eyes widening at the vehemence in Nyla's voice. "You know what I mean."

"No, this is important." Nyla gritted her teeth. "Leo will always be Seth's dad. No matter what. I need to hear you say it. That you'll never do anything to come between them or take Seth away or—"

"Nyla, Jesus." Mandi stopped walking. "Of course I'd never do that. Where is this coming from?"

She bit her lip, wondering if she'd said too much. She started walking again, not comfortable with Mandi looking at her like that. "I just don't want Leo to get hurt. *More* hurt. Or Seth, obviously."

"Neither do I." Mandi still hadn't let go of Nyla's arm, and she squeezed it tighter. "Seriously, is that what you think of me?"

"I don't know what to think." Nyla looked her sister in the eye. "I'm hurt you never told me what happened. I'm angry you'd do that to Leo. I'm frustrated that there's still this big secret hovering over us that feels like it might blow up at any minute. And I'm worried about Seth hating all of us if he finds out someday what we've hidden from him."

Nyla held her breath, praying her sister wouldn't realize she had more than one secret simmering under the surface. That Mandi's secret wasn't the only one threatening to burst out.

Mandi looked at her a long time. "Are you worried about Seth finding out on his own, or about you accidentally telling him?"

"Both!" She folded her hands under her arms and ordered her voice not to tremble. "Say he starts questioning things and gets his hands on a DNA kit. It'll crush him even more to know we hid it from him."

Mandi's throat moved as she swallowed. "And what if his aunt tells him?"

"You think I'm not worried about that every minute of every day?" Her voice sounded frantic and feral, but there was no way to rein it in now. "I hate that I'm so bad at keeping secrets. I hate it more than anything. Like, what the hell is wrong with me that I might spill something that hurts a child I love more than anything?"

"Okay, calm down." Mandi touched her arm. "Look, I get it. I remember your friend in first grade. Annabelle? The one with the abusive dad?"

Nyla blinked. "You knew?"

"Of course I knew." She squeezed Nyla's hand. "I always know what's going on with you."

Nyla held her breath until spots flickered in her field of vision. "Oh."

Mandi continued, missing Nyla's distress. "I assume that's why you picked a job where you're a mandatory reporter. You've got a built-in excuse to blab. To do some good with it."

"It's not just that." Nyla forced herself to take a steadying breath. "I've seen too many situations where people end up hurt because someone hid the truth. Cancer patients who try to spare adult children from seeing them suffer, but they end up hurting more because they don't get to say goodbye."

"Okay, okay. I get it." Mandi sighed. "Just give me some time, okay? I'm still processing it myself. Until you and Leo said it, I honestly didn't know for sure Leo wasn't Seth's biological father. Give me a little time to wrap my head around it, okay?"

The pleading look in her sister's eyes was one Nyla had never been able to resist. She nodded, then started walking again. Guilt pricked at her conscience. Here she was lecturing Mandi about being honest, while Nyla was hiding one whopper of a secret about Leo. Would Mandi be pissed? She'd find out soon enough, wouldn't she?

Unless it wasn't going anywhere. It couldn't go anywhere, right? They were just fooling around, nothing serious.

But as Nyla kept walking, she knew she wasn't fooling anyone, least of all herself.

• • •

Driving home with a belly full of ice cream, Nyla couldn't stop thinking about her conversation with Mandi. About her sister's confession that it felt awkward to see Leo date. How much more awkward would it be to see him date *Nyla*?

But no, that would never happen. They couldn't let it happen. It was just a couple kisses, not a relationship with a future. Nothing they couldn't wave off as hormonal impulse and pretend it never happened.

She was halfway to her house when she realized she didn't want to go home. Not to the quiet house without even a pet for company. Back when she'd dated Greg, they'd talked about getting a dog.

"Don't you think that's too much of a commitment for right now?" he'd asked, slinging his arm around the back of the couch as they snuggled up to watch some creepy detective show on Netflix one Friday night.

"Too much of a commitment?" she'd stared at the side of his face, wondering what nine years together was if not a commitment. "You mean walking it?"

When he didn't answer right away, she kept going. "Because I'd be fine with a cat, too," she'd said. "They don't need walks. They live longer than dogs, too."

From the way Greg had flinched, he didn't see that as a good thing. "Let's just wait and see."

That probably should have tipped her off that he was never going to propose. Never be the father of her children or the co-owner of a lovely little cottage with a white picket fence that she'd dreamed of.

"Dammit," she muttered as she swerved the car to avoid hitting a kamikaze chipmunk.

She wasn't annoyed with the chipmunk. It was anyone's guess if she was more annoyed with Greg from a year ago, or with herself for wasting nine precious childbearing years on a relationship with no future.

As she blinked herself back to the present, she realized she'd aimed the car toward Miller Pond. One of her favorite spots on earth, she'd learned about it the week after she and Greg split when Leo took her there with a gift he'd made just for her.

"It's a dartboard," Nyla had marveled as she stretched her fingers out to touch it. "With a photo of Greg's face on it."

"Excellent powers of deduction." Leo had handed it to her with a fistful of darts. "Time to get some closure."

And she had. He'd driven her out to this pond just east of the air base. Shallow at the edges and 50-feet deep in the middle, it was shaped like a lopsided heart and she'd never even realized it was there before then.

"Most folks don't," he'd explained as he propped up the dartboard against a tree. "I probably wouldn't either if I hadn't been flying over this spot for years."

As she eased her car along the dirt road now, she thought about that day. About so many other days where Leo had been there for her in a kind, brotherly sort of way. How had she gone from seeing him as a brother to seeing him as a guy she wanted to strip naked and lick from head to toe?

"Knock it off, Nyla." She said the words out loud, smacking a palm on the steering wheel to hammer home the point. "Stop thinking about him like that or you'll never shake the habit."

Pep talk complete, she parked the car in the small patch of dirt at the fringe of the trailhead. A plane glided low above her, coming in for a landing. She ordered herself not to think about Leo. He wasn't flying tonight, was he?

Leaning over to unlatch her glovebox, she pulled out the baggie of cracked corn she kept just for this. As she walked the half mile to the water's edge, the sun was sinking lower on the horizon, casting a warm, golden glow over everything. Ducks paddled the water's surface, the green-headed mallards quacking fiercely as she approached.

"Hey, guys." She sprinkled a handful of corn on the sandy shore, delighted as the noisy, feathered pack swarmed to claim their evening meal. "Don't crowd. There's plenty for everyone."

Of course, they didn't listen. She sprinkled some more corn, making sure the timid ones near the back got their fair share. "Come on, girls," she urged. "Push your way up here. There's some for you, too."

Catching sight of a smaller duck near the back with an injured wing, she took special care to toss a handful in her direction. "Don't be shy, sweetie. This is for you."

The duck waddled tentatively toward a scattered patch of yellow as two more zipped past her to get the feed. "Shoo," Nyla said, waving them toward another dusting of corn. "Let her have a chance."

She watched them eat, the cheerful quacking easing some of the tension from her shoulders. Feeding ducks had been her go-to form of therapy since she was little, and the source of Mandi's nickname for her. Her heart twisted as she thought about her sister, about their lifetime of family memories.

About the fact that she was healthy and alive because her sister gave her bone marrow, and how did Nyla repay that? By making out with Mandi's ex-husband.

Pathetic.

"Here you go." She spread another handful of corn, then glanced out over the pond. Several ducks paddled closer to the center of the lake, not hungry enough to make the journey all the way to shore to fight for Nyla's handouts.

She squinted toward another cluster of ducks, this one near the center of the pond. It was too far to see well, but was that duck hurt?

"Oh no." She dropped the baggie and ducks swarmed her feet. She reclaimed it without looking, not daring to tear her eyes off the wounded duck. A female, judging by her coloring. She lay flopped on her side, turning in a slow, helpless circle in the breeze.

Two other ducks paddled over, pecking at the injured bird.

"Stop," Nyla shouted, startling the ducks at her feet. "Leave her alone."

The bullies ignored her, though the ducks at her feet scattered. Should she call the Department of Fish and Wildlife? No one would be there at this hour, and it was getting late.

She had to do something.

Toeing off her sandals, Nyla glanced around. She saw no one. Rarely saw anyone here, actually. Without hesitating, she whipped off her T-shirt and tossed it on a flat rock at the water's edge. Her shorts went next, and she used them to cover up the bag of corn. Should she skinny dip?

No, she wasn't that brave. But she was in a hurry—she could see the bully ducks pecking the poor helpless body.

"Stop!" she shouted again, even though it was useless.

The ducks on the shore were having a smorgasbord with the baggie of corn they'd dragged out from under her clothes. She'd buy more duck food later.

With a deep breath, she charged into the water, wading fast to her shins, her knees, her thighs. Another breath and she plunged in, letting the inky liquid swallow her.

"Gah!" It was colder than she'd realized, and slimy, too. Algae blooms or muck or…well, she'd rather not think about it.

She kept swimming, legs churning, arms stroking the murky surface as she bobbed up once to check her course. Wow, it was farther than she'd realized.

Kicking harder, she picked up the pace. She had to get there fast. Maybe she should have planned ahead, brought her T-shirt to use as a net. Too late now, and besides, the duck seemed wounded enough not to put up a struggle.

"Hang on, girl." She wasn't sure if she was talking to the duck or herself, though she was feeling winded. Another twenty feet or so.

She bobbed up again, checking her progress. A cluster of six or seven ducks blocked her view, so she couldn't see the hurt one. God, had they already killed her?

Tears stung her eyes, or maybe that was pond water. She was almost there.

"Shoo!" she sputtered, splashing a handful of water toward the bully ducks.

A few glanced up, quacking their alarm at the crazy woman flailing toward them. "Go on, leave her alone."

The bullies turned and skittered away, quacking a few choice curse words. The injured one spun in a pitiful circle, completely motionless. Was she too late?

"Hang in there," Nyla called, breathing heavy. "I'm a nurse."

Like the duck understood. And like Nyla had any clue about a duck's medical needs. What the hell was she going to do with a wounded waterfowl?

But she had to try and she was almost there and *oh God*, the duck was definitely not moving at all.

Wait.

Nyla squinted, water clouding her eyes. She blinked hard, dog paddling the last couple strokes. The duck was stiff. The duck was immobile.

The duck was plastic.

"Son of a bitch."

A decoy, the kind hunters used. She reached out to touch it to be sure, and yep, no feathers. Just cold, wet molded plastic. Its feathers were painted, and damn realistic, she had to admit.

She stared at the fake duck, feeling like a fool.

No.

Grateful.

"This is good." The breeze splashed a wave into her face and she spit out water. "This is great. No injured duck."

The nearby ducks gave a few indignant quacks, vindicated from her false accusation.

"I'm sorry, okay?" She treaded water, making amends. "It looked real enough."

They quacked some more, clearly disagreeing.

Hell.

Still treading water, she weighed her options. She couldn't leave it out here. It was basically litter, and what if someone else launched a misguided rescue mission like hers?

She could hear her sister's voice in the back of her mind, teasing. "There is no one else on earth who would have done that."

Leo, she thought.

Leo would have done the same thing.

She grabbed the fake duck and tucked it under one arm. This was going to be awkward, but no more than stripping to her underwear to save a fake duck.

Rolling to the left, she started a slow sidestroke, moving clumsily with her new passenger. She concentrated on keeping her breath even, her strokes steady. She'd come in third for breaststroke at the state championships in high school, though admittedly she was rusty.

Focused on her breath, she forced her mind not to dwell on how far it was to shore. How there might be leeches or sewage or...*ew, no, don't think about that.*

The shoreline was closer now, but still pretty far off. She bobbed up to check, and that's when she heard it. Barking, distant but getting closer.

Woof! Woofwoofwoooofwoof!

A tank-sized golden retriever bounded across the beach, scattering sand and ducks with the force of its exuberant tail. Tongue lolling, the dog chased a cluster of mallards at the water's edge. The ducks flapped and quacked and took off into the sky in a tornado of angry wings. The dog gave chase, but lost interest in a hurry.

Woof! Woofwoofwooofwoof!

Nyla opened her mouth to yell, to startle it away from shore or maybe summon its owner. A slosh of water hit her in the mouth, sending her sputtering.

"Ack!"

The dog ignored her, focused on charging the last cluster of ducks toward the trees. Mission accomplished, the retriever stood wagging, searching for fresh prey.

Its ears pricked up. As Nyla stared, the dog gave a gleeful leap and tore off toward a flat rock.

The rock where she'd left her clothes.

"No! Doggie, *no!*"

Woof! Woofwoofwooofwoof!

Bounding toward her heap of colorful cotton, the dog snatched her blue T-shirt off the pile. Paws flying, it bounded down the beach, then turned toward the hill at the south edge of the pond.

Nyla watched helplessly as the dog charged up a bluff and then disappeared, its tail vanishing like a plume of smoke.

"Holy shit." Nyla gripped the plastic duck tighter, beelining it toward shore. She swam harder than she ever had, breaths coming in frantic bursts. Maybe that hadn't just happened. Maybe the dog dropped the shirt somewhere.

Maybe you're totally screwed.

Did she still have bags of Mandi's clothes in the car? No, dammit, she'd dragged those into the house yesterday. Of all the times to be efficient.

By the time she reached the shore, she was wheezing and panting and oh yeah, shivering on the shore in her panties and bra. She dropped the duck and looked around for the dog, praying its owner was nearby. Or not. Or yes, at least then she could get her shirt back.

But there was no one. Not even the ducks, quacking their laughter at her predicament. They'd all been scared away.

She looked down at the rock where she'd dropped her clothes, weighing her options as she assessed the faded cutoffs with a frothy glob of slobber on the fly. Fabulous.

Now what?

All right, at least she was alone. And at least her bra was the thick cotton kind, not lacy or see-through, though yeah, pale pink was kinda transparent with water.

Dammit.

She picked up the shorts, then dropped them again. Better to be commando than wearing wet panties under denim. With any luck, she wouldn't spot anyone on the trudge back to the car.

Hurrying to strip off her panties, she dropped them on the rock and stepped into the shorts. Oh, ouch. Wet skin and denim, not a good combination. The shorts got stuck on her wet thighs and she tugged harder, fighting to force them the rest of the way up her legs.

"Come on, work with me here." She tugged again, but the shorts weren't budging. Just wedged mockingly around her thighs like a denim tourniquet. "Dammit to hell."

"Nyla?"

She looked up and yelped. "Leo? What the hell?"

He stood frozen at the trailhead, face flushed as he stood staring in disbelief. "I'm wondering the same thing."

CHAPTER TEN

Leo blinked to clear his eyes, wondering if he'd suffered some kind of mild hypoxia coming in for that landing. Or maybe he'd inhaled trace amounts of ammonium phosphate dropping his load on the flank of that fire just now.

Those two things together might explain why Nyla was standing on the bank of Miller Pond wearing nothing but a wet bra, a band of denim around her thighs, and a look of total bewilderment.

"Shit." Leo grabbed the hem of his T-shirt and whipped it off, giving it a covert sniff before tossing it to her. "Here, put this on."

"Oh." Nyla gaped as the shirt fluttered to the ground.

It landed in a heap between them on the damp dirt, and they both bent to grab it at the same time. Their heads connected with a sharp *crack* and Nyla teetered to the side.

"Sorry." Leo caught her by the arms and pulled her upright, leaving the shirt on the ground. "Are you okay?"

She blinked a few times as if pulling herself from a daze. "Do I *look* okay?"

She looked pretty great to him, all warm curves and damp pink cotton. And, um…no panties, with her cutoff shorts wedged around her thighs. What great thighs, creamy and soft and—

"Shit." He'd already said that, hadn't he? He dragged his eyes to her face. "What—why—"

Why was he still gripping her by the arms, holding on like he was about to pull her damp, nearly naked body against his? He should definitely let go.

"What happened?" he finally managed as he dropped his hands to his sides and took a step back. "I thought I saw your car as I was coming in for the landing, but I didn't know you'd be—"

"Naked and wet and stranded topless in the mud?"

"Yeah, that."

Nyla shivered and he remembered his own T-shirt. Remembered he wasn't wearing one, either, a fact made clear by the slow detour Nyla's eyes took over his chest. With a tiny sound in the back of her throat, she grabbed the waistband of her cutoffs and yanked hard. That looked painful.

But she got them up, thank God, so she was covered now. She zipped up and fastened the button before squaring her shoulders and jerking her gaze back to his. "I was feeding ducks."

He nodded, not sure he was following. "I often get naked to do that."

"No, that's not what I meant." A wobbly smile tugged the corners of her mouth. "I mean, I was feeding ducks and I saw an injured one getting bullied and I thought it might die, so I didn't think."

"Sure you did." It was exactly what he loved about her. "You thought to rescue it, right?"

"Right, only it turned out it wasn't even a real duck."

She jerked a thumb toward the shore where a plastic hunter's decoy lay motionless on its side.

"Yep." Leo returned his gaze to Nyla. "That one's probably not needing any medical attention."

"I kinda got that." She looked down, checking the fly on her shorts to make sure she was covered. As covered as possible, under the circumstances.

Convinced she wasn't flashing him, she bent and snagged his shirt off the ground. She dropped something at her feet as he did it, and Leo stared at the wadded ball of pink.

"What is th—oh." Her panties. Probably a story there, too, but not one he deserved to know.

Nyla finished tugging his shirt over her head, then looked down at her chest. Which was definitely not where his eyes went, not even if her breasts were pressing round, damp circles into the white cotton.

"Dammit." She snaked her hands through the arms of his shirt, disappearing inside so he could see her moving around beneath the dampening fabric.

She twisted her arms behind her back and performed a complex acrobatic maneuver. The next thing he knew, she was whipping her soggy bra out through an armhole and dropping it on the rock next to her panties.

"Okay." What did a guy say to that?

"Sorry." She grimaced. "It's probably rude to go bare under someone else's shirt, but that wasn't going to work."

It was working just fine for him, but Leo kept his trap shut. "Problem solved."

Nyla dragged her fingers through her damp hair, then took a deep breath. "Let's start again. Thank you, Leo, for rescuing me."

"Thank you, Nyla, for rescuing that duck." He glanced at the prostrate plastic form lying at the water's edge. "For the intent, anyway. It's my favorite thing about you."

Nyla cocked her head. "That I nearly drowned myself for no good reason?"

"That you're kind enough to want to rescue a living creature in trouble." He shoved his hands into his pockets, since that seemed like a safe way to keep from reaching for her. "Not many people would do that."

"Thank you." She frowned at an empty plastic bag on the ground, a few flecks of dried corn clinging to an inside corner. With a sigh, she bent down and picked up the bag, then grabbed her wet underthings and shoved them inside. "Can we not speak of this again?" she asked as she straightened.

"Absolutely." He could keep his mouth shut, though he doubted she'd make it through the next family dinner without exploding.

Yet another thing he loved about Nyla, her openness. *Stop thinking the word "love" and "Nyla" in the same fucking sentence.*

He blamed the nudity. Or the fact that she was staring openly at his bare chest, the heat unmistakable in her eyes. At least he wasn't the only one thinking impure thoughts, though he couldn't decide if that was a relief or more trouble.

"You can keep that if you want." He gestured to the

T-shirt that hung nearly to her knees. "But I'm guessing I've got something that would fit better. Something your size."

She frowned. "You keep a stash of women's clothes in your truck? Are you a serial killer, Leo?"

He laughed. "I meant back at the air base. Lost and found gear. I'm pretty sure there's some women's things in there, plus tons of men's sweatpants and sweatshirts and towels and stuff. We always wash whatever ends up there or else it stinks to high heaven."

He was not making a very good case for why she should come with him instead of driving home braless beneath his T-shirt. A more logical move to be sure, but Nyla just nodded.

"Thank you." She bit her lip, looking down at the dress-like shirt. "I accept, since I need to stop at the grocery store on the way home and I don't want to go in like this." She hesitated, giving him a wary look. "Are there, uh—a bunch of smokejumpers hanging out in there?"

"I'll take you through the back door. There's an empty bunkroom right off that entry. We'll be very discrete, I promise."

Even if they weren't, the guys on the crew were smart enough to look the other way in a situation like this. Not that Leo had a ton of experience walking shirtless into the base with a half-clad woman beside him, but the guys here knew Nyla. They were respectful enough not to make a big deal about this.

"Come on." He paused, wondering if there were any

special requirements to hiking half a mile to her car without a bra. "I'll, uh—go slow."

A slow smile tugged at her lips. "My breasts thank you for your concern."

She folded her arms over her chest, which he guessed was meant to provide some measure of support. "Lead the way," she said as she toed her shoes on.

Leo turned, conscious of her right behind him, of the need to keep this casual and pretend it wasn't awkward. That he wasn't trudging along remembering how she'd looked in that transparent cotton bra, dragging those shorts up her thighs and over the curve of her back-side—

"Ducks," he blurted, forcing himself to refocus. "Did you know they can carry parasites?"

"Uh, yeah." She gave a funny little laugh. "I guess so."

Right, she was a nurse. Of course she knew stuff like that.

But he kept right on babbling, because it seemed like a better plan than silently struggling not to picture her naked under his T-shirt. "Yeah, so the ducks will leave the parasites behind in lakes and ponds and those cause this condition called swimmer's itch. If you want, you can shower off at the bunkhouse."

And now he sounded like a total creeper.

"Swimmer's itch, huh?"

"Yeah, the parasites that cause it are called schitosomes," he continued, aware he was blathering on but unsure how to stop. "Saw it on the Nature Channel. It's not dangerous or anything. Just itchy, but you can't be too careful when you're swimming in ponds and lakes and…and anywhere with ducks."

"Okay." Her voice held a twinge of amusement, so at least he was making her laugh. Probably *at* him, rather than *with* him, but he'd take what he could get. Anything to keep his mind off Nyla damp and beautiful and minus any underwear just a few steps behind him. Nyla with her perfect bare breasts moving beneath his shirt.

Only maybe they weren't moving, on account of her walking cross-armed and all. He needed to stop thinking about this.

Ducks. Keep talking about ducks.

"Remember that time you thought Pink Floyd was singing 'no ducks are hazards in the classroom?'" There, that was better than thinking about Nyla's bare body glistening with pond water.

Behind him, she gave a choked little laugh. "I blame the British accent," she said. "And for the record, I still don't hear it as *'dark sarcasm in the classroom.'* More like 'gloss room,' which I used to think had something to do with painting."

Leo laughed. "I love your sense of humor."

Goddammit, there was that word again. And he'd said it out loud this time, which made it worse. Thank God they'd reached her car. He rested a hand on the hood and turned as she caught up to him.

"Want to meet me at the air base?" He kept his gaze on her face, determined not to let it drop.

"Just get in." She popped open the door and slid into the driver's seat. "It's silly to make you walk."

"It's not that far." But he wasn't going to argue, so he ambled around to the passenger side and climbed in. The sedan's interior smelled like the vanilla air freshener she loved, with a hint of pond water and Nyla's shampoo. Roses, maybe, or strawberries? He'd never been great with scents.

But he'd always loved hers. Even when—

Goddammit. The L-word again.

He cleared his throat. "How'd family dinner go tonight?"

Nyla sighed and cranked the wheel to turn the car around. "Awkward."

"More awkward than normal, you mean?"

"A lot more." She bit her lip as she turned toward the air base. "Mandi spent the whole time worried I was going to go off like a geyser and start spewing secrets." She gave a small, indignant snort. "Like I'd do that in front of Seth."

He studied the side of her face, itching to touch the damp curl plastered against her cheek. "Just a guess, but I'm thinking my son's DNA isn't the main thing you're holding back?"

She swiveled to face him, nearly swerving off the road. She corrected quickly and aimed the car back toward the bunkhouse. "That's on my mind, obviously."

"Obviously." She did mean the kiss, right? Kisses, plural.

She shook her head as she crept along the narrow road leading to the back side of the bunkhouse. "I feel like I'm hiding something so huge and so...so...hurtful."

She choked on a laugh. "Can you even imagine how the family would react if they knew you and I had been... you know?"

He wanted her to say it. Wanted desperately to know how she saw it.

Just a casual kiss — *kisses*, dammit — or something more? Something with potential to lead somewhere.

"Yeah," he managed, a paltry answer. "I can see how it'd be weird."

But was weird the worst thing? He knew it was premature, and probably not a possibility at all. But really, would it be that nuts if he and Nyla got together? Unexpected, sure, but maybe not *that* weird.

Nyla bit her lip. "It just feels like a betrayal of Mandi, right?"

"Hell, no." He practically barked the words. "We're divorced."

She rolled her eyes. "I'm aware."

"And the divorce was her idea," he continued. Obviously, she knew that, too, but it was worth reiterating. "I mean, I didn't fight it, but the decision was hers."

So was the decision to cheat, though he knew better than to say that. Nyla was well aware.

"I hate Greg." She blurted it fast, biting her lip like she'd cursed in church.

Leo looked at her, wondering what he'd missed. "What?"

"My ex, Greg. I'm angry about how he handled our split, and angry that he wasn't straight with me for nine years. I have zero interest in rekindling things with him, but do you know how I felt when he started dating Wendy?"

"How?" The sick feeling in his gut told him he already knew.

"Horrible. Seeing my ex with another woman felt like someone ripped my heart out of my chest. Like I'd been kicked in the stomach, and I hated myself so much for feeling that way."

Oh. "I'm sorry, Nyla." He clenched his hands in his lap, not sure what else to say.

"I don't love him anymore. Haven't loved him for a long time. But it still hurt like hell to see him moving on so suddenly, and after telling me he didn't think he ever wanted to get married."

He nodded, seeing her empathy at work again. "And you're trying to spare Mandi that pain."

She pulled the car to a jerky stop in a parking space behind the bunkhouse, then turned in her seat to face him, brushing the wet curl off her face. "It's the least I can do, right? I owe my life to her. She gave me her damn bone marrow. I'd have died without her, and I repay her by making out with her husband?"

Hesitating, Leo reached out and caught one of her hands in his. "*Ex*-husband," he said softly, stroking a finger over her knuckles. "I'm not Mandi's property."

"I know that."

"I'm not anyone's property except my own," he continued. "Don't I get a say in this?"

Biting her lip again, she nodded. "Of course. I'm sorry, I don't mean to make you feel like a hunk of meat." Her gaze dropped to his chest again and color stained her cheeks. She jerked her gaze back up to his. "Sorry."

"Don't be." For ogling him. For thinking of him as something she might like to possess. None of that bothered him. Hell, he kinda liked it. "Come on." He unhooked his seat belt and pushed open the passenger door, needing to put some space between them. "Let's get us both dressed a little more appropriately."

She followed him to the back door of the bunkhouse as Leo pulled the keys out of his pocket. Only a handful of aerial firefighters lived here on base, plus a few Hotshots. Mostly younger rookies, and the bulk of them were out on a fire or probably raising hell in town if they weren't on duty. Still, he wanted to shield her from prying eyes.

As he pushed open the door, he used his body to block as he surveyed the hall. No one. No sound of anyone, either.

"Coast is clear." He held the door open and pointed to the lost and found closet. "Third door from the end. Help yourself to anything that looks like it'll fit."

"Thanks, Leo." She peered around him, hesitating at the threshold. "I really appreciate this."

"Don't mention it." He shoved his hands in his pockets. "Want a shower?"

She blinked. "Wh—oh, you meant alone?"

He laughed. "Yeah, alone." God help the images flashing through his brain. He took a few steps back. "Women's locker room is right there." He kept backing away, putting space between them. "I'll be in the break room." Or maybe in the men's locker room, taking a *cold* shower.

He'd backed halfway down the hall, so he turned around and kept walking past the bank of lockers, past the empty reception area and a row of empty rooms. He'd almost reached the end of the hallway when Nyla called out.

"Leo, wait."

He turned as she popped her head out of the lost and found closet. "Catch."

Her bare arm snaked out and tossed his T-shirt to him. His hands caught it by instinct as his brain fumbled to catch up. Was she topless?

"Found a jog bra." She laughed as the upper part of her body dipped out to reveal a well-fitted exercise top. "Must have been Janine's?"

"Uh, right." One of the female smokejumpers who'd transferred to the Alaska air base at the start of the season. "Sure, probably."

Stop staring. You've seen her in sports bras plenty of times.

They jogged together sometimes, and on hot days, that's how she dressed. Obviously, this was no big deal.

Only it was, and he couldn't stop staring.

Nyla just smiled. "There's a whole bin of stuff right here by the door that looks like it'll fit." She picked up a tank top and waved it at him. "Thanks again."

"No problem." Christ.

Forcing himself to turn around, he bypassed the

break room and made a beeline for the bathroom.

To force himself to stop staring.

To splash cold water on his face.

To remind himself that no matter what, no matter how much he might wish otherwise, Nyla was off-limits.

CHAPTER ELEVEN

Nyla finished rubbing herself down with a rough towel, confident she'd done her best to get rid of any pond parasites.

Not that she was worried about swimmer's itch. Her role on the hospital's Infection Control Committee kept her in the loop about community outbreaks, and she hadn't heard about infestations at local lakes and ponds.

But it was nice of Leo to worry. Nice that he'd hooked her up with the world's unsexist ensemble of a hot pink sports bra under a pale-yellow tank top advertising a brand of locally-produced cheese. The red terrycloth shorts she'd found were too big, but they fit fine with the waistband rolled over a few times. All in all, a hideous outfit.

It was perfect.

Because the last thing she wanted right now was to find herself feeling sexy and attractive and bold enough to seduce Leo. If having him play rescuer was her personal catnip, dressing like a clown college dropout was the equivalent of a cat owner snatching the squirt bottle to chase Fluffy off the counters.

"Stop being weird," she ordered her reflection.

Her reflection stared back with wild, wet hair and mascara rings under her eyes. She grabbed a wad of tissue and swiped at the smudges, wishing she'd thought to grab her purse. At least she had lipstick in there.

"You don't need lipstick," she told herself. "You need to stop thinking about looking good for Leo."

That part was easy, since she looked like hell. Okay, it was definitely time to leave the locker room. One last pep talk.

"Say thank you," she told herself. "If he offers a snack or a soda, just decline it politely and get home with your clothes and your integrity intact."

The Nyla in the mirror looked dubious, so she forced a cheerful smile and pushed open the locker room door. She'd been here a couple times with her sister when Mandi and Leo were just dating. He'd lived here at the bunkhouse that whole summer, flying off to fight fires when he wasn't with Mandi.

"It's such a sexy job," Mandi had confided to Nyla over girls' night drinks at their favorite bar. "Not super practical if we want kids, but neither is flying around the globe building water systems for third-world countries." Mandi had laughed, tossing her hair in that carefree way she had. "We're kinda perfect together, actually."

How much things had changed. For all of them, really.

"Leo?" Her voice bounced off the concrete walls as she made her way toward the break room. "Hello? Anyone here?"

Silence. Not even a response from one of the residents, which wasn't surprising. It wasn't the most welcoming space, all concrete walls and peeling pale green paint. She couldn't blame crewmembers for spending as little time as possible here when they were off duty.

"Leo?" She passed through the break room, pausing by the fridge. Maybe he was in the bathroom?

"Back here." His voice called faintly from down the hall.

Hesitating, Nyla followed the sound of hammering. As she reached the room at the far end of the bunkhouse, a funny ripple of nostalgia fluttered in her belly.

"Hey." She paused in the doorway of a bedroom, drinking in the sight of Leo crouched on the floor beside a metal bunk.

He looked up, spearing her heart with those warm brown eyes. "Hey, sorry." He stood up and set the hammer on the windowsill. "Came back here to see if my name was still on the wall and realized the reason no one's bunked down in this room all season."

She glanced at the bed, then wished she hadn't. Any horizontal surface made her think of sex, and with Leo standing right there—

"Someone broke the bed?" Her cheeks heated up as she tried not to picture all the ways a bed might get broken.

"Jelinski, probably." Leo snorted. "You met him, I think. Rookie jumper last season. Had a steady stream of women dropping by to visit."

"I went out with him once." Nyla shrugged as she registered the flicker of wariness in Leo's eyes. "I promise I didn't help break the bed. We never even kissed."

"Huh." He seemed like he wasn't sure what to say to that. Wasn't sure what to do with his hands, either, since he picked up the hammer again. She watched him toss it end over end, catching it each time. How did he do that? And how had she never noticed what great hands he had, big and strong and—

Nyla cleared her throat. "So…thanks again." She should definitely make a run for it. Only— "What did you mean about seeing if your name was still on the wall?"

"Oh, that." A flicker of self-consciousness moved across his face as he headed for the closet. "It's this tradition in the bunkhouse. Everyone signs their name if they stay here a season. Even when the rooms get painted, they skip this wall. There's names in here dating back to the eighties."

Nyla followed, curiosity clobbering self-preservation. She trailed Leo toward the closet, fascinated by the row of scrawled names on the inside wall.

"Wow." She trailed her fingers down the list, looking for Leo's familiar handwriting. "There you are." She leaned in, peering at the date. "Wow, has it really been that long?"

He stepped closer and pointed to the name right below his. "Remember this guy? Only jumped for two seasons and then took off on that wild journey around Australia."

"On a motorcycle." Nyla straightened, catching the wistfulness in Leo's eyes. "Was that part of the inspiration for Leo's Selfish Dream?"

"Nah, that was all my dad." He scrubbed a hand over his chin, eyes locking with hers. "He always wanted to do a big motorcycle road trip. Never even got the motorcycle.

That one in the picture with him belonged to a buddy."

She knew this, of course, just like she knew the scent of his skin, the way his T-shirt stretched taut over his chest. He stood so close, probably closer than he'd meant to. It was her fault for standing up so fast and pivoting to face him like she had.

But now, she couldn't step back. Her skin felt magnetized, tugged toward the steel of Leo's body. "I've always thought that was cool," she said. "Fixing up an old bike like the one your dad wanted. Having a goal like that."

He leaned against the wall, muscles flexing as he lifted his arm. "He had all these maps he used to spread out on the table. Campgrounds he'd marked, or detours he wanted to take so he could see some weird roadside attraction, like the world's largest vat of spaghetti." He laughed, but his voice had a distant, pensive quality. "He used to talk about it all the time, how he'd spend three or four years seeing the country."

Nyla swallowed, wishing she could offer a comforting hug. He'd put his T-shirt back on, so at least they'd have layers between them, but that hadn't stopped them last time, and besides, she wasn't that strong.

"Did it bother your mom?" she asked. "That he had this big dream that involved leaving her behind for such a long time?"

A shadow passed over his face. Faint, but it was there. "Probably. They were careful not to argue in front of me, but I heard them talking once. She asked how he could just take off like that, leaving the family for months. I was in my bedroom next door with my ear pressed up against the wall, trying like hell to hear them."

"What was his answer?"

Leo paused. "He said, 'that's why I'm waiting 'til Leo's out of school.'" He grimaced. "I know, right?"

"Ouch. Your poor mom."

"Yeah. I was just a kid, but even I knew that's not what she was asking. He must have figured it out, because there was this long silence and then he starts explaining. 'Don't worry, I'll come home all the time to see you,' he told her. He starts stammering and getting all flustered and I remember clear as day what my mother said."

"What did she say?" Nyla licked her lips. She hadn't done it on purpose, but when Leo's gaze dropped to her mouth, she felt a shiver of pleasure. "Was your mom angry?"

"That's the thing," he said. "She must have been hurt or at least a little disappointed. But she said, 'Joe, stop. It's okay. I've known since we met that you had this dream. I'm not going to be the one to steal that from you.'" His throat moved as he swallowed, but he didn't look away. "In the end, though, she's not the one who stole it."

Cancer. God, how she hated that word. "I'm so sorry, Leo."

He nodded once. "Thank you."

She loved that he didn't say "It's okay" or some other benign, soothing platitude people offer up to relieve discomfort. Leo was okay sitting with his hurt, feeling pain like a well-adjusted grownup. He was the toughest, strongest, most tool-wielding manly man she knew, and she'd never seen him hide his feelings. He'd cried at the hospital the day Seth was born, and before that, he choked up saying his vows to Mandi.

A tight knot formed in Nyla's throat and she swallowed it back. She'd never once seen Greg cry. Not a single time in the nine years they'd dated. Not even when they split up.

She took a shaky breath. "I should probably go."

"You probably should."

Neither of them moved. Nyla felt her heart pounding against her ribs, felt her palms slick with nerves. He wanted to say something, she could tell. He held back, jaw clenching with the effort.

Nyla couldn't hold back. "Would it be the worst thing?"

His eyes flashed, hot and dangerous. "What's that?"

He knew. They both did, she was positive. They'd been careening toward this moment for weeks. Months, maybe years.

Nyla bit her lip and felt a flicker of energy as his eyes dropped to her mouth again. "If we took this to the next level," she said softly. "Would the world end?"

She held her breath, knowing the answer. The world as she knew it, as they both knew it, would come to a screeching halt. If she kissed Leo again, if it led where she knew it would lead, they'd be past the point of no return.

Past sweeping this under the rug or insisting it was just a silly kiss. That it had only happened once.

But it had already happened more than once, and as Nyla reached out and put her hands on Leo's chest, she knew it was happening again.

"Nyla." His voice was ragged and hungry as his eyes locked with hers. "I thought you said we shouldn't."

"I know." She drew her hands across his chest, memorizing the hard flex of muscle as Leo closed his eyes. "But maybe life's too short to deny the things you want. Like your dad, waiting around for the right time to chase his dream. For a someday that never happened."

She was thinking of his father, but also of her parents. Her mom's lifelong wish to visit Europe, and her dad's steadfast refusal to get on an airplane. Her father's pleas that they buy matching kayaks and learn to paddle, and her mom's steadfast *hell no* until eventually, her dad stopped asking.

Is that what relationships were all about? A lifetime of pushing aside your own desires and being satisfied with the way things were?

Leo's eyes stayed closed. She could feel his heart hammering in his chest, the steady thrum pulsing through her palms.

"I want you." She said the words out loud, startling him enough so his eyes fluttered open. "Leo, I want you."

He groaned deep in the back of his throat. "Nyla."

She held her breath, palms still pressed against his chest. Leo made a choked sound.

Then his hands slid up her sides, tracing her hips, her arms, her shoulders, until they came to rest on the sides of her face. Fingertips skimming the hair at the edge of her temples, he looked into her eyes.

"Are you sure?"

She nodded, not trusting herself to speak. If anyone could find a way to ruin this moment with waterfalls of wasted words, it would be her.

So she stepped forward instead, going up on tiptoe to press her lips to his. He still cupped her face in his hands, and she could feel his heart galloping against her fingertips. Her lungs clenched tight as she reminded herself to breath.

"Leo." She whispered the word against his mouth, needing to remind herself what was at stake.

A longtime friendship.

Her sister's trust.

The simple structure of her nephew's world.

But all of that got washed away by the flood of feeling, the glide of Leo's tongue against hers. Sliding her hands from his chest, she moved them to his shoulder blades, pulling him tight against her.

Leo groaned. "You're killing me, Nyla."

She swallowed hard. "Is that a no? Because I could—"

"No." He shook his head, heat flashing in his eyes. "That's definitely not no. That's 'if you're sure, I'm locking this door right now and apologizing in advance that this is going to happen on a twin bed, because I honest to God can't wait twenty more minutes to drive home.'"

She smiled and stepped back, gripping the hem of her borrowed tank top. So much for an ugly wardrobe warding off sexual tension.

But it didn't matter. Nothing mattered but having

Leo's hands on her again, so she tugged off the tank top and reached for the front zipper on her borrowed sports bra.

"Wait, let me." Leo kicked the door shut and turned the lock, then hurried back to her side. "I've wanted to do this forever."

Forever.

She knew it was only an expression. That he'd been faithful in his marriage. That he'd never seen her as anything but a friend, a sister. Or maybe he had. Maybe she'd been fooling herself all along.

He was seeing her now, feasting his eyes on her as he slowly tugged the zipper of her borrowed sports bra. As her flesh spilled into his hands, he gave a groan of appreciation.

"Nyla." He sunk to his knees and breathed her name into the valley between her breasts. "You feel so good."

Closing her eyes, she laced her fingers through his hair as his tongue found her nipple. "Leo." She cried out as his teeth grazed sensitive flesh, then laved it with his tongue. "Don't stop."

His response was muffled against her skin as he teased and tasted, worshipping her with his mouth. Her brain skittered back to those first early months when he and Mandi dated.

"He's the best kisser," she'd gushed, leaning forward over the shared bistro table. "And his hands—"

"No." She croaked the word out loud without meaning to, blinking herself back to the present. Leo shot to his feet.

"I'm so sorry." He dragged his hands through his hair. "We can stop. Let me just—"

"No," she said again, and pounced on him.

This time when their mouths met, she left no room for second thoughts. She kissed him hard and deep and fierce with no space for questions, no room for doubts. As she backed him toward the mattress, he clutched her ass and boosted her up.

"This?" He broke the kiss, still holding her as he turned so her back was to the bed. "Is this what you want?"

She nodded, struggling to shrug off her bra as she held tight to his shoulders. "Please, Leo. I can't wait anymore."

His mouth found hers again, and with two quick steps, he was lowering her back onto the bed. The springs squeaked a little, and she said a silent prayer he'd fixed whatever the hell was wrong with the frame before she interrupted.

She clutched him desperately, nails digging into his back. She knew one of them might chicken out if they stopped kissing for even a moment. Her hands found the fly of his jeans, and she tugged at the zipper, conscious of the hardness straining soft denim.

"Jesus, Nyla." He released her lips only long enough to tug his shirt over his head. As he threw it aside, Nyla made quick work of shucking her borrowed gym shorts. No panties, thank God, so that was one less layer to worry about.

In an instant he was naked and stretched out beside

her, stroking his hand down her side. The space was narrow, but she welcomed it. They fit perfectly with their bodies pressed tight together, not a stitch of clothing between them.

Leo looked deep in her eyes. "Uh, this is probably the wrong time to admit I don't have a condom."

She bit her lip. "I do."

He smiled and stroked a hand over her hair. "Is that a nurse thing?"

She shook her head slowly, drawing her fingertips down his back. "That's an 'I've been thinking about this and wanted to be prepared' thing," she admitted, nodding toward the keys she'd set on the windowsill. "In that little coin pouch."

He laughed and reached for the keys, knocking them to the floor. Muttering a curse, he leaned down to grab them. Nyla let her gaze linger on the bunched muscles of his back, the curve of his glutes. He was impossibly well put-together, and she couldn't believe she was about to have him.

"Got it." Leo resurfaced with the condom, holding it up in triumph. Nyla reached for it, but he held it back. "In a minute. There's something I want first."

Her inner nurse teed up a lecture on the importance of using condoms from the very start of sexual activity, but before she opened her mouth, Leo rolled her onto her back and shouldered himself between her thighs and *ohmygod*, okay, the condom could wait a few minutes.

"Leo." She clutched the top of his head, marveling at

how well the man knew female anatomy. His tongue on her clit, circling, teasing, was almost too much to bear. Her brain darted to a dark corner, reminding her how he'd honed his skills.

Mandi. If Mandi knew—

But her selfish, desperate heart pushed back the thoughts and surrendered her body to sensation. She cried out as he stroked with the flat of his tongue. "Right there. Don't stop."

Humming in the back of his throat, he licked lazy circles around her clit, taking his time as her hips arched up off the bed and she whimpered her pleasure. How did he know just how to touch her, how to curl two fingers inside as his tongue worked magic on twelve dozen erogenous zones at once?

Or maybe she'd become one big erogenous zone, Leo transforming her body into a single buzzing, pulsing nerve. She gasped as his fingers stroked deep inside her, summoning her to the edge. Squeezing her eyes closed, she cried out as the first wave of climax crashed into her. "Oh God!"

He clamped one hand on her hip as he licked and stroked and carried her through crest after crest and *good lord*, how was it possible for an orgasm to last this long?

When she blinked her way back down to earth, Leo was kissing his way up her body. Dragging the back of one hand over his chin, he looked at her and grinned. "That," he said. "I've been dreaming of that for weeks."

She was still too mind-whacked to come up with

some witty reply. Just a sigh that came out sounding more like a moan, which made him smile again. Smile and lean down to dot a soft row of kisses along her collarbone.

"Please," she murmured, finding her voice again. "I want you inside me, Leo."

He drew back and grabbed for the condom. "Thought you might want to catch your breath."

She shook her head and reached down to help roll the prophylactic on. Not that he needed help, but she needed to touch him. Needed to feel him moving inside her as soon as humanly possible.

Letting her legs fall apart, she welcomed him into the cradle of her thighs, arms twining around his back. She reached down to guide him into her and found his hand already there, poising his thick length near her entrance.

"Inside. Now. Please." She was begging now, her whole body aching to feel him.

He drew the rounded head through her slippery cleft and Nyla hissed out a breath. She wanted him so much she saw stars behind her eyelids. She opened her mouth to whisper another plea, but the words burst into a sharp cry as he slid inside her.

"Ple—*yesssss*." Oh God, that felt so good. She clenched her thighs around him, pushing aside all her doubts, her fears. Nothing mattered but this moment, Leo angled up on his arms so he could watch her face as he slid into her.

"God, Nyla," he ground out. "You're so beautiful."

She *felt* beautiful beneath him, wanton and wild and

electric with his touch. Arching up off the bed, she gripped his hips with her thighs and held on for dear life.

"Don't stop," she panted, though there was no reason to think he might. He looked as enraptured as she felt, moving inside her with a rhythm she answered with a grind of her own hips. "Don't you dare stop."

He laughed and drove into her again. "Not until you come again." He bent to kiss her neck, drawing his tongue along the back of her ear. "If you want to, of course."

She shivered and arched up against him, already feeling the simmer of another orgasm. Unexpected, since she'd never been one to get off with plain old missionary.

But there was nothing plain or old about the way Leo made love. The precision of his movements, the way he angled himself just so to graze her clit with each thrust. She could feel herself going under again.

"Leo!" She shouted his name this time, not caring if an entire squadron of smokejumpers heard her.

He drove in hard, pushing her over the edge. She cried out and clutched at him, expecting him to follow her this time. To let himself go, shuddering with release.

But he wasn't done. The second she stopped trembling, he rolled to his back and pulled her on top of him. She blinked, disoriented as her body kept clenching around him. "Smooth move, Sayre," she murmured, leaning over to kiss him.

He kissed her back and gave her butt a tight squeeze. "I wanted to see you," he murmured, gliding his palms up her sides until he cupped her breasts. "To touch you like this."

She started to move, marveling at this new angle. How was the man still rock hard? Thank God for the stamina of older men, not that he was much older than she was. But how astonishing to have sex with someone so adept at giving pleasure, so conscious of just how to touch her.

Don't think about how he learned that. Don't think about how—

"Stay with me, Nyla," he urged, squeezing her butt again. "I can see those wheels turning in your brain."

She blinked and refocused, then bent to kiss him again. "I'm right here."

And she was. Closing her eyes, she lifted her arms to touch her breasts. She'd never been this bold in the bedroom before, but she'd never been with a man who made her feel so…so…

"Gorgeous." He hissed the word like a prayer as Nyla circled her hips. "You're the most beautiful woman in the world."

This time, she didn't let her brain dwell on how many women he'd assessed. It was only the two of them, locked in each other's eyes.

"Oh." She gasped as her eyes fluttered open at the stroke of Leo's thumb. He grinned up at her, circling the pad of it over her sensitive nub as she rode him faster. "Leo, God."

"That's it. I can feel you gripping me."

So could she. Tiny pinpricks of light burst behind her eyelids as she sucked in a breath and ground down onto him. The tip of him hit something deep inside her and she shattered.

"Fuck!" It was Leo calling out this time, Leo grabbing her hips and driving into her as she came hard again, his climax spurring hers. She rolled her hips, intent on milking every ounce of pleasure from the moment. She felt him pulsing, saw his eyes wide with dazed wonder as they crested higher and higher still.

When they both came down, she was still breathing hard as he rolled to his side and got rid of the condom. He was kissing her, touching her, murmuring words she could barely make out as she came down from her sex-sated haze.

"Nyla."

Her eyelids fluttered open as he said her name, and she met his gaze to find him smiling. "That was amazing. Remember that, okay? As your brain starts racing again, I want you to promise you'll remember how fucking magical that just was. Promise me?"

She nodded, not sure she could form real words anyway, but certain she could keep that promise.

Because right now, she was positive that even if she lived six more lifetimes, she would never shake the memory of this moment with Leo.

CHAPTER TWELVE

Leo drove home in a sex stupor, replaying the conversation with Nyla in his head.

"Stay," he'd urged, kissing his way from her neck to her shoulder as she sat up in bed. "Not here, I mean. Come home with me and spend the night."

She'd turned and smiled at him, wriggling into the borrowed sports bra before kissing him once on the mouth. "Aren't you forgetting something?"

"Please?" he'd asked hopefully, already imagining what it would feel like to wake up with Nyla in his arms.

She'd laughed and bounced off the bed, rummaging on the floor for her clothes. "Your son, goofball. Isn't he getting dropped off at nine?"

Crap. He'd almost forgotten, which wasn't like him at all. He prided himself on being a devoted dad, the guy who remembered every baseball practice and parent-teacher conference. "I suck," he'd admitted as he rolled off the bed to search for his pants.

"Don't feel bad." She'd turned to face him, fully dressed as he stood naked with his pants in hand. "Last month Mandi totally forgot Ryan's mom was bringing him home at ten after they stayed to watch the other team in the finals at that tournament outside Seattle. We were halfway through a second bottle of wine when Seth came bounding through the front door."

She'd clamped her mouth shut then, a guilty look passing over her face. "Shit. I didn't mean to tell you that."

"It's okay." God, she was adorable. Pants located, he'd tugged them up over his hips and buttoned his fly and stepped closer to kiss the warm spot at the base of her neck. "You're right, it does make me feel better knowing I'm not the only parent shirking my duties for an evening of pleasure."

"Mmmmm." She'd melted against him then, seeming to forget her haste to get gone. "When can I see you again?"

"Tomorrow?" Too fucking eager, but so what? "Or how about Saturday night? Ryan's mom drew driving duty for Sunday's tournament, and they're leaving late that evening. We could order sushi, stay up all night, wake up together Sunday morning. I'm not due at the game until late in the day on Sunday."

She'd moaned again as he tugged aside the strap of her tank top to kiss the sensitive spot he'd found on her left shoulder. Kissing it again, he drew in a breath as she stepped away. "You're forgetting brunch," she murmured with her eyes closed.

"Brunch?"

"At my parents' house." She turned and put a hand on his chest, then stepped back. "Remember? Dad's hoping you can help fix Mom's pizzelle maker so she can do those special Polish cookies."

Right. Fuck, he really was losing it. "We're planning Seth's graduation party and your dad's surprising your mom with her early birthday gift."

"Bingo."

He'd dragged a hand down his face then, struggling to get a grip. "Sorry I'm being a shitty dad. Shitty ex-son-in-law, too."

Nyla had stepped closer then, pulling him in for a kiss. "You're the best guy I know. Best dad, best…well, everything." Kudos to her for dodging the ex-son-in-law bit. "How about when you come back from the tournament? Mandi's got Seth, and we can decompress from the awkwardness of brunch."

"Deal." He'd kissed her one last time, then let her go.

He could still taste that kiss on his drive home. Glancing at his watch, he was startled to realize Seth would be home in thirty minutes. Not that Seth wasn't old enough to let himself in and be alone for a few minutes, but still. Leo made it a point to be there when his kid got home whenever possible. It wasn't like him to forget.

He let himself in through the garage and spent a few minutes filling Howie's kibble dish and assuring him he was the best cat in the universe. After shoving a frozen burrito in the microwave, Leo ambled down the hall to check himself in the mirror.

Whoa. His T-shirt bore two smudgy boob prints in the middle of the chest. Probably where dust settled on wet cotton before Nyla ditched her damp bra. The thought of Nyla's breasts—all of her, really—sent blood surging south all over again. He tossed the shirt in the hamper and pulled on a clean one as Seth came banging through the front door.

"Hey, Dad!" He hollered his greeting from the kitchen, the smack of the fridge door making it clear he'd beelined straight for food. "Yo! Anyone home?"

"Duh." Leo ambled down the hall, doing his best not to look like a guy who'd been naked with Aunt Nyla an hour ago. He scrubbed a hand over his chin. "Didn't you eat at Ryan's?"

"Yeah, but I'm starving. Oh! Burrito." He yanked open the microwave door just as the timer dinged.

"*My* burrito." Leo grunted and grabbed another one from the freezer, throwing it on a plate as Seth laid claim to the first one. "You're stealing my dinner, punk."

Seth laughed and took a monster bite out of the first one, yelping the way he always did when he didn't bother letting it cool. "Hot!"

"One of these days you'll learn." Leo hit some buttons on the microwave and set it humming again. "Milk?"

His son swallowed a mouthful of burrito and shot him a hopeful look. "How about Coke?"

"How about it's late and you don't need all that caffeine and sugar." He poured a glass for Seth and one for himself, pausing to grab a bowl of grapes from the fridge. "Eat your fruit." He shoved the bowl in the space beside Seth, then grabbed his burrito from the microwave and sat down beside his kid.

Seth grinned around a mouthful of food. "Thanks, Dad."

Dad. Even after twelve years, the word never ceased to thrill him. It never lost its shine, not even knowing what he knew about DNA and the guy in Uganda.

A cold lump formed in his gut, and he swallowed it back with a big gulp of milk. "How was practice?"

"Great." Seth shoved a fistful of grapes into his mouth and started to talk, but Leo silenced him with *the look*. Grinning around his grapes, Seth chewed and swallowed and tried again. "Ryan's mom was late picking us up, so she took us to McDonalds for dinner and then we went to the batting cages."

"Because you didn't get enough baseball today?"

Seth laughed. "No such thing."

Leo grabbed a cluster of grapes, leaning back in his chair as he plucked them from the stem. "My dad and I used to hit the batting cages every Sunday. Same ones, over on Division Street."

"No kidding?" Seth shoved a trio of grapes in his mouth, looking thoughtful. "Was Grandpa Joe a lot different from Grandpa Bob?"

Leo took his time answering. "Yeah, I guess. My dad was more into sports and camping and stuff like that. A lot taller than Bob, but they both love fishing. You have the same laugh as my dad."

Which was weird to say. His father never met his only grandson, and now that Leo knew they shared no DNA, it made zero sense for them to share that. Biology was weird and Leo had a lump in his throat, so he fumbled for a way to change the subject.

But Seth wasn't done. He was looking down at his plate with a furrow between his brows. "I wish I got to meet Grandpa Joe. He sounds like a cool guy."

"He was. I wish you could have known him." The lump was getting thicker in Leo's throat, and he forced it back again with more burrito.

"Hey!" Seth bolted straight in his chair, grinning again. "I almost forgot. I'm asking Aunt Nyla to come to career day."

Leo lifted an eyebrow. "What, a dad who flies air tankers isn't cool enough?"

Seth laughed and picked up his plate to lick off a gob of melted cheese. "Nah, this one's just for medical people. They asked for doctors and paramedics and nurses. Besides, you know how Aunt Nyla loves that stuff."

"She does." The thought of Nyla sent Leo's brain careening down carnal pathways again.

What would happen if they actually dated? If they made it public, let the whole world know they were together. A real relationship, not something hidden in the shadows.

His brain tripped down that path, imagining them vacationing together, moving in, maybe getting married.

Would Seth still call her Aunt Nyla?

Would family dinners be even more awkward?

Hell, maybe he wouldn't be invited anymore. God only knows how Ted and Laurel might react to Leo being passed between their daughters like a hand-me-down shirt.

The thought made him glum, and he downed the rest of his milk like he was chugging a beer.

"Did I do something?"

Seth's question caught him off-guard. "What do you

mean?" Leo asked cautiously.

"You're acting kinda weird. Like maybe I'm in trouble or something."

Leo took his time responding. "Did you do something to deserve to be in trouble?"

His kid started laughing, then grabbed another fistful of grapes. "I'm the best kid in the universe. You know that."

"I think I saw that on the evening news," he mused, standing to clear his plate. "Must be what that crowd is for outside, folks clamoring to get your autograph."

"It's rough being a celebrity." Seth picked up his own plate and glass. "I can see tomorrow's headline already—'Seth Sayre loads his own dishes in the dishwasher without being asked.'"

"Atta boy." Leo ruffled his son's hair, feeling a sharp stab of emotion behind his ribs. "How about you? Everything going okay at school?"

"Yeah." A faint blush crept up his kid's neck. "There's this girl I like—I told you about her last week, remember?"

"Sahalie, yeah."

Seth grinned. "I might ask her to the end-of-school dance."

A wave of emotion socked him in the gut and he took his time replying. "Look at you, growing up so fast."

"Next week I'll be borrowing the car."

Leo laughed and stood up to clap his kid on the shoulder. "Let me know if you want to practice asking Sahalie out. Or, you know—if you have any questions about girl stuff."

Seth blushed. "I will."

"I love you, buddy."

"Love you, too, Dad." Seth wrapped his arms around him and squeezed hard, making Leo's ribs crack. "I'm gonna go to bed now, 'kay?"

"Don't forget to pick up your towel off the floor," he reminded him. "Oh, and I left Grandma's birthday card on your desk."

"Already signed it this morning."

"Shoulda known, considering you're the best kid in the world."

"Universe, Dad. *Universe*." Seth laughed as he turned and loped down the hall to his room.

God, he really was growing up fast. The sharpness wasn't easing up in Leo's chest, so he put the milk back in the fridge and grabbed himself a beer. He glanced at the thermometer on the wall, noticing it was still warm enough to sit outside.

Popping his beer open, he slipped out through the sliding door and out onto the deck. He'd built that deck himself more than ten years ago, with Mandi following behind, sealing and staining the boards. They'd cracked beers together afterward, celebrating their hard work.

Was Nyla right? Would his ex-wife be hurt if he moved on with her sister? A small, secret, petty part of him couldn't feel bad about that. Wanted Mandi to feel the sting of seeing him in a happy relationship when she'd cast him aside.

But that wasn't fair. He hadn't been happy in their

marriage, either. Not near the end, anyway. Hell, if he was being honest, he almost couldn't blame her for screwing around. He'd been so wrapped up in work back then, and she'd tried to get his attention.

"Maybe we could have a picnic this weekend," she'd said, boosting herself up on the counter in the garage where he was working one summer afternoon. "We haven't done that in ages."

"Can't," he'd said, barely looking up from the part he'd been working on for his mom's car. "The new head gasket came in. I want to get this put in right away."

She'd looked at him a long time, a gaze he'd felt even though he hadn't looked up. "I think it's wonderful how you're always doing things to help other people," she'd said slowly. "Putting everyone else first, that's great. I just—" She'd stopped herself there, and Leo had looked up to see her pressing her lips together.

"What?" he'd asked, without really wanting the answer.

"Never mind."

"What?" He was getting impatient.

"Nothing."

He'd been married long enough by then to know "nothing" was always something. "What is it, Mandi?" He probably hadn't done a good job of keeping the irritation from his voice, and he'd seen a flash of pain in her eyes.

She'd hesitated a long time, choosing her words carefully. "I just never knew, when I married a guy who puts everyone else's needs before his own, that I wouldn't count as 'everyone' anymore. That I'd become part of you instead."

Before he could say anything, she'd slipped off the counter and drifted into the house. He'd stared at the door for a long time, wondering what the hell to say to that.

In the end, it hadn't mattered. He'd said he was sorry and took her on that damn picnic. Probably acted like an asshole about it, which he wasn't proud of.

Two weeks later, she'd gone to Uganda.

Nine months later, they had Seth.

Now, Leo ran a hand over the knotted porch rail, reminding himself to re-sand it. To buy another couple gallons of sealant and get things spiffed up again. There was never enough time in the day, not lately.

He sighed and tipped his head back, swilling his beer as he looked up at the stars. Somewhere on the other side of town, maybe Nyla was doing the same thing. Maybe her body still hummed with pleasure, just like his was now. Maybe she was wondering the same thing he was about where they were headed and what sort of future they could have together.

Maybe, just maybe, there was a chance he'd get it right this time.

• • •

Leo ambled along the sidewalk in front of his ex-in-laws' house at eight Sunday morning, toolbox in hand. He had a bottle of bubbly in the other hand as he walked past Mandi's car, which saved him the awkwardness of deciding if he needed to shake hands or hug his ex-wife as she opened her car door and unfolded herself from the driver's seat.

"Seth make it out okay last night?" she asked by way of greeting.

"Yep. Ryan's dad had the motorhome all tricked out in team colors."

"Nice." She smiled, but it didn't quite reach her eyes. "Did he remember his glove this time?"

"Yep. I stapled it to his hand."

She laughed, but it sounded forced. He stood frozen on the sidewalk, waiting for her to say whatever the hell was on her mind.

He didn't wait long.

"Look, I'm worried about Nyla."

His lungs froze in his chest. Shit, she knew. "Yeah?"

"Just—you know, that she'll blurt something out about this Seth situation before it's the right time."

Leo let out a long breath. He considered his words carefully, wondering what she could read on his face. "When is the right time?"

"I don't know. Soon?" She twisted her purse strap around her wrist. "I just…I'm not sure how Mom and Dad will react, but I feel like maybe Seth should know before they do. And I'm not sure Seth's ready to hear something like that yet."

He didn't disagree. Part of him wanted to, but she was right. No twelve-year-old wanted to hear his mother banged someone besides his dad. Hell, twelve-year-olds probably didn't want to hear about *any* sex involving their parents, but especially not adultery. "Understandable," Leo said slowly.

He patted himself on the back for not saying the snarky stuff out loud, but Mandi must have seen it in his eyes.

"Don't start." She sighed, looking more tired than he'd seen her in a long time. "I know I screwed up and caused all this, but I don't think Seth should suffer the consequences, and before you say I should have thought of that before I opened my legs, *I know*."

Her words came out so rushed that it took him a moment to catch them all. He watched her face, waiting to see if she had more to say. "You done?"

She looked down at the ground, then nodded. "Yes. Well, not quite." She met his eyes again. "I'm sorry, Leo. Really, I am."

"Good. And I agree with you."

She blinked. "You do?" Her forehead creased in a frown. "Wait, you mean the part about me screwing up?"

He laughed and shifted his grip on the champagne. "That's not what I meant. I agree it's not the right time to tell everyone. I don't know when it'll be right, but not yet."

Her shoulders slumped with relief. "Then we're on the same page."

"Sure." He glanced toward the house. "We should probably get inside."

"Of course." She bit her lip. "So maybe we should work together to keep Nyla from blabbing? She means well and all, but we both know she can't keep a secret to save her life."

Hearing Nyla's name sent a jolt of electricity through him, and he wondered if Mandi saw it on his face. "Yeah, okay."

"All right then. And Leo?"

"Hmm?"

"For what it's worth, I never stopped loving you."

His heart seized up like a bad engine. "What do you mean?"

She glanced at the house and Leo saw the curtains move. Great. Ted and Laurel probably thought they were witnessing a reconciliation. They'd have the champagne popped before he got through the door.

Mandi turned back to him. "Look, I know they want us to get back together, but that's not what I'm talking about."

"Good." An asshole response, but he had to be honest.

She didn't flinch. "As the father of my child, the man I spent more than a decade with—that matters to me, Leo. Even if we're not together, there's still no one in the world I'd rather raise a son with. I hope you know that."

He nodded, not sure what to say to that. In the back of his head, he heard the echo of Nyla's words.

"Seeing my ex with another woman felt like someone ripped my heart out of my chest. Like I'd been kicked in the stomach, and I hated myself so much for feeling that way."

He forced out the words he knew she needed to hear.

"I care about you, too. And you're a good mom."

Tears glittered in her eyes, but she blinked them away. "Come on." She touched his hand, nodding at the bottle. "Want me to carry that?"

"Sure." He released his grip on the champagne, letting her take it from his hands. "Ready to do this?"

He wasn't sure what he meant, but she laughed and nodded. "Operation keep Nyla's trap shut? Absolutely."

She turned and skipped ahead of him, up the walkway and toward the house, as her mom swung the front door open. Laurel gave him a knowing smile, probably planning their second wedding ceremony in her head.

With a heavy feeling in his gut, Leo trudged the rest of the way to the door.

CHAPTER THIRTEEN

Nyla hated running late.

She hated even more that she'd kinda done it on purpose.

But she was being responsible. If she'd shown up on time — or God forbid, *early* — she risked having her mother read everything on her face. The sex with Leo, Mandi's secret affair, the sex with Leo, Seth's biology, the sex with Leo, her father's birthday gift, and obviously, the sex with Leo.

"God." She sat in her driveway, banging her head on the steering wheel a few times, annoyed with herself for grinning. This was serious stuff, and now she was ten minutes late for brunch.

"That's a blessing, at least." She needed to stop talking to herself in the driveway. A neighbor walked by — old Mrs. Henshaw with her toothless poodle — and Nyla waved and tried to pretend all was normal.

As if.

She'd slept with her ex-brother-in-law and nothing would ever be normal again.

Was it wrong to feel tingly about that? The whole thing was bad, clearly, but also maybe good?

She started the car and drove carefully to her parents' place, braced for a scolding from her mother for being tardy. Better than the grilling she'd have gotten if she were there on time, so she called it a win.

As she pulled up along the curb, her belly flipped over at the sight of Leo's truck just ahead of hers. And okay, Mandi's car. Another flurry of butterflies flapped in her gut as she wondered what Mandi might read on her face.

The weekend Nyla lost her virginity, she'd come down to the breakfast table in her favorite flannel pajamas. She felt different, glowy and happy and bursting with secrets, but she'd been sure she'd hidden it well.

Mandi—home for Christmas break—had taken one look at Nyla's face and stood up from the table. "We'll be right back." She'd grabbed Nyla's arm and hauled her up the stairs into her bedroom. "Tell me everything," Mandi had whispered, bouncing on the bed. "How was it? Did you come?"

God, how embarrassing.

But also nice, to have someone who cared. Someone who didn't judge, and who knew her enough to coach her on how things were supposed to work and how she shouldn't get frustrated if sex wasn't as perfect and synchronized as it was in the movies.

"I'm happy for you, Duckie," Mandi had whispered as she hugged Nyla tight. "He's a good guy and I'm glad you used protection."

Nyla sighed and glanced at her parents' house. Call it a hunch, but she didn't think things would go the same way now if Mandi knew about her and Leo.

With a deep breath, she opened her car door and grabbed the bowl containing her favorite spinach and strawberry salad. She'd tucked the feta and the honey-lemon dressing in little mason jars in her purse, so she'd need to remember it later. The honey was from Guatemala, procured by Mandi from some farmers' collective in a village where she'd volunteered earlier in the year.

Deep breath. You've got this.

As she made her way up the walkway, the door flew open and Mandi greeted her with a smile. "Hey, Duckie! How's it going?"

Nyla smiled back, grateful to her sister for heading off their mom's scolding. "Good. Sorry I'm late. I got busy making salad and I lost track of time and—"

"It's fine, no worries." Mandi grabbed the salad bowl and thrust a champagne flute into Nyla's hand. "Have a mimosa."

"Oh. Thank you." She took the crystal flute as Mandi ushered her into the house. "Everyone's outside, but I wanted to show you something first. Come on, it's in the guest room."

"Okay." She sipped her mimosa, enjoying the sweet tang of orange juice spiked with plenty of champagne. She didn't usually drink in the mornings, and especially not on an empty stomach, but the beverage was cool and delicious, so she followed Mandi through the kitchen with a pit stop to tuck the salad in the fridge.

"Shouldn't I say hi to Mom and Dad first?" Nyla glanced outside, stomach flipping when she spotted Leo seated across from her parents. He was holding an electric wire and talking to her dad, pointing at the prong end with one long, thick finger.

Nyla swallowed hard, unable to take her eyes off him. *Dammit.*

"This will only take a second." Mandi grabbed her arm again and dragged her toward the guest room as Nyla struggled to keep a grip on her drink.

"This is really good." She took another sip as Mandi pulled the bedroom door shut behind her. "Is this fresh-squeezed juice?"

"Yeah, I did a whole bag of oranges before you got here." Mandi bent down and hauled a cardboard box out from under the bed. "Remember these?"

Nyla peered down at the box of VHS tapes. "Are those all the videos Dad took when we were little?"

"I found them when I was cleaning out my office. I totally forgot I rescued them when they did that big garage cleanout ten years ago." Mandi stood with a tape in each hand. "Don't you think Mom would love watching them again?"

Nyla sipped her drink. It was going down fast. "Do they even have a VCR anymore?"

"I bought one at Goodwill." She smiled and set the tapes aside. "I thought maybe we could watch these while we eat. Remember that one Dad took of us at the beach with Mom when we were little? I still can't believe she wore a bikini, or that she—"

"Wait, I thought we were here to plan Seth's graduation party." Nyla took a tiny sip of mimosa, reminding herself to take it slow. "When's Dad giving her the surprise?"

"After brunch. We can do all of that later. Or whenever." Her sister's gaze skittered toward the window, and Nyla looked, too.

Leo was standing now, cordless drill in one hand as he laughed at something her mom said. Her stomach rolled, and she wondered if she could blame it on champagne. On anything but the way she felt around Leo.

As she watched, he set the drill down and stretched, exposing a swath of muscular abdomen. Her mouth watered as she remembered what it felt like to run her tongue over —

"Gotta hand it to Leo," her sister said, jolting Nyla's thoughts from the gutter. "He keeps himself in good shape."

"Guh," said Nyla, and drank more mimosa.

"You okay?"

Nyla nodded, mouth full of orange juice and champagne. "Great!" she gurgled. "Fantastic."

She dared another glance out the window and watched her mother pointing to something on the pizzelle maker, which was spread out on the table like a gutted fish. "Did they get that fixed?"

Mandi shrugged. "I think so. Leo was tinkering with it earlier."

Leo. Since when did the sound of his name send goose bumps rippling up her arms? Or the sight of those muscular shoulders, the forearms she'd felt braced on either side of her as he drove in deep and —

"Ack." She coughed as the champagne went down the wrong pipe.

Mandi caught her arm. "Shit, are you choking again?

I can get Leo in here to—"

"I'm fine, I'm fine." She waved her sister off, eyes watering. "I just forgot how to drink, that's all."

"You sure you're okay?" Mandi looked dubious. "Let me get you a glass of water. Stay here."

"I'm really fine." She tried to grab her sister before Mandi darted away. "I'm really okay and I'd like to go out and see Mom and D—"

But Mandi was already out the door, so Nyla polished off the rest of her drink and carried the flute out into the kitchen. As she set it on the counter, Leo came through the sliding glass door with a mimosa in one hand.

"Hey, I thought that was you." He set his glass on the counter and studied her face. "Everything okay?"

"She choked on her drink." Mandi handed her a glass of water and gave Leo a look Nyla couldn't read. "Everything's fine. You got the pizzelle maker working again?"

"Yeah, it was just a frayed wire, so I showed them how to replace it. She should be able to make the cookies for graduation like Seth wants." He looked at Nyla with concern. "You sure you're okay? You look a little flushed."

"I'm good." She gulped her water and tried not to look at him. God, this was awkward.

"I'll go see if Mom and Dad need refills." Mandi stepped back from the sink and gave Leo another odd look. "You got this?"

"Yep."

Got what? Nyla glanced from her sister to Leo, not

sure what was going on.

But one look into Leo's brown eyes and she found herself not caring.

"Hey," he murmured as Mandi slid the patio door closed behind her.

"Hey back." She glanced outside again. "Is there a reason you two are keeping me away from Mom and Dad?"

He gave her a sheepish look as he scrubbed a hand over his chin. "Maybe?"

"What? Why?"

He started to lean in, then seemed to think better of it. He took a step back and shoved his hands in his pockets. "Mandi's worried about you bursting and saying something about Seth. About…you know."

Yeah, she knew. And she tried not to feel irritated, since her sister had a point. "I can keep quiet." She glanced down at the counter, noticing her voice didn't sound too confident. "I'm pretty sure."

Leo smiled, hands still in his pockets as his gaze swept her face. "I missed you," he murmured. "The other night was amazing."

Heat flooded her cheeks, her neck, her arms. She was burning up all over, and sure everyone could see. Even her parents from twenty feet away on the patio.

"Yeah." She dared a glance at him and felt her cheeks grow hotter. "It was pretty great."

Leo studied her face. "You look kinda tense. Want the rest of my mimosa? I barely touched it."

"I'm not sure that's—"

"I'll throw in a cherry, since I know that's how you like it."

He turned and rummaged through the fridge, and Nyla summoned the strength not to stare at his ass. Or not. God, he had a great butt.

"It's fine, I don't need—okay." She shut her mouth, deciding she really did want another mimosa. It would give her something to do with her mouth besides blab or drool over Leo. "Thank you."

"No prob." He located the jar of maraschinos and plucked out two with his bare fingers. "Don't tell your mom."

She rolled her eyes. "Because I'm awesome at keeping my mouth shut."

He smiled and her stomach flipped again. "You've got this. I believe in you."

She nodded and sipped her drink, since that seemed safer than talking. "Thank you," she said when she came up for air. "The cherries make it better."

"They always do." He studied her face, searching for something. "How about you? You good?"

She nodded and took another sip. "I'm good. I can handle this."

She was pretty sure, anyway.

Mandi floated through the door again and Nyla took a step back, even though she wasn't standing that close to Leo. She felt electrified and magnetized, like she'd slam into him if she stood too close.

"How are Mom and Dad?" she asked, hurrying to fill the silence. "Are they hungry or thirsty or should I go out and visit with them or—"

"Drink." Mandi tapped a fingernail against Nyla's glass. "You need to chill out a little. Relax, okay?"

"Okay." She wondered if Mandi thought this was still her first mimosa. She didn't seem to notice the cherries.

Mandi was busying herself making more mimosas, adding the champagne and pouring orange juice from a pitcher. Nyla glanced at Leo, who was doing a great job of acting normal.

Why the hell couldn't she manage that?

She turned back to Mandi, needing to keep her eyes off Leo. "I'm really fine, you guys. I can do this. I can shut up and stop talking and not make a big deal about Seth or Uganda or Dad's gift to Mom or—"

"Breathe." Leo's brow creased with concern. "You're good, Nyla. Just breathe, okay?"

Mandi rinsed a couple champagne flutes and glanced out the window again. "They're in one of those moods again."

"Which one?" Nyla glanced at her parents and took another sip of her drink. The cherries really did make it go down easy.

"The mood where they're dropping hints about me and Leo getting back together." Mandi grimaced and looked at him. "Sorry, I know it's awkward."

He shrugged, not looking at Nyla. "I'm used to awkward."

Nyla swallowed hard and set her flute on the counter. Then she picked it up again because she wasn't sure what else to do with her hands. Grabbing Leo seemed appealing, and what if she really did that?

"Can I go see Mom and Dad now?" She looked at her sister, because that was easier than looking at Leo. "I'll keep my mouth shut, I promise."

"Of course. I'm not keeping you." Her gaze flicked to her ex-husband. "One of us should probably stay with her at all times, right?"

Nyla rolled her eyes, which made her a little dizzy. "I don't need a babysitter, you guys." Only maybe she did. She was feeling kinda woozy.

Leo took a step closer and she shivered. "I've got you."

She shivered again, then worried it was too obvious. "Brrr!" She gave an exaggerated shudder, playing it up for Mandi's sake. "Dad must have the air conditioning cranked again."

Mandi eyed her curiously. "You sure you're okay?"

"I'm great! Perfect." She chugged the rest of her drink and set the empty flute on the counter. Clapping her hands together, she put on a bright face. "I'm great!" She'd already said that, hadn't she? "I'm ready."

Leo studied her again, then nodded at Mandi. "I'll head back out there. See you in a few?"

"Yep!" Nyla chirped, even though she wasn't sure he was talking to her. "See you soon." Did she sound a little slurred? She should stop saying words with the letter *S*.

Sealing her lips together, she turned back to her sister. Mandi was busy arranging filled champagne flutes on their mother's silver tray. "I made you another one."

She handed the glass to Nyla. "Hopefully, number two will take the edge off."

Nyla took a sip and wondered why the hell her sister was talking about going to the bathroom. Number two? She did have to pee, but—

"Oh. You think this is my second—".

But Mandi wasn't listening. She was muttering to herself and tapping at her phone. Nyla sipped her drink, deciding it was easier that way. Besides, she didn't want to rat out Leo for being impolite and not finishing his drink. See? She could do this. She could totally keep a secret.

"Boys," Mandi muttered, tucking the phone into her pocket. "He remembered his glove but forgot his cup. I should probably let him learn his lesson by getting hit in the nuts, but then I'd never have grandchildren."

Nyla nodded and pressed her lips together, not trusting herself to comment on procreation or testicles or sperm or really anything at all.

"You all right?" Mandi frowned.

Nyla nodded and looked away, afraid of what her sister might see on her face. Leo was back at the table, easing into the chair beside her dad. His long legs kicked out in front of him, muscular arms folded across a chest that was big and broad and—

"Ack." Nyla cleared her throat, choking back the urge to comment on any part of Leo's body. She forced herself to face her sister. "I'm good."

Mandi picked up the tray of mimosas. "Sorry I'm making you feel like you need a babysitter."

"It's okay." Really, it was. Or maybe not. Her head definitely felt fuzzy.

"I'm remembering that time you tattled on yourself for coming home after curfew," Mandi continued. "You were so sure you'd be found out, so you blurted out this whole story about going to a party and trying beer for the first time and sneaking in through the window. Remember that?"

Nyla sighed, feeling defensive. "I was sixteen. I have much better control now."

Maybe not with her third mimosa half gone. She should probably come clean with Mandi about that, but her sister started talking again.

"Okay, what about last Easter?" She balanced the tray in both hands and started toward the patio door. "Mom was looking everywhere for that gravy boat, and you sat there for an hour like you wanted to explode. Then what happened?"

Nyla sighed and trudged after her sister. "I knew she wouldn't really care that Dad accidentally gave it away," she muttered as she reached for the door. "And I thought it was mean to let her keep searching."

"Exactly." Mandi gave her a good-natured hip bump, miraculously keeping all the champagne flutes balanced while Nyla's sloshed over the rim.

She licked the side of her glass, not wanting things to get sticky. "Point taken," she muttered, and followed her sister out the door.

All this walking was making her head swim. How much alcohol was in a mimosa, anyway? She should have paid more attention to her sister mixing the drinks.

Focusing instead on putting one foot in front of the other, she did her best to walk a straight line from the door to the patio table. She was doing a good job, too, until her mother called out.

"Shut the door, Nyla. You're letting flies in."

Right. She forgot about that.

She turned around carefully, conscious of her head spinning. This was not good.

But okay, she could handle it. She was an adult woman, capable of managing her alcohol. So what if the glass wobbled a little in her grip as she pulled the door shut? Champagne flutes were hard to hold, dammit.

As she turned again, she noticed Leo's eyes on her. His gaze followed her slow, cautious path to the table. Was he checking her out, or making sure she didn't fall over? Social cues were so hard to read sometimes.

She sipped her drink as she wobbled to an empty chair. As she glanced at her mother, she saw her mom flick a look from Mandi to Leo and back again. God, would she ever get over this idea they'd reunite? Someone needed to clear that up once and for all.

She dropped into an empty chair, then realized she'd made a bad choice. She was right next to Leo, with her father on the other side.

Shit. "Did I say that out loud?"

Leo looked at her. "What?"

"Shit."

He gave her an odd look. "Um, yeah. I guess you did."

"Dammit." She looked at her mother. "Sorry. I don't

usually curse in front of my parents."

Her mom gave her a funny look. "Are you okay, sweetheart?"

"Excellent." The word came out a little slurred in the middle, but she was pretty sure no one noticed. Glancing down at her drink, she discovered there was less than a tablespoon left. Might as well finish it off.

Setting her glass down, she turned to her father. "Hi, Dad." She reached over and gave him a side hug, which felt a little awkward. Had she forgotten how hugs worked? "How are you?"

"I'm fine, sweetie." He hugged her back, totally normal, totally not suspicious of anything. Not the sex with Leo or the stuff with Mandi or the fact that his younger daughter might be a tiny bit drunk.

Nyla. Nyla was the younger daughter. God, she was thirsty.

Stop it. Get it together.

She forced a bright smile for her father. "How was golf yesterday?"

"Really nice." Her father smiled and gave her a wink. What was that about?

Oh, right. Her mother's birthday gift. He hadn't golfed, he'd gone to pick up the luggage set he'd be giving her as part of the gift. *Got it.*

She winked back, or tried to. She couldn't remember how winking worked, so she closed both eyes and opened them again fast. The backyard spun.

"It's fun, isn't it?" her dad whispered.

She leaned close and whispered back. "What's that?"

"Having a secret."

"Definitely." Wait, did he know about the sex?

No, of course not. He was talking about the cruise, the trip to the Bahamas. Her mother was going to shit herself.

Grinning, Nyla looked at her mom. "Hello."

Nothing to see here. Act normal.

A giggle slipped out, but Nyla covered it quick.

Her mom frowned. "Something wrong, sweetheart?"

Mandi telegraphed a weird, frantic look at Leo. What was that about?

"That's a great manicure, Mom." Mandi grabbed their mother's hand a little roughly. "I love that color!"

"It's sparkling plum." Their mom held out a hand so they could admire it. "Seemed too young for me, but your father talked me into it. Said it's sassy."

"Sassy," Nyla repeated, giggling. She picked up her champagne flute, then remembered it was empty.

"Here." Her father nudged his glass in front of her and held a finger to his lips. "You know I can't stand these things. Take mine."

"Thank you, Daddy." She picked up the flute and took a drink, trying to recall if she still called him daddy. Was that their thing, or was that something she'd read in a Katee Robert novel about the woman who seduced her ex-father-in-law?

Which was waaaaaay worse than sleeping with an ex-brother-in-law. It was in the rules or something.

All these sex thoughts sent her gaze skittering over to Leo. He was watching her oddly, a crease between his brows. "Want me to take that?"

"My drink?" She gripped the stem tighter and took a swig in case he tried to wrestle it away. "Nope. Mine."

"Ooh-kay."

He didn't look thrilled, which was his problem. He had his own drink anyway, so she shouldn't need to share.

"Nyla, tell me about career day." Her mother's question yanked her attention off Leo, which was a good thing. "Seth says you'll be speaking?"

"I'm looking forward to it." There, that sounded sober. Mature and sober, just like she ought to be.

Everyone kept looking at her expectantly, so she decided to keep going. "Last time I did it I drank too much iced tea before it was my turn to speak, and then I got up there and talked and talked and talked, and pretty soon I had to pee, and then I laughed at something one of the kids said, and I might have peed myself a little, but it was okay because I had a pantyliner since my period was due that day. It's like clockwork, you know."

She clamped her mouth shut. Dammit. Now she'd gone and blown her cover.

Or not. They were all still looking at her, but everyone was smiling. That was good, right?

Mandi laughed, but her laugh sounded weird. "Oh, Nyla. You're so funny."

Nyla threw her head back and laughed because that's what you did when someone said something funny. Someone touched her shoulder, and she turned to see Leo patting her on the back.

Touching her, which he probably shouldn't do in public like this. Or maybe they did do this? She couldn't remember if they touched in public.

"It's not my boob," she pointed out helpfully.

Leo blinked and drew his hand back. "What?"

"Nothing." She clamped her lips shut, determined not to say anything else.

Then she opened them again because it was hard to drink a mimosa with her mouth closed.

She gulped it down fast, needing to make it gone. All gone, down to the bottom. When she set the empty glass on the table, he was still watching her.

"That's still your first, right?" He frowned at the empty glass. "You already ate the cherries?"

Another giggle slipped out, but she covered it. "Funny." He didn't really think she'd had just the one drink, did he? She wasn't sure anymore how many it was. Let's see, the first one Mandi gave her, the one from Leo with the cherries, the one from Mandi in the kitchen, the one from her father…that was three? No, four. Or was it five?

She had to stop staring at Leo.

Tearing her eyes off him, she focused on the big blue bowl in the middle of the table. Mmm…watermelon. Her favorite.

She reached for it, grabbing a handful of the cheerful little balls.

"Nyla." Her mother frowned across the table. "There's a spoon. And those are for brunch. The quiche is still baking."

"Oh. Okay." She shoved the melon balls in her mouth fast in case her mom tried to take them away. Juice dribbled down her chin, and she looked for a napkin to wipe it off.

"Here." Leo handed her the hankie from his pocket, fingers lingering on the back of her hand. "You want to maybe go for a walk or something?"

"I'm good." She hiccupped and covered her mouth. "I could use something to drink."

Her mom stood up and started gathering glasses. "I'm getting myself a fresh mimosa if anyone wants one."

Nyla glanced at her empty flute and tried to recall if she wanted one. Mandi frowned at her across the table. "You finished your second already?"

Nyla laughed and nudged her father's empty glass back in front of him. "Don't worry, Daddy. I won't tell."

She meant the drink he'd slipped her, not the cruise. She should probably clarify. "Not about Mom's present. The birthday cruise to the Bahamas."

Mandi gasped and Nyla slapped a hand over her mouth. *Oh shit.*

Her mother froze, a champagne flute in each hand. "What was that?"

Nyla shook her head frantically, hand still clamped across her lips. "Nothing, Mom." Which came out sounding like "Mwffing wom" because it was hard to talk through fingers.

"Sorry." She pried her hand off her mouth. This was bad. This was very bad.

Everyone was looking at her now and no one was

saying anything. That was even worse.

"Seth!" she blurted. "We should talk about Seth!"

Mandi's flew wide. "Um, I think we should—"

"Don't worry!" Nyla stood up on legs that didn't work right. She made her way to Mandi's side of the table and leaned down to whisper. "I wasn't going to say anything about the affair. *Graduation*. That's what I meant. We're here to talk about Seth's graduation, right?"

She plunked down in the empty chair beside Mandi, satisfied she'd fixed things. Why was everyone looking at her like that?

And Leo, what was up with that weird look on his face?

Oh no. "I didn't whisper, did I?"

Mandi sat frozen, her face white as a sheet. Nyla looked at her mom, who'd gone to stand beside their father. She was glaring at Dad, hands on her hips like she did whenever Nyla got in trouble for talking too much.

"Affair?" her mom demanded. She was glaring at her husband, Nyla's dad, who was also her mom's husband. Family stuff was so complicated.

"*Affair?*" Her mom was practically shouting, which made Nyla's head hurt. "Who had an affair?"

Leo stood up, knocking his chair over. "Let's get some air." He caught Nyla by the arm and hauled her to her feet, his hand warm and strong on Nyla's arm. "We'll be right back."

But she didn't need air, she was already outside. She needed to fix this fast. "Wait, no. I've got this." She tugged her arm free, stumbling a little.

Leo caught her and his hands felt so good on her arms, so warm and strong and *right*, and she knew she needed to say something to make this okay. To distract them all from Mandi's secret and her dad's secret and *for crying out loud*, why did everyone have secrets?

"We're sleeping together!" The instant she yelled it, she knew she'd found the answer. Everyone stopped talking and stared at her.

Looping her arms around Leo's waist, she squeezed tight. "That's right, we're *screwing*. Dunking the donut. Hiding the hot dog. Baking the potato."

She wasn't sure that last one was a thing, and she also wasn't sure they got it. She gave Leo another squeeze to underscore the point. "Boinking," she added.

Mandi seemed to shake herself from some kind of daze. She looked at Nyla, then Leo, then back to Nyla. "You're not serious."

Leo was looking down at her like he wasn't sure where she'd come from, but maybe he'd like to send her back there. She let go of him, recognizing something wasn't right, and she was the reason.

"Um," Leo said. "Right, so about that…"

Mandi gasped and slapped her hands over her mouth. "You've got to be kidding me."

On Nyla's other side, her mother was still shouting, but it wasn't about Leo. "I knew you were having an affair with that floozy from your office." She was yelling at Nyla's dad, hands on her hips. "That tramp with the big hooters and the skirts cut up to her coochie."

"Laurel, no." Her father looked frantic. "We're going on a cruise. To the Bahamas!"

"You're taking that bitch on a cruise when I've waited forty-three years to go somewhere, *anywhere*—"

Her mother drew her hand back and Nyla saw in a flash what she meant to do. Her mom was going to slap her dad and she couldn't let that happen. She wobbled toward them and dove, tackling her mom like she'd seen people do on TV.

They landed in a heap on the grass, her mother's dress flying up as Nyla fell on top of her. A strange buzzing in the back of her brain told her she'd just screwed up again, but she couldn't make out what all the voices were saying.

Mandi shouting at Leo.

Leo shouting at Mandi.

The neighbor lady shouting at her father over the fence and her mom screaming and flailing and Nyla should probably get off her and *oh God*, this was all going wrong.

She rolled over in the grass, falling on her back with her face tipped toward the sky. The soft blanket of green engulfed her, cradling her with its light, feathery blades. The grass felt so cool, so welcoming, that she let her eyes drift closed.

Tomorrow.

She'd figure it out tomorrow.

It's the last thought she had before she passed out.

CHAPTER FOURTEEN

Leo watched Nyla's eyes flutter open. Braced for the worst, he grabbed the big silver bowl Laurel had handed him before he walked in here.

"Leo?" She started to sit up, then winced. "What time is it?"

Setting the bowl on the nightstand, he grabbed a bottle of water and twisted the top off. "A little after noon." He handed over the water. "Drink."

She didn't argue, and also didn't puke, which he took as a good sign. Gripping the bottle with a hand that looked none too steady, she tipped her head back and drank. And drank. And drank.

If there was one thing he'd learned today, it was that Nyla had a tremendous capacity for fluids. Impressive, really. Everything about her impressed him, right down to how she'd fought so hard to fix things in spite of the mimosa sabotage.

By the time she set the bottle down, it was half empty. Nyla looked at him and winced. "What happened?"

He wondered if she already knew the answer and wanted him to confirm it. Or deny it, which he couldn't do.

Leo took a deep breath. "Well, you told your mom about her birthday gift." Might as well start with the easy stuff. "She's excited about the cruise." Once she stopped yelling about Ted's secretary, anyway.

Nyla nodded, then winced again. "That's not the only thing I spilled, is it?"

"You held on to your glass like a champ." Might as well give some positive feedback. "But no. Uh...there were other beans spilled."

He glanced at the bowl, poised to hand it to her if she looked ready to hurl. Once she heard everything, odds were good she'd need it.

"What else?" Her voice was strained and hoarse. "Tell me, Leo. What else did I say?"

He sighed. No sense stalling any longer. "You might have mentioned Mandi's affair. Your parents know I'm not Seth's biological father."

That last part had come after, thank God. Once Laurel and the neighbor stopped yelling, once Mandi stopped freaking out, they'd all sat down with the rest of the champagne and hashed it out.

Nyla, blessedly, had slept through the worst of it.

"God, no." She closed her eyes and rested her head against the tufted headboard. "Was it bad?"

"It wasn't awesome." No sense beating around the bush. "Your parents freaked about the DNA thing. Everyone was so heated up and mad and it took them a few minutes to sort out who was related by blood and who wasn't and whether Seth was even related to them."

That part stuck in his craw. Who the fuck cared whose DNA Seth carried? Ted and Laurel apparently. But they still had their grandson, and Leo...well, Leo had a gross feeling in his gut knowing things might have gone differently if they'd discovered their precious grandson didn't have Franklin blood pumping through his veins.

That pissed him off.

He realized Nyla was watching his face, eyes glittering with tears. "Hey." He reached for her hand. "It's okay. I'm not mad at you."

"You should be." She blinked a few times, fighting back the waterworks. "I'm so sorry, Leo. I have no idea how that happened."

"I do." He threaded his fingers through hers, then reached up to tuck a curl behind one ear. "It's not your fault, okay?"

"Of course it's my fault." Her disgust was palpable. "God, I drank so much. More than I've ever had in my life, even in college."

"That's at least half my fault," he insisted. "Maybe more. Mandi and I had the same idea thinking you were too tense and wound up. That maybe if you had a drink, you'd relax and be less apt to blow."

She snorted and looked down at the quilt covering her legs. "And how'd that work out?"

"Not great." He grabbed the water bottle off the nightstand and took a drink, then handed it back to her. "Drink. You'll feel better."

"Where have I heard that before?" But she lifted the bottle to her lips and took a healthy slug. When she set it down, she looked at him with wary eyes. "That's not all of it, right? I spoiled the vacation surprise and violated my nephew's privacy and ratted out my own sister, but that isn't everything."

She must have already known. Deep down, she remembered. Leo still felt like a dick saying it. "Right," he said slowly. "There's more."

He waited for her to say it. To put the pieces together and react however she was going to react.

Nyla just stared at him. Stared like her tongue didn't want to form the words. "I told them," she said softly. "I told them about us, right?"

Us.

Was it wrong he heard the word with a capital letter? A grand proclamation, an official title out there in the open for all to see.

He couldn't read her face, so he nodded. "Yeah. Yep, you did."

Nyla closed her eyes, making it harder for him to read her. Was she horrified? With herself, or with the fact that other people knew about this thing, this magical thing, that had burned bright in the center of his chest for weeks.

When she opened her eyes again, her expression had softened. "So that's it." She licked her lips. "They know."

Was he imagining things, or was that a glimmer of hope in her eyes? The world hadn't collapsed around them, and here they sat with their fingers laced together in this soft, fragile space.

"They know." He held the next words back until he couldn't anymore. "I'm glad."

He watched her face, gauging her reaction. Surprise. Confusion. And again…hope?

"Glad?" She asked like she wasn't sure she'd heard right. "Glad I blurted out everyone's secrets, including yours?"

"Maybe the delivery could have gone better," he admitted. "But yeah. I'm glad we don't have to hide it anymore."

Her blue eyes held his, searching, assessing. She looked down at the water bottle in her hands, then brought it to her lips again. She drank until it was empty, then set it on the nightstand. "I see."

Watching her face, he felt his heart vibrating like a plucked string. This could go so many ways. She could panic and hide and say this was over. Too much drama, too much work.

Or she could see things like he did. A fresh chance for them both, damn the weirdness of it all.

"Nyla," he murmured. "It's going to be okay."

"Yeah?"

The uncertainty in her voice nearly broke his heart. He didn't feel uncertain. He felt happy. Awkward, sure, but oddly grateful for the chance to make a go of this.

That's assuming she wanted to. Did she?

He really couldn't tell.

She closed her eyes and rested her head against the headboard. "I don't remember much. I know I said a lot, and I remember maybe the family isn't thrilled about us dating." She opened her eyes, wincing again. "I didn't say dating, did I?"

"Nope." He fought back a smile, knowing this wasn't funny. Not at all. "You didn't say dating."

Again, he choked back laughter, fighting for his straight face. But come on, how could he not be charmed by what she'd said? Sure, she'd been drunk. Definitely not thinking clearly.

But she'd stood there and laid claim to him in front of her mother, her father, her sister—hell, even the neighbor. That had to mean something, right?

She was looking down into her lap, but he could see the wheels turning in her head. When she looked at him again, she had a question in her eyes. "Is there anything else?"

"What do you mean?"

"Anything else I should know?"

I love you.

The words crept unexpected into his brain. They didn't make sense. Not something he'd ever thought, not with her. Not in the way he meant them now.

But they were true and real and right there on the tip of his brain, laid bare for him to see. Could she see it?

He swallowed back the thought, not wanting to scare her. It was way too soon. "Look, this is awkward," he said. "We've got some conversations ahead of us that are going to be uncomfortable."

Being drunk had saved her from the grilling she'd get later on. He wished he could protect her from it, but he couldn't. Not always.

"Here's the thing, though," he continued. "You let the air out of the balloon. You got us out of hiding, and honestly, I'm happy about that. I really am glad."

It was the second time he'd said those words, and he

could see in her eyes that they'd registered this time.

"I'm not sure how I feel," she said softly. "I hate that I did it this way. I feel like a jerk and my head hurts and I keep having flashes of things I said and I want to go hide in the bathtub and never come out." She licked her lips, eyes locked on his. "But you're right. There's a bright side."

He nodded, hoping like hell she meant the same thing he did. That whatever this was between them, it wasn't just sex. There was a whole other level beyond this, and he wanted to go there with her.

Was he hoping for too much? Maybe she wanted to tuck tail and run the other way. Hell, he couldn't blame her. This was complicated enough.

"What's the upside?" His voice croaked, and he wasn't sure he wanted the answer.

"That we don't have to sneak around. We can be open about this." She bit her lip. "If we want to."

He wanted to. God, did he want to. "That sounds good to me."

She looked down at their hands clasped together. The tiniest smile tugged the corners of her mouth. "Did I really say 'hiding the hot dog' to my parents?"

"Yep." He grinned, no longer able to fight it. "You did. Want us all to pretend you didn't?"

"That's okay." She looked up again. "On a scale of one to ten, how pissed is Mandi? Or my parents? Or—"

The door swung open, and the question died in her throat. Leo blinked up at his ex-wife. Her eyes were red, her nose was running, and her hands were clenched at her sides.

Bad signs, all of them. He knew that better than anyone.

Mandi's gaze flicked to their intertwined fingers and she made a choked sound. "Nice. Am I interrupting something?"

Nyla pulled her hand back and drew a deep breath. "I'm so sorry."

Mandi blinked hard, not looking at him. She wasn't looking at anyone. Her gaze fixed on the wall a few inches over Nyla's head. "I guess I deserved that, didn't I?" She flicked her gaze to Leo. "Was this your way of getting me back?"

"What?" He had no clue what she meant.

She flicked her wrist, impatient. "I have an affair, so you fuck my little sister. Tit for tat?"

Nyla flinched, and Leo felt his blood boil. "That doesn't even make any sense."

"No?" Mandi crossed her arms over her chest, a move Leo knew was meant to hide her shaking hands. "It makes perfect sense. You know how much my sister means to me. You know I'd do anything to protect her, and what do you do? You seduce her like some kind of a—"

"Stop." Nyla's voice cracked Mandi's sharp words, strained but strong. "It wasn't like that."

Mandi whirled on her. "So what was it like? Explain it to me."

Nyla looked at Leo, floundering. "It just happened."

The words sounded feeble, helpless. But somehow,

they found their mark. Somewhere deep down, Mandi recognized them as her own. He watched her shoulders slump in defeat.

Part of him relished seeing his ex-wife knocked off her pedestal.

Part of him felt like an asshole.

All of him wanted to reach for Nyla, to get her out of here as fast as possible.

But she wasn't done talking. "You have every right to be angry," Nyla said. "Not because I slept with Leo. I don't regret that, not even a little, and I'm not going to apologize for it." She glanced at him, summoning courage, then met her sister's gaze head-on. "But I am sorry I hid the truth from you," she added. "I'm sorry I didn't tell you what I was thinking and feeling and *doing*, because that's not what sisters are like. Not us. We tell each other things."

She let the words hang there between them, red-tinted bubbles filled with so much meaning. He said nothing, watching emotion play out on his ex-wife's face. Sadness. Anger. Regret. Pride, stinging and sharp.

When Mandi's gaze slid to his, her spine seemed to dissolve.

"You're right." Mandi sank down onto the edge of the bed, ignoring Leo to reach for Nyla's hand. "I should have told you about the affair."

Told *Nyla*?

Uh, okay. Or hey, maybe if she'd never had the affair in the first place?

But saying that wouldn't be helpful. Not now. There

was so much he wanted to say, but he kept his mouth zipped. If there was one lesson he'd taken from his marriage, it was knowing when to shut the fuck up.

"I'm so sorry." Nyla was crying now, too. "I didn't want to hurt you. I know how much I hated when Greg moved on, and to have it be your own sister—"

"Duckie, no." She gripped Nyla's hand, and Leo wondered if they'd notice if he left the room. "You're right, I'm pissed. I'm hurt and I'm confused and I've got so many questions that I don't think I want answers to. Not anytime soon." She glanced at Leo, her expression hardening. "And I've got things to say to you that I definitely shouldn't say."

"Right." He stood up, recognizing his cue to leave. "I should give you two some privacy."

Mandi took a shaky breath and stared him down. "Let's drive together."

"What?"

"To Seth's game. It'll give us a chance to talk."

That sounded as appealing to him as shoving hot barbecue tongs up his nostrils, but he found himself nodding. "Sure. Sounds good."

Even Nyla looked surprised. "Really?"

Mandi took a deep breath. "We can be adults about this, right? Talk things over like grownups?"

"Yeah, of course." He wasn't so sure about the grown-up part, but he was game to try. He shifted his gaze to Nyla's and something melted in his chest.

"You okay?"

She nodded, fingers still twined with her sister's. "I'm

good." She choked on a laugh. "Well, not good. My tongue feels like sandpaper and I still think I might puke."

Mandi swiped a tear from her eye and laughed. "I can make you my famous hangover remedy. Don't tell Mom and Dad."

Nyla rolled her eyes and grimaced. "Because I'm definitely the best person to keep a secret." Her eyes slid to Leo and her smile turned warmer. "So I'll see you later?"

He nodded, recognizing he'd been dismissed. "Yeah, sure. I'll call when the game's over." Gaze shifting to Mandi's, he shoved his hands in his pockets. "Want me to drive?"

"Sure."

He turned to go, reaching for the doorknob as he braced himself to face their parents. There would be questions. Judgment. Probably anger.

Then Nyla's voice rang out behind him and he stopped. "Leo?"

"Yeah?" He turned to see her watching him with something in her eyes that looked like love. His heart squeezed tight in his chest as he held his breath.

"I'm glad, too."

A slow grin spread over his face. He nodded once, then turned and walked out the door.

• • •

Hours later, he was driving down the highway with his ex-wife. It was the last place in the world he wanted to be.

"Thanks for driving." Mandi flipped the visor down, rubbed a spot of grease off the mirror, then flipped it back up. "I'll buy dinner."

"It's no big deal." Honestly, he'd rather be driving than sitting in the passenger seat, twiddling his thumbs and wondering what the fuck to say to his ex-wife. Was there a reason she wasn't saying anything? Probably letting him squirm, a passive-aggressive tendency he'd used a time or two in their marriage.

God, I was an asshole.

He let the silence stretch out until he couldn't take it anymore. "You wanted to talk?"

From the corner of his eye, he saw her turn toward him. "I think we should. Don't you?"

He didn't know what to think, so he concentrated on changing lanes, on waving to the trucker in the red ball cap to make sure he wasn't in the guy's blind spot.

Several seconds went by. Minutes, maybe. Mandi fiddled with the radio dial, then turned it off. "So. You and Nyla, huh?"

And there it was. For some reason it felt good knowing this was awkward for Mandi, too. "Yeah. Me and Nyla."

That felt good, too, saying it out loud. Not giving a fuck who found out.

Mandi sighed. "I guess I should have known."

He jerked his gaze off the road, blood pressure rising. "What the hell is that supposed to mean?"

"Relax, Leo. All I meant is that you're good together."

"Oh." Wait. What?

"Don't look so shocked," she continued like she hadn't just thrown him for a loop. "All these years, the two of you liked the same TV shows. You laughed at the same jokes. Hell, you had way more in common than the two of us ever did. It makes sense."

"I—" Shit, what the hell did he say to that? "I never thought of her that way. Not once, not while we were married."

"Of course not." She waved a hand, whacking the visor she'd left down. "That's not what I meant. I'm just saying, I see how it could happen."

He fixed his eyes on the road again, not sure what to say. "That's it?" It had to be some kind of trick.

"Well, no. There's more to it than that." She rummaged in her purse and came up with something in a wrapper that crinkled. He glanced over to see her break a granola bar. She offered half to him and he took it.

"Thanks." He bit into it, sending a spray of crumbs across his lap. The peanut-buttery taste reminded him of road trips with Seth when he was little, and it took him a few beats to collect himself. "What do you mean? More to what than what?"

"What?" Mandi nibbled the treat, looking a bit like a hamster. "Oh, with Nyla? Well, for starters, what's Seth going to think?"

"We haven't gotten that far."

"I see."

He glanced over at her. "And what's Seth going to think about Uganda?"

She flinched, then nodded. "Point taken."

"So we agree we've got some awkward shit to tell our kid. *Our* kid." He gripped the wheel harder, needing to emphasize the point. "And that we don't have all the answers about how or when to say it."

"Agreed."

Leo snorted. He couldn't help it. "If only we'd agreed on more shit when we got married."

"You wish we were still married?"

"What? No!" He swerved, nearly running them off the road. "Jesus, no."

Mandi laughed and shoved the rest of the granola bar in her mouth. She finished chewing, then shoved the wrapper into her purse. He should give her credit for that, for not stuffing it in his overflowing trash bag.

Dusting the crumbs off her lap, she looked at him. "Let me ask you this," she said. "Where do you see this going with Nyla?"

"Is that your business?" Even before the words were out, he regretted them. "Sorry. You're right. I know we agreed we'd talk about this when one of us got serious about someone we were dating."

Mandi gave him a level look. "Yeah. We also talked about coming to an agreement about the right time to introduce our son to anyone we dated. Guess that's out the window here."

He started to defend himself, then stopped. It wasn't a jab, just a fact. Maybe he should stop expecting everything to be an attack. He glanced over to see her staring out the window at the trees. "It wasn't about hurting you," he said softly. "Or getting back at you.

Whatever you said back there at your folks' house, that's not what this was about."

"I know." She turned to face him. "People say shitty things when they're hurt."

Wasn't that the truth.

He took a deep breath and loosened his grip on the steering wheel. "Look, I really don't know what's going to happen. We're having fun, enjoying each other's company."

Mandi made a noise halfway between a laugh and a snort. He decided to ignore it.

"My point is, I don't know what's in the future." He focused on the road, pausing to pass a slow-moving farm truck. "I guess that's the good thing about dating when you're older. You don't have to worry about time-lines and ticking clocks and what age you're supposed to get married or buy a house or whatever shit people put on themselves in their early twenties."

She turned to face him, eyebrows lifting. "For you, maybe."

"What does that mean?"

"It means Nyla's never been married." She folded her hands on her lap, eyes narrowing slightly. "Yeah, she owns her own house, but she's never bought one with somebody. She hasn't planned a wedding or kept an ovulation calendar or registered for sheets at Target."

"Why would she want to register for sheets at Target?" As far as he knew, she had plenty of sheets.

"Jesus, Leo, you're so dense sometimes."

"What?" He did a mental rewind through the conversation, wondering what he'd missed.

Mandi sighed the way she did when reminding Seth for the thousandth time not to forget his baseball jersey. "It means you're at different places in your life. It's fine for you to be all 'we'll figure it out,' but Nyla's a woman in her thirties. She doesn't have that luxury."

"Kids. You're talking about having kids?" Shit, he hadn't thought about that.

"I'm talking about all of it," she said. "You've got your own ticking clock. Six years until Seth's ready to graduate, and then you're living for you. You're off on your motorcycle, traveling the world, doing all the things you've spent your whole life wanting to do. That's great, but what does that mean for Nyla?"

"Fuck, Mandi. I don't know." His blood pressure was rising again, so he took a few calming breaths. "We've barely started dating. Christ, we've slept together *once*."

At the edge of his vision, he saw her shoot him a withering look. "I don't need details about your sex life with my sister, thanks."

"Well hell, you're backing me into a corner here." He took a few more deep breaths. "I appreciate your concern."

"No, you don't."

He didn't. "I'm glad you're looking out for Nyla." That much was true. "I care about her, too. A lot."

She didn't say anything right away. "I can see that."

"Then will you just trust me?"

More silence. He glanced over to see her watching him with a look he couldn't read at all. A look he'd spent his whole marriage trying to figure out, and never had.

"Don't hurt her." Mandi bit her lip and looked out the window again. "I know you think I'm a bitch, and maybe I am. But I love my sister more than anything, and I swear to God, Leo—if you break her heart, I will rip off your balls and shove them down your throat."

He laughed. He couldn't help it, the words were so ridiculous.

But she looked at him sharply and he stopped laughing. "Understood."

"I mean it, Leo. Nyla deserves the world. She deserves a guy who respects and cares for her and has dreams that don't depend on crushing hers. That wasn't Greg."

"It wasn't Greg." At least they could agree on that.

As silence stretched out, he wondered if she wanted him to say it was him. To promise forever, that he'd love, honor, and cherish Nyla forever.

He adored her, maybe even loved her. No way he'd tell Mandi that before Nyla, but he felt pretty sure it was true.

But forever? They hadn't gotten that far yet.

"I won't hurt her," he said again. "I'll be careful."

"Good."

As he gripped the steering wheel, he prayed to God that was enough.

CHAPTER FIFTEEN

"Thanks, Mom." Nyla gripped the bowl of melon balls, still feeling like an ill-behaved teenager. "Have a good night."

She started to step back from the front door but should have known her mother wouldn't let her off that easy.

"I still don't see why you couldn't find someone else." Her mother sighed and leaned heavily against the doorframe. "Someone without so much…baggage."

Nyla gritted her teeth. They'd been through this already, at least a dozen times since Mandi and Leo left. "They were never getting back together." That's what this was about, after all. "I'm sorry, but it wasn't happening. Not ever."

Her mother sniffed and turned to deadhead petunias in the hanging basket by the door. "I just think families should be together. They have a son together. Mandi may have made some mistakes, but—"

"Mom, give it a rest." Nyla shifted her grip on the bowl, wishing she could flee. Wishing Leo were still here, even though she didn't wish this particular moment on him. "They've been divorced for years. They're in different places now."

Her mother looked at her. "And you're in the same place? You and Leo?"

"I don't know yet." That was definitely her cue to go. "We'll talk more later, okay? I love you."

"I love you, too." Her mother closed her eyes a moment. "I only want what's best for you. You and Mandi both."

"I know that, Mom." And she did know it. As she got into her car and buckled her seat belt, her mom was still on the front porch, waving. Her dad had gone to bed already, an early riser to his wife's night-owl ways. They'd always been like that, at opposite ends of the spectrum. Somehow, they'd made it work.

She drove home in a fog of fatigue, still fighting the effects of the hangover. The alcohol was out of her system, replaced by a thick syrup of guilt. What the hell had she been thinking, drinking like a damn teenager?

No, not a teenager— God help her, Seth would be one soon. She'd been drinking like an irresponsible, totally careless adult. It was no one's fault but her own, even if other people had given her the drinks. No one pinned her down and poured champagne in her mouth.

"I'm never drinking again," she muttered as she turned down the street toward her little bungalow.

As her headlights swept the driveway, she gave a sharp gasp. Leo? Or a truck that looked a lot like his. She stomped the brake, idling at the curb.

From the depths of her purse, she heard her phone buzz. Fishing it out, she glanced at the screen.

Leo: Just got back. You home?

She smiled and texted a reply.

Nyla: Right behind you.

He was already out of his truck before she hit send. She tapped it anyway, then eased into her driveway right beside him. As she stepped out, he stepped forward and pulled her into his arms.

"I missed you," he breathed into her hair. "So much."

"I missed you, too." She squeezed him tight, so grateful to be here with him, grateful they didn't have to hide anymore. "How was the game?"

"A slaughter," he said. "They lost every inning, but Seth had a good attitude about it. Mandi's taking him out to the all-night diner for banana splits, so he's probably forgotten the game by now."

She didn't want to talk about Mandi. Or Seth, for that matter, though she loved the kid.

Even more, she loved the feel of Leo's arms around her, the thrum of his heartbeat as he held her tight to his chest. She pressed her face against the center of it, breathing him in. He smelled like grass and soap and, inexplicably, peanut butter.

She drew back and smiled up at him. "I can't believe you came."

He grinned wickedly, and she knew the next words out of his mouth before he said them. "Not yet. But give me ten minutes naked with you and—"

"That long?" She grabbed his hand and pulled him toward her door, all traces of hungover brain fog vanishing. "I'll have you know I've got a king-size bed. A vast improvement over the air base. No more twin bed."

And no more hiding. Just the two of them, at her place, not even thinking about what happened if Mandi dropped by. Or her parents or Seth or—okay, maybe not Seth. They weren't there yet, but soon.

For now, it was just them. "Wait. Melon balls."

Leo frowned. "Is that like blue balls?"

"Very funny." She opened her car door and pulled out the bowl her mother had given her. "Sustenance for later," she said, shoving it into his hands as she turned toward the house.

She was on the steps in six strides, and yes, she counted. That's how eager she was to be inside with him, alone and naked. Fishing her keys out of her purse, she fumbled her house key into the doorknob. Her hands were shaking, which made no sense. This was Leo, the guy who'd fixed her garbage disposal and watered her tulips when she went on vacation.

But everything was different now. She felt it in her bones as she flicked the porch light on and stepped inside. He followed her in, setting the bowl on the entry table. He started to reach for the light, but she stopped him.

"Wait. Let me." She left him standing there as she rushed the bowl to the kitchen and shoved it in the fridge. She hurried back, moving in moonlight that streamed through the window. "I don't want lights," she murmured as she slipped her arms around his waist. "We've seen each other a thousand times. A million times over the years. Right now, I want to *feel* you."

It sounded corny and maybe didn't even make sense. But as he pulled her close, she knew he got it. This was new and different and strange and magical, and she wanted to experience every breathless touch without the clutter of eyesight.

Leo kissed her, tunneling his fingers in her hair as he backed her toward the bedroom. She clawed at his shirt, dragging it over his head as they crashed into the coffee table.

"Oops." She giggled as her shirt got tangled on her elbow. "So much for grace and romance."

But it was romantic, just in a different way. The flicker of headlights through the slats in her blinds, the soft symphony of crickets outside, the spicy vanilla scent of the candle she'd burned that morning. Was that only ten hours ago? It seemed like years, like another lifetime when they had to hide and pretend and worry who might know.

"Nyla." He breathed it against her mouth as he unhooked her bra, whispering her name like a prayer. "You feel so good."

He felt unreal, all rippled muscle and springy hair and solid, warm skin under her palms. They'd reached the bedroom and she fought the urge to turn on a light. This was instinct, pure and simple, a human craving for touch. For *Leo's* touch.

Turning in his arms, she backed him toward the bed. With a giggle, she drew back and set the heel of her hand against his chest. His heartbeat thudded through her palm as she smiled up at him. "You," she whispered.

"Me." He kissed her again. "And you."

Nyla sighed, then pushed him back onto the bed. He tumbled with a lot more grace than she would have, pulling her down on top of him. He still wore jeans, and she ground against him, straddling his hips to feel the thick hardness between her thighs. She'd lost her own pants somewhere back in the living room, so only a thin strip of lace separated her from him.

She needed more.

Sensing her hunger, Leo rolled her onto her back and stripped off her panties in one motion. They flew through the darkness to land with a crash as they knocked something off the dresser. She didn't care.

All she cared about was getting his jeans off, tugging the zipper as his tongue grazed hers. Her fingers slipped into his boxers and she wrapped them around his shaft, making him moan against her mouth.

"Nyla. God."

She couldn't stop. Her body was someone else's, wild and wanton and hungry for his heat. They were both naked now, rubbing against each other in dizzying combinations. Forearm against breast, tongue against biceps, his thigh between her parting legs to brush her *right there*.

"Oh God." She practically came right on the spot, moaning as she ground against him.

"You're so wet." He kissed her deep and hard, hips angling between her thighs as her legs fell apart. She fumbled in the dark for her nightstand drawer, praying she had more condoms. Had she stuck the last one in her coin purse the other day?

Fingers closing around cellophane, she drew her hand back with a squeak of triumph. "Score," she giggled, and set to work sheathing him with it.

Leo groaned as she took her time rolling it on, stroking him, swirling a fingertip through the wetness at his tip. "Nyla."

She loved how he said her name, not expecting a response. He was back between her thighs, the head of his cock slipping through her wet folds. She gasped, wrapping her thighs around him to draw him inside.

In the darkness she looked up at him and saw his gaze fixed on her face. "You're so beautiful."

Then he slid inside her, making her cry out with pleasure. "*Leo*." She clawed at his back, breathing him in, memorizing the planes of his shoulder blades with her palms.

He drove in deeper and she arched up to meet him, closing her eyes. She felt him everywhere, the tips of her toes, the lobes of her ears, and deep, deep inside where no one else had touched before.

She cried out again as he rocked into her, moving faster now. They moved together like they'd choreographed this, like every motion had a purpose. Like they knew every inch, every molecule of the other body. Maybe they did.

Maybe they'd always known, deep down, this was how it should be.

The orgasm crept up fast, snatching her breath away. She bit down on his shoulder and said his name. "Leo," she breathed. "Oh God, Leo."

He knew without asking, without her telling him, what to do. Sliding an arm under her hips, he pulled her up and against him as he rocked into her. Stars burst behind her eyelids as he hit that spot, right there, yes, yes, *yes*!

Leo moaned, too, and she knew from how he tensed in her arms he was chasing her climax with his. He thrust into her again and again, breathing in her ear, whispering how good she felt, how he wanted her, loved her.

Loved her?

As her orgasm ebbed, she blinked herself back down to earth. Had she heard right? She couldn't hear anything with her pulse pounding in her ears. Her hand splayed on his chest as he rolled off, and she felt his heartbeat thudding with the same rhythm.

"Wow." She breathed the word softly, not sure if she meant the sex or what he'd said.

Or had he said it?

Force of habit, maybe, years of being married and making love to the same woman, her sister, *oh God—*

"Nyla." He touched her hand in the darkness, rolling to his side to pull her against him. Nuzzling his face in her hair, his breath felt warm against her neck. "I love you."

Holy shit.

She blinked again, no longer questioning. She was certain of it now, more sure than she'd been of anything in her life.

"I love you, too." She turned in his arms then, giggling self-consciously as her thigh stuck to his and her arm tangled in the sheet. He got rid of the condom and she nestled against him, too flabbergasted for words.

Except those three.

"I love you." She said it again, her voice stronger this time, surer. "So much, Leo."

She saw his smile in the darkness, felt the drumming of his heart against her chest. White flashed in the dark, his teeth, he was smiling as he looked down at her.

"I love you." His voice rumbled deep in his chest. "Now what do we do about it?"

CHAPTER SIXTEEN

I love you, now what do we do about it?

Of all the wrong-ass things he could possibly say to Nyla in bed, that one took the prize.

But she didn't bat an eyelash. "I think we should take it slow." Even with the room in semidarkness, his eyes had adjusted enough to see her cheeks flush. "Well, maybe not the sex part. We don't need to take that slowly."

He planted a kiss on her shoulder, and another at the curve between her neck and collarbone. "That ship's sailed."

"Thank God." Another blush, which he caught as she ducked her chin. "Is this where I make a crack about the motion of the ocean?"

He grunted and snuggled her close, loving the feel of her warm and naked beside him. "Okay, but I might not laugh. Not because it's not hilarious, but I'm still catching my breath."

She stirred against him, making him wonder if he could go again this soon. He might not be twenty anymore, but Nyla somehow turned him into a horny teen.

"Are we doing this now?" she asked, and it took him a second to drag his brain back from the sex zone. "The talk about future and defining the relationship and all that—is that the conversation we're having?"

He couldn't tell from her tone how she felt about the

prospect, so he took his time answering. "Maybe?" Another kiss on her shoulder. He couldn't seem to stop kissing her, touching her warm, damp skin. "I mean, we've spent weeks dancing around and trying to pretend nothing's happening. Now that we don't have to pretend anymore, seems like a good idea to figure out where we stand."

What the hell was he doing initiating "the talk" like this? For God's sake, this wasn't like him. Not that he had a huge track record of dating, getting married so young and all. But if he weren't lying here with his dick out, he'd suspect he'd lost it somewhere.

Maybe that was toxic masculinity talking. He'd seen a TV show about it, and never wanted to be one of those guys who dodged emotional shit. He was old enough, secure enough to have a conversation like this.

Nyla stirred again, hand tracing his hip like she loved touching him, too. "Okay," she said. "Well, it's no secret I wanted to get married. That I totally expected Greg and I would tie the knot and make babies and live happily ever after and all that." She winced and met his gaze. "Sorry. That's poor form to bring up an ex in bed, isn't it?"

He planted a kiss at the edge of her ear. "My ego can handle it."

"Mmm." She arched into him as he kissed his way down the column of her throat and into the warm space between her breasts. "What were we talking about again?"

"I forget." No, wait. He was the one who started this conversation. He could damn well get a handle on his sex drive. One last kiss and then he came up for air. "You wanted to get married and have babies. Past tense?"

She hesitated. "With Greg, yes. I'm glad we didn't get married." Another hesitation, longer this time. "I absolutely, positively made the right choice giving him that ultimatum, and he made the right choice when he turned me down."

A flash of emotion in her eyes told him the wound wasn't quite healed, but he understood. He still had sore spots from his own divorce. They'd always be there, part of the fabric that made them who they were.

Leo kept his eyes on her face, processing her words. "So you want those things still? Marriage, kids, the white picket fence?"

Nyla bit her lip. Leo studied her, braced for an answer he wasn't sure he wanted to hear. He'd done the marriage thing and it hadn't worked. He was more than halfway through raising a kid. Did it make him an asshole to have doubts he'd want to do it again?

"Yes," Nyla said softly, and Leo's breath caught in his throat.

Wait. He hadn't asked his question aloud.

She was answering the other one, the question of whether she saw marriage and kids in her future.

"I see." He tried to keep his voice steady, his breath even.

She was still biting her lip, so he leaned down and kissed it. She relaxed against him, twining her fingers in his hair.

When he drew back, she looked less tense. Still, the

worry stayed in her eyes. "I've always pictured myself as a mother," she said. "A wife. The whole nine yards. When I imagined my future, that's always what I've pictured."

"I understand." And he did understand. God knows he had specific ideas for how his future would unfold.

And God knows they needed to get this out in the open. Make sure neither of them had expectations the other couldn't meet. "Do you think that—"

"You know what?" She rolled to her side, tightening her grip on his hip. "I might not be ready for this conversation yet. This is still new and my brain's fuzzy and I'd just like to lie here and bask in the afterglow a bit."

"Of course." He was such an asshole. "I'm sorry."

"For what?"

"For being the jerk who rained on the parade."

"You didn't. Not at all." She kissed him again, then smiled. "Besides. That's the thing about parades."

"What's that?"

She grinned wider, nails digging possessive little crescents into the muscles of his backside. "There's always another one coming."

"Damn straight," he said, and rolled her onto her back.

• • •

In the morning, Leo got up at seven and padded to the kitchen. He dragged Nyla's old waffle maker off the top of the fridge, pleased he knew where she kept it. He set to work making batter, mixing eggs and flour and sugar as he hummed along with cheesy eighties music he'd asked Alexa to play at a low volume.

Nyla had worked early shifts at the hospital for years, seldom sleeping in even on her days off. This morning she didn't work until nine, and Leo wanted to surprise her with breakfast in bed.

He rummaged in the fridge for syrup, sniffing something that turned out to be strawberry compote. Perfect. He'd just located the powdered sugar when her voice rang out behind him.

"Mmm, sausage rolls!"

He turned to see her padding into the kitchen, wearing a green robe belted at the waist. Her dark curls were rumpled, cheeks flushed with beard burn.

Leo's breath stalled in his chest. He'd never seen anyone so beautiful.

Also, she wanted sausage?

Dragging his gaze off her, he jerked a thumb at the fridge. "I didn't see any sausage in there, but there's bacon. You're craving sausage rolls?"

"No, the song." She hummed along with a few bars of the Starship tune jamming through the sound system. "We built this city on sausage rolls?"

Leo's guts melted into a puddle of warm goo. "God, I fucking love you." Yeah, the song was about *rock and roll*, not sausage rolls, but how goddamn charming was that? "Ready for coffee?"

"Oooh, yes, please." She stretched up to grab a green-and-white mug from the cupboard, then filled it herself from the pot. "And I love you, too."

He poured a big glob of batter in the waffle maker and closed it up, setting the timer to get it crispy the way she liked. Then he turned to Nyla and pulled her into his arms. "Thank you for last night."

She laughed and nuzzled against him, setting her mug on the counter. "Are you thanking me for something specific?"

"The sex. The snuggling. The sleepover. Take your pick."

"All of the above, thanks."

Somehow they wound up kissing, with Nyla boosted up onto the kitchen counter, robe parted while Leo's hands roamed. Her front blinds were wide open, so he scooted her along the cool quartz to score some privacy behind the cupboards.

God, she felt good. Warm and soft and all his. He could get lost in her sweetness, forgetting the family complications and the complex conversations from last night. This was all that mattered.

"Mmm." She gripped the back of his head as he explored downward, tongue circling her nipple before he moved down to her navel. He kept going, kissing his way down, parting her thighs…

Ding!

"Dammit." Leo groaned and straightened up. "Cock-blocked by a Belgian waffle."

Nyla laughed and rearranged her robe. "Now there's a good song title."

Leo groaned and adjusted his jeans, wishing he'd

stayed in his boxers. It would be so easy to pull out his cock, slip inside her, and—

"I'll set the table." Nyla hopped off the counter, still grinning as she grabbed plates from the cupboard.

He watched her move, willing his hard-on to go down as he flipped the latch to open the waffle maker. He split the thing in two and divided it between plates. A handful of grapes on each plate—he was such a dad—and a quick detour to throw some bacon in the microwave.

Moments later, they were sitting down to breakfast like an old married couple. Unease churned his gut, but he pushed it aside and swallowed some coffee.

"This is amazing." Nyla shoveled a bite of syrupy waffle into her mouth and grinned. "Even without the sausage rolls."

He grinned and offered her an extra slice of bacon. "In case it helps ease the pain."

"Thanks." She took the bacon with a wink. "For the record, I know that's not what the song's about."

He looked up from dousing his waffle in strawberry syrup. "But only because someone told you?"

"True." With a shrug, she swirled a slice of bacon through the strawberry syrup. Leo tried not to cringe at the gross combination. "Mandi had to break it to me in high school. For what it's worth, I think sausage rolls make a much better subject for a song than rock and roll does."

"Can't argue there." Hearing his ex-wife's name made him cringe again, though hopefully he kept it on the inside.

Would it always be weird like this? Maybe with time, it wouldn't end up feeling like his ex was seated at the breakfast table with them, her shrill laugh filling the room as she snagged the funny pages and poured the last of the coffee.

Leo picked up his mug and brought it to his lips. As he glanced out the window, his hand froze in midair.

"Oh shit." He slammed down his mug and stood up. "Is that Mandi's car?"

Nyla spun in her chair, jaw dropping as the passenger door flew open on Mandi's sedan. As Leo watched in horror, his son bounced out and came loping up the walk.

"Oh no!" Nyla jumped to her feet and gave Leo a frantic look. "What now?"

The doorbell chimed and Leo's heart cannonballed into his gut. "I can't hide," he hissed. "He must have seen my truck by now."

Nyla looked down at her robe as the doorbell chimed again. "Hang on."

She sprinted toward the bedroom, leaving Leo alone in the dining room as Seth banged on the door like the impatient preteen he was.

Back in the driveway, Mandi's door opened and she slipped out of the car with her sunglasses on top of her head. She took her time strolling up the walk, long ponytail trailing behind her. As she passed the front window, her gaze shifted to the living room where Leo stood. Her eyes flew wide as they locked with his.

Oh shit, she mouthed.

Exactly.

He could think of no good excuse for why he'd be at Nyla's this early on a weekday. He tried and failed, never much good at lying.

As Mandi jerked her gaze off his and joined Seth on the doorstep, Leo swallowed hard. Would his ex throw them under the bus and make a big deal of this?

On the other side of the door, he heard Seth's voice asking why Dad's truck was here. So much for making an escape. He couldn't hear Mandi's answer, but the doorbell chimed again.

Jesus.

Where the hell was Nyla? As he scanned the living room, his gaze snagged on her T-shirt crumpled by the coffee table. Shit. Where had he tossed her bra? He wasn't sure they'd made it to the bedroom before he'd wrangled it off her.

With Seth still pounding—of all the times for the lessons in persistence to sink in—Leo kicked the T-shirt under the couch and headed for the door. He'd almost reached it when Nyla rushed in. She'd thrown on a pair of sweatpants and a hoodie, but her hair was still rumpled. The flush in her cheeks had little to do with her sprint from the bedroom, but at least she was here, leaning close to whisper in his ear.

"What should I say?" She smoothed her hair back and reached for the doorknob. "How about you're here to fix my sink?"

"Maybe." Leo dragged his hands through his own hair, pretty sure it was standing up in spikes from Nyla dragging her fingers through it. "My toolbox is in the truck."

"We'll improvise." Nyla pasted on a smile and yanked the door open.

Sunlight streamed in and Seth stood grinning on the front porch. "Geez, Aunt Nyla. Were you taking a dump?"

"Seth!" Mandi shot him a glare. "Not funny."

"Kinda funny," Nyla admitted, swinging the door wide. "You're here for the body parts?"

Body parts?

Leo tried to play it cool as his kid trudged through the door with his ex-wife right behind. He glanced quickly at his shirt, checking for lipstick from last night. *All clear.*

Mandi gave Nyla an apologetic shrug. "*Sorry,*" she mouthed over Seth's shoulder before clearing her throat. "Did we get the day wrong?" she asked. "Seth said you offered a bunch of anatomical models from the hospital. Some sort of loaner program for their biology unit?"

"No, it's fine." Nyla folded her arms over her chest as Leo watched his son's gaze land on him.

The way Seth's eyes brightened flooded Leo's chest with warmth, even as his face flushed with embarrassment. "Hey, bud."

"Dad!" Seth rushed forward and threw his arms around him. "How come you're here?"

Nyla sucked in a breath, then exhaled a stream of words. "Oh my gosh, it's been such a hectic morning! I was doing dishes, just—um—washing my coffee mug, you know? And the water stopped working and I haven't even showered yet or washed my hair or anything, but I remembered Leo knows plumbing, so he came by to check it out. Isn't that nice of him?" Her blue eyes darted from Mandi to Seth to Leo, imploring them to buy it. "So weird," she added weakly, brushing a loose curl off her forehead.

Mandi tucked her chin into the collar of her fleece jacket, but not before Leo caught her knowing smirk. "I texted we were on our way," she said. "You must have been…snaking the drain?"

Leo coughed as Nyla's cheeks went pink. "Yeah, uh, Nyla made me breakfast. Waffles to say thanks for fixing the shower."

"Sink." Nyla winced. "I mean, the plumbing in general. They're all sort of connected, right?"

Seth cocked his head. "Was it something with the main line?" He looked at Leo. "Remember that time we had to shut off Grandma's water because she flushed Bob's dentures down the toilet and the pipe exploded and there were turds all over and—"

"I'll go get the body parts." Nyla backed toward the hall, wisely removing herself from the temptation to blurt out exactly what she'd been doing with Seth's father all night. "They're around here someplace."

"Cool." Seth ambled over to the table. "Can I have this bacon?"

"We are not here to raid Aunt Nyla's breakfast." Mandi put her hands on her hips, slipping into mom mode. "We're already late for school. And you wouldn't be hungry if you'd gotten up in time for a full breakfast."

"Whatever. I've got granola bars in the car."

Leo stepped between his son and Nyla's bacon. "I hope you've got more than a granola bar."

"He ate a banana already." Mandi shot him an exasperated look. "Maybe this time he'll drink his milk instead of leaving it in the car to rot."

"Okay, Mom. Jeez."

A crash from the guest room made Leo turn toward the hall. "Everything okay?"

"Fine, I'm good," Nyla called back.

Leo started to turn back to his family, then stopped as his gaze locked on something pink and lacy. Shit.

Nyla's bra, draped over the lamp in the corner, swaying lightly in a gust from her heater. Outstanding.

He glanced at Seth and Mandi, who were still bickering about breakfast. Leo took a few steps toward the lamp. If he could just grab it and stuff it in his pocket and—

No. Bad idea. Getting caught shoving Nyla's lingerie in his pockets would be worse than not touching it at all.

He stopped, halfway between his kid and the dangling bra. Now what? As Mandi took a breath from scolding, she glanced at Leo. Her gaze flicked to the lamp and stalled.

"Uh, Seth." Mandi edged sideways and pointed at a photo on the opposite wall. "Don't you think it's time we update this one?"

With his kid focused on the family portrait, Leo lunged for the bra. Too fast, and he felt his feet tangle in something. He glanced down as he fell, recognizing the belt he'd searched for this morning.

"Dammit." His knees hit the ground and Leo snatched the belt by its buckle and frantically threaded it through his beltloops.

As he lurched to his feet, Seth turned back around. His gaze dropped to Leo's hands on his belt buckle. "You gotta go?"

"Huh? Oh, yeah—in a sec."

Seth shrugged, seemingly unperturbed by the thought of his father taking off his pants in someone else's living room. Mandi, meanwhile, was losing her shit. She kept laughing, then covering it with fake coughing.

Seth turned back around. "If you get sick, we can't go to Haiti," he pointed out. "Remember what you said? We both have to take our vitamins and stay away from sick people."

Mandi nodded and dropped her sleeve from her face. "Got it."

Leo cleared his throat. "So, you're still in that science unit, huh?" he asked. "The one with the medical stuff?"

"Yeah, it's pretty cool." Seth glanced back at the bacon, thankfully more riveted by pork than by the bra Leo hadn't managed to grab. "Mom checked my grade online this morning and I got an A on that last test."

"Good job," Leo said. "I know you studied hard."

"Yeah, thanks." He cocked his head at Leo. "Mom said she hated math and science, but you're pretty good at it, huh?"

Leo nodded and did everything in his power not to

look at Mandi. "Yeah. Yep. Lots of chemistry and biology. Came in handy studying forestry."

"Cool." Seth edged closer to the bacon. "Hopefully I got it from you."

"What's that?"

"Science stuff." Seth wiped his hands on his jeans. "Maybe I got your science skills instead of Mom's so I can get into med school."

Leo nodded, applauding his kid's ambition even as the bottom dropped out of his stomach. "Sure, you can be anything you want."

Mandi cleared her throat. "Aunt Nyla always had a great mind for STEM. You should have seen the science project she did for—"

"Here they are!" Nyla swooped back down the hall, a big box clutched to her chest. As she moved into the living room, one corner of the box caught the lamp cord. The lamp wobbled, swaying on its base like a drunk pirate.

Leo watched in horror as the pink bra dropped into the box. Nyla's mouth fell open as she looked down at the box of plastic hearts and kidneys and now a lacy pink brassiere wrapped around a hunk of plastic meat.

"I've got it." Mandi rushed over and plucked the bra from the box, then tossed the garment down the hall toward the bedroom. "Wow, those are really something."

"Um, thanks?" Nyla looked down at the box, cheeks stained with color. "That, uh—"

"I swear I'm going to buy you one of those drying racks." Mandi scooped the box from Nyla's arms, tossing her hair as she strode toward Seth and grabbed his arm. "I'm telling you, they make all the difference when you're washing delicates."

"Guh," said Nyla.

Seth was still fixed in his spot by the table. "Are you sure I can't have that bacon? There's like three pieces and they're just sitting there getting co—"

"Take it!" Leo and Nyla blurted at the same time.

Leo couldn't look at her. Just shoved his hands in his pockets and wondered how the hell it got so hard to act normal. How could two people be such terrible liars?

"One piece." Mandi stepped into the center of the room, blocking Seth's view of the lamp. "Eat it fast, because we're running late." She shoved the box at him as Seth inhaled the bacon. "Take your body parts, too."

"Thanks." Seth finished chewing, grinning as he headed for the door with the box of parts in his arms. "Thanks, Aunt Nyla."

"Not a problem," she squeaked.

Seth turned back to his dad. "You're coming at five, right?"

"Yeah." He cleared his throat. "Be ready to go when I get there. No horsing around after practice."

"I know." Seth gave a dramatic sigh as he pushed through the door with the box in his arms.

"Have a good day at school," Leo called, his voice oddly tight with emotion. "Love you."

"Love you, too!" Seth yelled as he headed down the steps with the door wide open. "Say hi to Grandma."

Grandma. Right, shit, he was due at his mom's house

at nine. How the hell had the morning gotten away from him?

One glance at Nyla and he remembered all over again. He'd do it again, too, if he could just get her alone.

Mandi watched Seth amble toward the car, waiting until he was out of earshot to turn back to Leo. "I hope you remember this the next time I ask to change up the schedule."

He nodded once. "Thanks." He usually accommodated schedule changes, but yeah, he was sometimes a dick about it. "I owe you."

Mandi grinned and looked at Nyla. "You suck at sneaking around."

Still grinning, Mandi pulled her sister in for a hug, cupping a hand around Nyla's ear to whisper something Leo couldn't hear. Sister stuff, probably, but it made Nyla flush bright red.

"I hate you." Now grinning herself, Nyla pushed her sister away. "You're such a jerk."

Mandi laughed and headed for the door. "Be good, kids!"

And then she was gone. Leo watched the car back out of the drive and move down the street. He stared at the space where it had been, bewildered by everything that had just happened.

He turned back to Nyla. "Did my ex-wife just help hide my hookup from our kid?"

"No." Nyla grinned and stepped closer, hooking her fingers in his belt loops. "My sister just saved me from embarrassment with my nephew."

"Huh." Leo pulled her close, still shaking his head in disbelief. "That could have been bad."

"No kidding." Nyla tipped her head back to peer up at him. "You think he suspected anything?"

He shook his head. "What kid is going to believe his dad's hooking up with his aunt?"

Nyla winced and dropped her hands. "Are we going to end up on one of those weird talk shows, throwing furniture?"

"God, I hope not." Leo shuddered. "I've got a bad shoulder. Throwing chairs would irritate it."

Nyla laughed and glanced back at the table. "Want me to reheat that?"

"Nah, I've gotta run." He glanced at his watch. "I promised my mom I'd come fix her gate. She's expecting me at nine."

"Is she expecting you to show up in a T-shirt that smells like sex?" She grinned and pressed her nose to his chest, making a big production of sniffing. "Maybe it's okay."

He plucked at the shirt's arm hole and did his own covert sniff. "I might have an extra in the car."

"I love a guy who plans ahead for sexy sleepovers."

He laughed and pulled her into his arms. "Sorry about this."

"About what?"

"The awkwardness with Mandi and Seth." He brushed a kiss on her temple. "Having to run off so fast."

Nyla tipped her head so the next kiss landed on her mouth. "And for leaving me without a morning quickie?"

His dick twitched, and he wondered if maybe he could text his mom about being an hour late.

"Go on." She swatted his butt. "I have to get dressed for work anyway."

"Need help undressing?" Maybe he didn't need to be there right at nine...

Nyla laughed. "I can't be late today. There's a staff meeting first thing."

"All right, all right." He kissed her one last time, then drew back. "Have I mentioned I love you?"

Her eyes crinkled as she grinned. "I love you, Leo."

"One more." He stole another kiss, then he grabbed his keys off the table by the door. "Sorry to stick you with the dishes."

"Only fair, since you made breakfast and then gave me credit for it in front of your kid." She backed toward the hall. "I'll text you after my shift."

"Sounds good." He watched her move, hating that he had to leave. She blew him a kiss, then vanished into her bedroom.

With a sigh, Leo turned and headed out the door.

The drive to his mom's house went quicker than it would have from his own place, so at least he wasn't late. He parked a block away and rummaged around for a clean T-shirt, but came up empty-handed. He found a stick of deodorant in the glovebox, which he didn't remember putting there. He wasn't in a position to be picky.

Smearing some on, he glanced in the rearview mirror to check his hair. Christ. He smoothed it back, then started the truck again. A neighbor came out scowling, dismayed by the strange man putting on antiperspirant in front of her house. Leo gave a friendly wave before continuing to his mother's house.

His mom was already outside watering flowers when he pulled into the driveway. She looked up and waved, smiling as he parked.

"I wasn't sure you were still coming." She turned off the spigot and began coiling up the hose as Leo approached.

"I've got that." He took the hose from her, surprised by its weight. He needed to remember to buy her one of those lighter nylon kinds.

After coiling it up on the hook, he pulled his mom in for a hug. "Sorry I'm a couple minutes late. Got caught up with Seth."

Not a total lie, but his mom sniffed him as she drew back. "Whose perfume is that?"

"New deodorant." He took a step back and hoped she couldn't read anything odd on his face. "How've you been?"

"Fine, dear." Her brow furrowed. "I thought Seth was with Mandi?"

"He had to swing by the house and grab something." No need to mention it was Nyla's house. He was getting better with the fibs.

His mom peeled off her gardening gloves. "How was brunch with the Franklins?"

"Good." He thought about Nyla's drunken confessions and fought the urge to grimace. "We made some headway on planning Seth's graduation party."

"Graduation party." She made a funny little huffing noise and shook her head. "When I was Seth's age, we only had graduations for high school and maybe college. None of this 'kindergarten graduation' or 'middle school graduation' and whatnot."

Leo leaned against the house and shoved his hands into his pockets. "I think it's cool."

"Oh, absolutely." She wiped a hand over her brow, then grabbed the front of her shirt to flutter it for air. "I wish they'd had that when you were little. He was so sick by the time you were in high school, and it would have been nice if your father could have—" Her voice broke, and so did Leo's heart.

He started to reach for her, but she swiped at her eyes and waved him off. "Sorry to be a silly old woman."

"You're not silly."

She gave a watery laugh. "But I'm old?"

"You don't look a day over twenty-one."

"Thank you, dear." She took a shuddery breath, still fighting to keep her smile. "You need to work on your skills if you ever want to date again."

"I'll keep that in mind."

She breathed a wistful little sigh. "I just meant your father would have loved to see you graduate. Not just high school, but college. It's a big deal being the first in a family to have a degree."

Leo nodded, pride blooming in his chest. He'd been damn proud he'd not only paid his own way through school, but for Mandi's grad school after they married.

He'd tried to be a good husband, a good provider, *a good guy*.

A lump formed in his throat and he swallowed it back. "I always wanted to be like Dad."

"You are, sweetheart. So much." She was blinking back tears again, and Leo wished he hadn't said anything. He should have talked about baseball or Seth or gardening.

But his mother wasn't ready to let things go. "I miss him so much, sometimes. Bob's a wonderful man. But it's different with the father of your children."

"Yeah, I get it." Did he, though? He loved being a dad, couldn't imagine never having Seth.

But was he an asshole for looking forward to his kid-free future? Days of sailing down the highway, wind blowing his sleeves as he rode 'til he got sleepy and then camped where he felt like it. Ate dinner out of cans, answered to no one but himself.

His mother must have mistaken his wistful look for something else and pulled him in for a hug. "He'd have been so proud of you." She squeezed hard, then let go to look him in the eye. "You really are like him."

"Good." His chest swelled with pride, even as his heart ached inside it. "He was such a great guy."

"The best." She sniffled and wiped her eyes with her sleeve. "Always putting everyone else first."

Leo took two deep breaths, remembering his ex-wife's words of frustration.

"I just never knew, when I married a guy who puts everyone else's needs before his own, that I wouldn't

count as 'everyone' anymore. That I'd become part of you instead."

"He sacrificed so much for everyone else," his mom continued. "I just wish—" She shook her head. "Never mind."

"You wish he was still here?"

"Yes, but that's not what I meant."

She studied him a long time. So long, Leo began wondering if that was the end of her thought.

Then her eyes softened and she tried again. "I wish he'd spent more time doing the things he loved." She held up a hand as if to stop him, though Leo had no plans to do that. "Don't misunderstand me—he loved you," she said. "More than anything in the world, he loved being a dad. But sometimes I think about how little time he spent doing the things he wanted. That motorcycle trip was always something to be done *someday*. Fishing the Salmon River or maybe even Belize instead of little ol' Miller Pond. All the things he put off for another time."

Leo nodded, throat feeling tight. "Guess he didn't know he wouldn't get that other time."

"That's true." She went back to fanning herself, blinking hard to get rid of the tears. "It's such a shame."

He nodded again, feeling like a puppet. "I like to think he was still happy."

"I know he was, sweetie." She glanced up at the sky, looking for rain, maybe. "But I always wonder if he could have been happier. Maybe if he'd had more freedom instead of working all the time, his body wouldn't have given out the way it did. Maybe he could have made it through another round of chemo."

Leo nodded, not sure what to say to that. "I guess we'll never know."

"Gah! Look at me being weepy and silly. Come on." She grabbed his sleeve and towed him toward the house. "The gate can wait. Let's get you fed before we start chores."

He didn't have the heart to tell her he'd eaten already, and he didn't have the balls to tell her he'd done it with Nyla. She liked Nyla well enough, but the Franklin family...

"Did I tell you Ted and Laurel are taking a cruise in the Bahamas?"

"Good Lord." His mother pivoted on the back porch and rolled her eyes. "Honestly, that family. Any excuse to throw money around."

Yeah. That.

"They're not so bad."

Another eye roll from his mother. "I'm just glad you're free of them. I can't wait until Seth's grown and you can stop having to do all those family dinners and whatnot."

Leo sighed inwardly and pulled open the door for her. "After you, Mom."

She smiled and shuffled into the house, pausing to pat his cheek. "Such a good boy."

He swallowed back the lump in his throat and followed her into the house for his second breakfast.

CHAPTER SEVENTEEN

"I think that covers it for what it's like being a nurse." Nyla tugged the ends of her stethoscope, grateful for the prop as she scanned the sea of preteen faces. "Any questions?"

A few kids glanced at each other. Some looked bored. Some looked like they might want to ask a question but hadn't determined yet if it was the cool thing to do.

Her nephew, God bless him, threw her a rope. "What's something funny that's happened to you as a nurse?"

Nyla grinned and threw the kid a mental high five. "Well, there's a lot I can't tell you because of HIPAA. Anyone know what HIPAA is?"

Seth raised his hand, of course, but she looked around for someone else. A slouchy white kid in ripped jeans—a floppy-haired punk Nyla pegged as the class smart-ass—called out from the back of the room. "Is that like a female hippopotamus?"

"Exactly," Nyla deadpanned. "You should see the size of the enemas we have to give them."

That earned her a few snickers, while a couple leaned over to ask classmates what "enema" meant. Nyla glanced at the teacher, hoping she hadn't crossed some line, but Mrs. Hernandez was laughing right along with them.

"It's about patient privacy, right?" This from a tall Black girl in pretty green top.

"Exactly right." Nyla rested a hand on the teacher's desk. "HIPAA is something we follow in healthcare to provide patient privacy, so it limits the kinds of things I can share with all of you. But I'm sure I've got a story or two that keep the people involved anonymous."

Of course, she did. Seth himself had heard a few of them, but she took her time scooping up the box that held plastic body parts as she pondered the best ones to share with a middle school audience. Her most amusing ones tended to involve foreign objects in random orifices or bizarre drug-seeking behavior. Entertaining for twelve-year-olds, but maybe not appropriate for the classroom.

She set the box of organs on the desk and leaned against the counter beside it. "Let's see, once I had a patient who came in complaining he'd gotten something in his eye." She winked at Seth, who'd heard this one before. "I got him up on the exam table with the light in his eyes and said, 'open wide.' And the guy opens his mouth, big as you please, and says, 'aaaaaaaaahhhhhhh.'"

That one got a few laughs, plus a few groans. Tough crowd. She'd come prepared to talk about nursing as a profession, but not so much the funny stories.

"This one's not mine, but there was a case in Mexico City about five years ago where a teenager got a hickey from his girlfriend." Another glance at the teacher, since Nyla wasn't sure twelve-year-olds even knew what hickeys were, let alone expected someone to broach the subject in class. Mrs. Hernandez lifted a brow, but waved Nyla to keep going. "Anyway, the guy died."

"Died?" Now the floppy-haired kid was sitting up straight, pale face flushed behind his freckles. "No way. From a hickey?"

"Yep." Nyla scanned the room, seeing she had their attention. "For those who don't know, a hickey is a bruising of the skin that results from sucking on it until tiny blood vessels break. Usually on the neck or arm or someplace like that."

"What? Why?" God help the sweet-faced blond girl looking horrified in the front row.

"Varying reasons," Nyla said. "Sometimes, just to be funny. It's not usually fatal, but in this case doctors believe the hickey resulted in a blood clot that traveled to the patient's brain and caused a stroke."

There, let that sink in for a bit. She wasn't usually one for scare tactics, but might as well give them a reason to think twice about the kind of stuff that gets teenagers into trouble.

A hush fell over the classroom, and since she didn't want to end on a low note—

"How about a nurse joke?" she offered.

A blue-haired kid in the front row sat up a little straighter. "What did the nurse say when she found a rectal thermometer in her pocket?"

Nyla grimaced. She should have been specific about who got to tell the joke. "What did she say?"

The kid grinned, pleased with himself. "Some asshole has my pen!"

The class burst into laughter as the teacher stood and clapped her hands to get the kids back under control. "Language, Ryan," she said. "Remember our talk about being on our best behavior for guests?"

Nyla fought back a grin, not wanting to encourage the kid. She'd have to remember that one, though. "Why do nurses bring red magic markers to work?" she asked.

No one had an answer, though a few kids looked leery. Probably hoping for something dirty.

A raven-haired girl in a white soccer jersey that set off her bronze skin tossed a lifeline from the middle row. "Why do they bring red magic markers to work?"

Nyla crossed her arms over the chest of her favorite purple scrub top and grinned. "In case they have to draw blood."

That got her a few more groans and even a laugh from the teacher. "Okay, I have a question." Mrs. Hernandez stood up and joined Nyla at the front of the class, crossing her legs as she leaned back against the cupboards. "Are there any common fibs you have to tell patients? Things like, 'this really won't hurt all that much' when you know it's going to be really painful."

Nyla bit her lip. Did Mrs. Hernandez see right through her and know she was the worst liar ever? But no, that's not what she meant.

"I'm not actually very good at fibbing," Nyla admitted, keeping her eyes off Seth. Nearly two weeks had passed since he'd caught her with Leo that morning, and she still felt weird about it. Still had trouble meeting his eye at family game nights, though Lord help her, she'd managed to keep the relationship under wraps.

"Let's see," she said, still fumbling for a fib. "Okay, so sometimes new babies that are born are really cute and it's easy to tell the new parents, 'you have such a cute baby' or 'what beautiful eyes she has.'"

"Ah, I see." Mrs. Hernandez smiled. "So, what do you say when it's an ugly baby?"

Nyla grinned back and delivered the punchline. "We say, 'oh, she looks just like you.'"

The students laughed, and so did Mrs. Hernandez. Before anyone could throw another question at her, a loud trill signaled the end of sixth period. As kids stood and began to file out, Seth approached. His hair flopped over his forehead, which must be in style now. He wore a cheerful grin and a green flannel shirt she was pretty sure belonged to Leo at some point.

"Good job, Aunt Nyla."

"Thanks, kiddo." She ruffled his hair, earning a grunt of protest as Seth shot an earnest look at the girl in the soccer jersey. The girl smiled, face softening around angular cheekbones as she shouldered her backpack.

Ah, young love.

Nyla threw an arm around Seth. "For the record, you definitely weren't an ugly baby."

"That's what I hear." Seth rolled his eyes and slipped another glance at the girl, who seemed to be lingering by the door. "Mom swears she had a nurse who asked to send my picture to some baby model company."

"Your mom's not lying." Nyla gave herself a mental slap for the word choice, but kept going. "It's true, I was there when it happened. The L&D nurse had a sister who worked for some modeling agency out of L.A. She swore you were the prettiest baby she'd ever seen."

He had been, too. Nyla still remembered walking into the birthing suite an hour after delivery. Mandi had been asleep, but Leo stood cradling the infant against his chest, crooning softly to the bundle in his arms.

He'd looked up as Nyla walked in and his whole face glowed with love. "He's so perfect," Leo had murmured, tears glinting in his eyes. "The most perfect thing I've ever seen."

An ache had settled deep in her chest, a yearning she'd never felt before. Something desperate and hungry and howling to be filled.

She blinked herself back to the present and squeezed Seth's shoulder. "No lie," she said, holding up one hand as though swearing an oath. "Honest to God, I've seen hundreds of newborns in my career, and I've never seen one as cute as you."

"Aww, shucks." He gave a mock bow, then glanced at the girl lingering by the door. "Hey, Sahalie—you going to the dance on Friday?"

He scampered away to catch up to her, throwing a wave at Nyla as he fled.

Still smiling, she began packing up her props that hadn't made it into the box yet. A stray liver, a left lung, a coil of small intestine.

Mrs. Hernandez grabbed a gall bladder and tucked it in the box. "Thanks again for coming today."

"No problem. It's fun."

"You actually just gave me a really great idea for our unit coming up."

"Bad nurse jokes?"

The teacher laughed. "Tempting, but no. I think I'll have the kids bring baby photos."

Nyla looked up from the pancreas she'd just grabbed. "What's the lesson?"

"Genetics." Mrs. Hernandez turned to grab a lung off a desk, missing Nyla's sharp intake of breath. "I just sent home the permission slips. We're doing finger prick tests to learn about blood typing. It could be fun to put up baby photos of the students to let them guess who's who."

A cold ripple churned in Nyla's gut. "Blood typing?"

"It's a new unit this year, very exciting." Mrs. Hernandez dropped a lung into the box unaware the floor had just shifted under Nyla's feet. "We got a grant from the state to buy the kits. It's a great learning opportunity."

Nyla nodded, speechless as she stood holding her box of plastic body parts. "It does sound like they'll learn a lot." She swallowed hard, knowing exactly what Seth stood to learn.

Knowing this was about to change everything.

• • •

"Why the hell are they doing this in middle school?" Leo sat down hard on the edge of his couch, softening a bit as Howie the Wondercat jumped onto his lap. He stroked a hand down the soft orange fur as Nyla watched with envy.

She wouldn't mind having that hand on her. Four weeks had passed since they first slept together, and she couldn't seem to get enough of him since then. Who the hell was this wanton woman thinking about sex at a time like this?

Commanding herself to pay attention, she positioned herself beside the coffee table halfway between her sister and Leo.

Mandi sighed and sank into the chair opposite him. "We have to tell him," she said. "I don't want to, but I'd rather he hear it from us than learn about it in front of all his friends."

Nyla looked from Mandi to Leo, trying not to let her gaze linger too long on Leo. He looked damn good with his shirtsleeves rolled up to his elbows and a smudge of grease on his forearm. He'd been out flying the new air tanker near the Mt. Baker Wilderness today, and the image of him in the cockpit had her knees feeling squishy. Hesitating, she sat down at the opposite end of the sofa.

Mandi rolled her eyes. "You can sit next to each other. Jesus, Nyla. I already know you're bumping uglies."

Nyla winced and glanced at Leo. "At what point does this stop being weird?"

He shook his head, still hung up on Seth's school situation. "Probably not anytime soon."

That shouldn't sting, and she knew he didn't mean anything by it. But yeah, this wasn't ideal. She looked to Mandi. "Do you want me to be part of it? Telling

Seth, I mean."

Leo stroked Howie from head to tail, frowning the whole time. "How would that go down?"

Ignoring her ex-husband, Mandi looked at Nyla. "What, you mean like be my moral support?"

That wasn't what she'd meant, but sure. "I could be moral support for both of you," she said. "But mostly I was thinking he might have questions about genetics. Medical stuff that I could help answer."

Leo shook his head slowly. "That's not the kind of thing he'll want to know. He's a kid, he doesn't give a shit about chromosomes and blood types. He'll want to know exactly how his mother ended up having sex with someone else while we were still married."

"For God's sake, Leo." Mandi stood up, eyes blazing. "That is not what *my son* is going to focus on."

Leo flinched like he'd been slapped. Nyla held her breath, not sure whether to reach for him or stay out of this. No good would come from leaping into the middle of a fight.

But this was her sister. Her lover. Her *family*.

"Um, guys." She waved a hand, desperate to ease the tension. "Maybe if we focus on—"

"*Your* son?" Leo's jaw clenched as Howie leaped off his lap with a sharp chirp. "*Your* son, Mandi? That's the card you're gonna play? I don't care what the goddamn DNA says. Seth will always be just as much my child as yours, and if you think I'm going to step back and let you stomp all over that—"

"I'm not stomping on anything!" Mandi clenched her

fists at her side, tendons straining in her neck. "For God's sake, that's not how I meant it! I'm saying I know my kid, and the last thing he's going to focus on is our sex life."

"*Your* sex life." Leo threw his hands up in the air. "In case you forgot, I wasn't there for Seth's conception."

Mandi glared at him. "Oh, I haven't forgotten."

"Guys, stop!" Nyla leaped to her feet, clambering onto the coffee table like a bouncer in a bar fight. "This isn't helping anything. Will you please quit yelling?"

Now they were both glaring at her, the two people she loved most in the world. Her sister, her best friend, the woman who'd literally saved her life.

And Leo, sweet, kind, sexy Leo. The best man she'd ever known.

She looked at him, knowing he was most likely to see reason. To take a deep breath and calm down so they could talk this through like three rational adults.

His brown eyes met hers, searching. Then he closed them and nodded once. "You're right." He sat down on the couch, jaw still clenched tight. "You're right, this isn't productive."

Mandi took a shaky breath and sat down, too. "I'm sorry, okay? I really didn't mean that the way it came out. I know Seth's your son, Leo. He always will be."

Leo nodded, staring down into his lap. Again, Nyla ached to reach for him. Was it her place as his lover to do it?

Or her place as Mandi's sister to sit tight, to let them sort this out however they needed. She looked to Mandi.

The helplessness on her big sister's face nearly broke her heart.

"Okay, so back to the details." Nyla spread her hands on her knees and slipped into helper mode. "The lesson's in two weeks?"

"Less than that," Leo muttered. "Ten days? They're doing it right before school ends."

And right before Mandi and Seth left for Haiti. Not ideal, especially not for Leo who'd find himself separated from his son at the exact moment that son got a buttload of shocking news dumped on him.

"Okay, so…." Nyla trailed off and glanced at Mandi. "What's best here?"

Her sister blinked, throat moving as she swallowed. "Leo's right," she said softly. "I'm the one who's going to come out looking like the bad guy here. If you're willing to be there, Nyla—I'd like it if someone had my back."

She nodded as her heart twisted in a tight little ball. "I'll be there." She put her hand on Mandi's and squeezed. "Wherever you want to do it. Whenever you think it should happen."

She could feel Leo's eyes on her. Could hear the questions in his head about how this might all shake out, and whether she had *his* back, too. She glanced at him and held his gaze.

I love you, she channeled as best she could. She didn't move her lips at all, but he nodded like he'd heard her.

"Agreed," he said. "Nyla should be there. Seth trusts her, and there's gonna be shit we can't explain. The sort of stuff that's best explained in medical terms."

Nyla turned back to her sister. "All right. We've got that part decided. When do you—"

"Wait, no." Mandi swallowed, gaze shifting to Leo. "Your mom. I think Helen should hear this, too."

"What?" Leo looked dumbfounded.

"I'm serious." Mandi's brow furrowed. "Seth shares things with her that he doesn't tell anyone else, and besides—it'll give him an ally who's not all tangled up in this triangle. Someone who's not banging his dad. No offense, Nyla."

"None taken." Mostly.

Leo sat blinking and bewildered. "You want to do this in front of my mom?"

Mandi gave a defeated sigh. "Not really, but it seems like the best option. Is that a problem?"

"No, I just—" He dragged his hands down his face, shaking his head. "I'm surprised, that's all."

Mandi blinked hard the way she did when fighting back emotion. "She's going to find out eventually, so maybe it'll help if she and Seth go through this together. It'll be like ripping the Band-Aid off clean."

"Okay," Nyla said, coming around to the idea. "So Leo's mom?"

As Howie launched himself onto her lap, Mandi began to scratch his ears. "She hates me anyway, so it's not like this will change things."

Leo frowned. "She doesn't *hate* you—"

"She's disappointed in me." Mandi rolled her eyes. "Wasn't that the word she used? When we broke the news to her about the divorce and she asked whose idea it was and I admitted it was mine?"

Shaking his head, Leo rested his palms on his knees. "This is different."

Nyla wasn't so sure this would be any better, and it might be a lot worse. It wasn't her place to say it, so she settled for steering the conversation back on track. "I think that's brave," she said. "Having Leo's mother there, I mean."

Gratitude flashed in Mandi's eyes. "This way, everyone who needs to know will know, and Seth will have his whole family to turn to with questions."

"It makes sense." Nyla squeezed her sister's hand, touched by the gesture. Having Helen there would make things way worse for Mandi, and she knew it.

But her sister was right, it would cushion the blow for Seth and give Leo an ally with no ties to his ex-wife.

Searching Leo's face, she waited for him to respond. "What do you think?"

He held her gaze for a long time. Slowly, he reached out and took her other hand. "I think I love you," he said softly. "So fucking much."

Mandi gave a choked little laugh. "Holy shit." She made a weird gulping sound and squeezed Nyla's fingers tight. "You guys are serious? I thought you were just screwing."

Nyla watched her sister's face to gauge her reaction. "Yes," she said. "I love Leo. And, um…apparently, he loves me."

Mandi scooped up the cat and deposited him on the coffee table as she stood. Her smile looked forced, and Nyla could have sworn she saw tears glittering in Mandi's eyes. "Oh my God." Mandi's laughter sounded real enough, but choked with other emotion. "I'm happy for you, I am. But I just—fuck, this is weird." She turned away and swiped a hand over her eyes as she headed for the kitchen. "This calls for vodka."

Leo glanced at Nyla as Howie leaped onto his lap. Nyla shrugged as Leo called out to Mandi. "You know where it is."

"Still the freezer?" She didn't wait for a reply. Just marched into the kitchen, leaving Nyla alone with Leo.

She turned to see him watching her. "You okay?" he asked softly.

"Yeah. You?"

He nodded and squeezed her fingers. "A little scared. What if he hates us? If he feels like he's not my kid anymore, you know?"

"He could never feel that way." She knew it was true, deep down in the pit of her soul. "You'll always be his dad, Leo."

He nodded, though he didn't look fully convinced. "I really love you."

"I love you, too." She smiled and tightened her grip on his fingers. "And I promise we'll get through this together."

Mandi bustled back into the living room, carrying three shot glasses brimming with clear liquid. Handing two of them to Nyla, she sat down with one in her hand.

Leo held his aloft. "What are we drinking to?"

"To families." Mandi thrust her glass in the air. "The

good, the bad, the messy, the complicated, and the totally fucked-up."

Nyla didn't ask which they were. Maybe all of the above. She clinked her glass against her sister's, then Leo's. He was watching her with curious eyes. "You good?"

She nodded as her stomach rolled. "A little queasy, but yeah."

Taking a tiny sip of her vodka, she swallowed back the weird feeling in the pit of her gut. As Mandi and Leo tipped their heads back to down the liquid in a gulp, Nyla covertly dumped hers in a plant, belatedly realizing it was a fake one.

Sorry, Ficus.

Darting a glance at Leo, she threw in another silent apology as she set the empty glass on the table and folded her hands on her lap.

CHAPTER EIGHTEEN

The next weekend, Leo stood with his hands in soapy water as his mother and Seth laughed in the next room. He glanced at the clock on the wall and a dart of anticipation shot through him. Ten minutes until Mandi arrived with Nyla.

That was the plan, what they'd all agreed to last week. Leo would invite his mom and Bob for a pre-graduation party. Mandi would stop by for dessert, a plot made easier when Seth himself suggested it.

"We're having cream puffs, right?" Seth had asked. "Because you know that's Aunt Nyla's favorite and—"

"You want to invite her?" Leo couldn't believe it was so easy.

"Yeah, could we?"

"Absolutely." And since Nyla and Mandi had a standing dinner date the last Saturday of every month, it made sense for them both to swing by after. Nice and easy.

Only now it didn't feel that way. Leo's gut hunkered heavy in his abdomen like he'd swallowed a brick. He kept catching himself wanting to text his ex to call the whole thing off.

God. What if Seth got angry? With Leo, with his mother, with the world in general?

Or worse, what if it completely crumbled the kid's sense of self? What if he cried or felt lost or confused or heartbroken? It was the worst feeling in the world, knowing his son was hurting and that there wasn't anything he could do to fix it.

"Is everything okay, sweetheart?" His mother's voice pulled Leo from his thoughts, and he nodded as he ran the skillet under cold water. "Just finishing up the dishes."

"Want me to dry?" Not waiting for an answer, she stepped into place beside him and grabbed the red dish towel. "Dinner was excellent. I understand Mandi's stopping by?"

"Yeah, Seth wanted her here." Leo cleared his throat. "Actually, um…we're going to be sharing some kind of important news, so—"

"You are *not* getting back together." She banged the pot down hard on the counter and stared at him. "Leo Josiah Sayre, please tell me that's not what's happening."

"Shhh!" Leo choked back a sound somewhere between horror and laughter. "I promise you on my son's life that's not what it's about. Cross my heart and hope to die."

"Thank God." His mother went back to drying, stealing glimpses at him every few seconds. "Is this something I should be prepared for? You're not putting me in a nursing home, are you?"

"Mom, you could probably bench press me." He leaned over and kissed her cheek. "Is there a reason you always go for the worst-case scenario?"

"I'm a mother," she said. "We're always prepared for the worst."

"And I'm grateful for that." He handed her the big steel mixing bowl and cleared his throat. "Seth might need you, okay? The news we're giving him, it'll probably shake him up a little."

"Understood." She pressed her lips together. "You're not going to give me some advanced notice?"

Hell, maybe he should tell her early. They'd all agreed not to, but he couldn't recall why at the moment.

He'd just opened his mouth to say it when the doorbell chimed.

Shit.

Adrenaline surged through him, his body seized by the same sensation he felt the first time he jumped from an airplane into a dark, smoldering forest.

Voices rang out from the front of the house—Mandi, Nyla, Seth, Bob. Leo swallowed back the words that were surging up his throat and replaced them with others as he looked at his mother.

"Thanks for being here." He reached up to tuck the mixing bowl back into the high cupboard. "And for being my mom."

She smiled and patted his belly. "It's the best thing I could have done with my life." Then she turned and walked into the living room.

Leo drained the sink and wiped his hands on a dish towel, stalling for time. Nyla's voice rang out from the living room, soothing his racing heart. He was damn glad to have her here, even if seeing her would make his heart race in a different sort of way.

He took his time joining the party, needing a few

minutes to compose himself. *God*. This was it. The moment that would change everything.

He took one more deep breath and headed into the living room. "Hey, guys. Good to see you."

He gave Nyla a hug, trying to recall if he used to do that. Yes, of course he did. Why was it so hard to remember how to act normal around family?

When he let go, she flashed an encouraging smile and sat down on the loveseat beside Mandi. They'd planned this, too, where everyone would sit, only Seth had parked himself in the easy chair instead of on the sofa between his grandparents.

That was fine. It was all fine. They could still do this. Why were his palms sweating?

His mother was handing out creampuffs, the pillowy lumps taking up the whole surface of Leo's best salad plates. Should he offer everyone milk? That wasn't in the plan, but maybe he should improvise.

Or maybe he should just sit the hell down and try to be calm.

"She made some chocolate ones just for you, Dad." Seth grinned with a face covered in powdered sugar. "Aunt Nyla gets one, too."

"This looks great, Mom." He took his plate and flicked a gaze to Nyla, ignoring the way his heart flipped over in his chest.

Nyla blushed and glanced away, and Leo tried to focus on his cream puff. The flaky pastry, the perfect, fluffy whipped cream, sent him spiraling back in time. Back to childhood birthday parties when his dad was still alive.

Back to Seth's sixth birthday with a fat candle in the center of his boy's dessert as everyone sang and clapped and—

"So, Seth." Mandi took a deep breath. "There's something we've been wanting to talk to you about."

Leo stilled with the cream puff on a plate in his lap. His heart thudded in his ears as Nyla shot him an *oh shit* look.

They were doing this. Just diving right in.

Mandi glanced at him, and Leo remembered that was his cue. He shifted the plate on his knee and looked at his boy. "Right, son, uh, your mother and I talked." What else? "Um, we decided you're old enough now to have some important information."

Seth took a big bite of cream puff and chewed, looking wary. "Adult stuff?"

Mandi's throat moved as she swallowed, though she hadn't taken a bite of her pastry. "That's right, adult stuff. First, we want you to know we both love you very, very much."

"Very much," Leo echoed as his stomach balled into a tight knot. "And nothing's ever going to change that."

"Shit." Seth winced. "I mean, *shoot*."

Mandi frowned. "Seth, that's not—"

"Wait, no, don't tell me." Seth looked at him and Leo felt his gut tighten. "You told Mom?"

Leo blinked. "Told Mom what?"

"That I like Sahalie." Seth frowned and stuck a finger in the center of his cream puff. "You know Mom's gonna make a big deal about this and we only kissed the one time, but—"

"Whoa, whoa, whoa." Leo held up his hands. "That's not what this is about. We're happy that you like a girl."

"Or a boy," Mandi put in helpfully. "Either would be totally fine with us."

Bob leaned forward on the couch, looking earnest. "Or maybe someone who's non-library. That's okay, too. We're your family and we love you."

Leo sighed. "The word is *non-binary* and absolutely this family supports all forms of sexual identity and gender expression and we'll embrace anyone you happen to love." Shit, they were getting way off track. He glanced at Nyla, not sure how to reel this back in.

Nyla gave a helpless shrug. "Sahalie must be the girl from science class?" She offered Seth an encouraging smile. "Very smart. Pretty, too."

Leo closed his eyes. This was definitely not going according to plan. He needed to do damage control, make sure Seth knew he hadn't betrayed his confidence. He shifted his gaze to Mandi. "For the record, I never breathed a word about Sahalie, right?"

"Confirmed." Mandi lifted one shoulder. "But I knew there was someone special on your radar. Moms *always* know."

Leo held his breath and did his best to keep from looking at his own mother. "Right, okay, so this isn't about Sahalie."

"It's not?" Seth picked up his cream puff and took a huge bite. "Is it about what I said to Coach Albright?"

Christ, this was not how the conversation was meant

to go. Leo raked a hand through his hair, belatedly realizing he had whipped cream on his fingers. Great.

"What did you say to Coach Alb—you know what? Never mind." He shot another look at Mandi. "Your turn."

At the end of the couch, Bob leaned forward again. "Wait, this isn't one of those interventions, is it?" He nudged Leo's mom with his elbow. "I saw it on *Dateline*, how teenagers these days are into drooling."

"Drooling?" She shot an alarmed look at Leo. "Is this true?"

Leo closed his eyes and felt his last shreds of sanity slip away. "Jesus, I have no idea."

Seth heaved a sigh. "It's *Juuling*, Grandma. And no, I'm not juuling. That's for losers and druggies."

Leo opened his eyes in time to see Seth's eyes dart to Mandi. "Wait, is this about the vanilla extract? Because I swear I didn't drink it even if it has like a bunch of alcohol in it and Ryan said his brother got drunk off it this one time. But seriously, I was just putting it in a milkshake and I knocked the bottle over and I thought you'd get mad so I filled up the rest with water and—"

"Okay, Seth, no." Mandi shook her head. "This isn't about the vanilla extract."

Leo dragged his hands down his face, wondering how they'd gotten so far off the plan. He totally believed the kid about the vanilla, but that was hardly the point. "Seth, you're not in trouble," he said. "This is actually something personal we're wanting to share with you."

"Personal?" The kid looked leery now. He finished chewing his creampuff and glanced at Nyla. "Is this about you and my dad?"

Nyla blinked. "What?"

One corner of Seth's mouth quirked up. "Yeah, I mean…he wasn't really fixing your shower, right?"

Nyla's mouth fell open. Her hands flew up to cover it, but there was no mistaking her response.

Holy shit.

"Seth." Mandi was in full-on mom mode now. "You know better than to make assumptions about other people's personal business—"

"No, it's okay." Leo glanced at Nyla, who flashed him an alarmed look.

But hell, he wasn't okay lying to his son. Might as well be honest. He took a deep breath and looked at Seth. "I mean, yeah. You're right." He watched his son carefully. "Aunt Nyla and I have been…dating."

"Okay." Seth took another bite of creampuff.

What?

Leo looked at his mother, steeling himself to fend off the attack on Nyla's family. Or a flurry of accusations about secrets and responsibility and—why was she smiling?

"I'm glad that's out in the open." His mother licked powdered sugar off one fingertip and nodded at Seth. "Honey, how do you feel about it?"

Seth shrugged and chewed his dessert. "Cool."

Cool? That's it? Weeks of anxiety and stress and hiding and all his kid could come up with was *cool*?

Leo looked at his mom. "You're not upset?"

"Why would I be upset?" She shot a look at Mandi before her gaze settled on Nyla. "You're lovely, dear. And much better-suited for my son than your sister was."

Nyla flushed bright pink. "Um, thanks?"

"Hey." Mandi frowned, then seemed to reconsider. "I guess I can't argue with that."

"Nor should you." Leo's mom sat up straighter on the couch. "Not the simplest situation in the world, but I trust your judgment, son." One more flicker of disdain for Mandi. "Generally speaking."

Leo took another ragged breath. Could it really be this easy? He looked back at his kid, gauging his reaction. Was he just playing it cool? "You're sure you're okay with this? You want to talk about—"

"Grownup stuff?" Seth gave a dramatic shudder. "Uh, no. Gross."

Leo bristled. "Actually—"

"No, it's fine!" Nyla flipped a curl off her forehead. "Next subject please."

Seth grinned. "It's cool, seriously. I mean, I love you, Aunt Nyla."

"I love you, too." Nyla's eyes filled, and she swiped at them with her sleeve. "Sorry. I don't know why I'm getting all emotional."

Leo hesitated, wanting to reach for her. Damn this stupid seating chart plan.

Focus.

They still had bigger issues to cover. "Okay, so, that's out in the open." He took another breath, preparing himself for the tougher stuff ahead. "So, uh…there's actually something else."

His mother folded her hands on her lap. "Well get to it already."

"I'm *trying*." And failing, apparently. He glanced at Mandi, trying to remember how they'd agreed to do this.

Mandi sat stiff on the edge of her seat. She looked a bit green, which was weird because so did Nyla. Maybe something they had for dinner. Wasn't there a salmonella outbreak recently at Carousel?

His ex-wife's gaze darted around the room, her face getting paler by the moment. She looked from Nyla to Bob to Seth, her expression growing more frantic as her gaze shot back to Seth.

She sucked in a ragged breath, then let it out on a sob. "I had an affair, okay?" The words flew out like flaming darts as she covered her face with her hands. "It was horrible and wrong and a mistake I'll regret for the rest of my life, but I can't regret it completely because the end result was you, Seth." Dropping her hands, she looked at Seth. "That's what we've been trying to say. Your dad, he'll always be your dad. But he's not your *dad*…biologically. You know?"

Seth stared at her in silence. Leo braced for rage. For tears, for questions, for anything.

"You mean…I'm not adopted?"

Leo blinked. "What?"

Seth swiveled to look at him. "I mean, I found out a couple years ago that I couldn't be your kid, but I thought maybe I wasn't Mom's kid, either, and—" He shrugged, glancing at Leo's mom. "Grandma said that wasn't true, but I didn't know what to believe."

Leo gaped at his mother. "You knew about this?"

"Well of course I did." She folded her arms over her chest. "Seth came to me that summer he went to camp. They did some blood type experiment, part of the science unit. After he got back, we looked things up on the internet."

Bob nodded beside her. "Amazing what you find on the world wide web. Did you know you can hear a whale's heartbeat from more than two miles away?"

"Okay, um." Jesus, what the hell? He looked back at Seth. "Wait, so you knew all this?"

"Sort of." Seth shrugged and looked at his mom. "I didn't know that part. The stuff you just said. Affair?" For the first time, a flash of confusion appeared in his son's eyes. "That's not good."

"It's not, you're right." Tears filled Mandi's eyes and she blinked them back. "Honey, you've been holding on to this for how long?"

Seth scuffed his feet on the carpet and shrugged. "I don't know. A year, maybe?"

"Baby, you know you can talk to me about anything." Mandi got up and knelt by Seth's chair, murmuring words Leo couldn't make out, which was fine. They needed to have this moment.

Turning to his mother, Leo shook his head. "You seriously knew about this? And you didn't think to tell me?"

"Seth swore me to secrecy." His mom anchored her

hands on her knees. "My word is my bond."

"I understand, but…" Leo dragged his hands down his face. "What if *I* hadn't known?"

"But you *did* know." Her gaze slid to Mandi, and she lowered her voice. "I don't like that she trapped you with a child the way she did. I love Seth dearly, you know that. But still. You never had the chance to make your own choices."

Trapped? Leo gripped the arms of his chair. "Mom, I never felt that way."

"She took away your option to leave," his mother insisted. "Children are blessings, and Seth is the best kind of blessing. But having a child complicates things."

"Mom, stop." Leo could feel his hackles rising. "I love Seth no matter what. Even if I'd known about the biology, it wouldn't have changed that he's my son."

"Of course, dear. We all love Seth." Her voice had risen again, so she tamped it back to a whisper. Not that it mattered, since Seth and Mandi were absorbed in conversation. "I just think Mandi took advantage. Knowing you're a good, upstanding, responsible man who'd never leave, even if his wife was absolutely *not* the right sort of woman for—"

"Um, that's my sister." Nyla waved a hand, keeping her voice low. "I appreciate that you're okay with me dating your son, but can you please not bash my sister?"

Helen sighed and crossed her arms. "Fine. All I'm saying is that we have every right to be *disappointed* in how Mandi handled things."

Leo decided to let it drop, since he had more

important things to deal with. He glanced at Seth who was thankfully still focused on his mom. "Let's stop that line of discussion," he said. "What's done is done."

His mother gave another snort of disdain and shot one more look at Mandi. "She's right about one thing," his mom murmured. "Moms always know. And I knew from how you acted, how carefully you watched him, that you'd already found out. Or maybe you'd always known."

"I didn't," he said, shaking his head. "I mean, I did, but I didn't always, and—never mind." This was hardly the issue to dwell on.

He looked back at Seth, who was giving his mom a hug. Something twisted in Leo's chest as he watched Mandi stand up and wipe her eyes before returning to her seat.

Leo took a few deep breaths and looked at his son. "Um, okay. Seth—do you have any questions for us?"

Seth shrugged. "I dunno. Like—you're still my dad, right?"

"Absolutely. Always." Goddammit, this was hard. "I don't care what your DNA says. I will always, *always* be your father."

"Okay." Seth had a slightly blank look on his face, the one that told Leo his boy was still processing. It took a while sometimes. Seth was like him in that way, needing hours, sometimes days to come to terms with his emotions. He'd be ready to talk later, and when he did, Leo would be there.

Seth glanced at Nyla and his expression brightened

just a little. "So like, do I still call you Aunt Nyla?"

She darted a quick look at Leo as she recognized the train had changed tracks. "Of course. Your mother is my sister, so you and I—we're blood-related. And anyway, you're my nephew no matter what."

"Yeah, I know, but this thing with my dad." Seth waved a hand, hair flopping over his forehead. "Like if you get married and stuff. Or you know, if you guys have a kid—is it my brother or my cousin?"

Mandi made a choking sound. Bob snickered. Leo's mom made the *tsk-tsk* noise reserved for anyone who got caught swiping cookies off the cooling rack.

And Nyla—

Oh shit.

She'd gone ghost white, swaying a bit in her seat. Leo bolted off the couch. "Are you okay?"

She wobbled to her feet, bracing herself on the back of the chair. "I'm okay, I'm good, I'm fine."

She didn't look fine. Leo touched her arm. "You don't look good. Was it something you ate? I know sometimes dairy—"

"Yes, I'm sure it's something I ate." Nyla smiled through gritted teeth, knuckles white as she gripped the back of the chair.

"Duckie?" Mandi touched her arm. "The food at Carousel can be such a gut bomb. I'm kinda queasy myself."

Was it Leo's imagination, or did Nyla throw her a grateful look? "That's totally it." Nyla offered a weak smile. "Um, excuse me. I'll be right back."

She turned and bolted for the bathroom.

CHAPTER NINETEEN

"Duckie? Can I come in?"

The soft rap on the bathroom door forced Nyla to lift her face from the edge of the porcelain altar. A fresh wave of nausea hit her, and she took a few deep breaths before answering.

"I'm good! You're totally right about the burger." She reached for the glass of water she'd had the good sense to set on the floor between her first and second bout of barfing. "You were smart to order that chicken dish."

"Nyla, I *know*."

A flutter of fear moved through her. She took her time flushing, rinsing her mouth, and spitting carefully in the toilet. Her legs felt glued to the floor, and she took a few deep breaths to get her voice right before replying. "Tell everyone I'll be out in just a sec. Sorry to wreck the party."

"They're outside, sweetie. Leo suggested they walk to the park to see that new picnic pavilion. No one's in the house but me."

Thank God for Leo. Nyla closed her eyes and took a few more steadying breaths. Then she pushed to her feet, legs shaking as she made her way to the door. She pulled it open, then turned to fill the water glass again.

She said nothing as Mandi stepped inside and locked the door. As Nyla rinsed her mouth, Mandi reached out and caught a fistful of curls at the nape of Nyla's neck.

"Spit," Mandi said. "I'll hold your hair."

Nyla obeyed, then swished and spit some more until the waves stopped rolling through her belly. Mandi put the toilet lid down, then folded a towel and spread it on top.

"Have a seat." Mandi perched on the edge of the counter and pulled a packet of Saltines from her sleeve. Tugging up her top, she wrestled a green soda can from her waistband. "I brought you some crackers and a ginger ale I found in Leo's fridge. That always helped me when I was—you know."

Nyla nodded, since that was easier than trying to speak. She should probably start denying it. She hadn't taken a test yet, so it was easy to plead ignorance.

But who the hell was she kidding?

Mandi held out a cracker and Nyla took it, nibbling the edge carefully. Once she'd finished, she accepted the soda and swallowed a few cautious sips. Thank God it stayed down. That wasn't the case the last couple days.

"So." Mandi's eyes brimmed with sympathy. "How far along are you?"

Nyla swallowed another sip of ginger ale, buying herself some time. "I don't know for sure. I haven't taken a test."

Mandi nodded like she expected that answer. "I get it. It took me weeks to get the guts to grab a test at the Dollar Store, and even then, it took six more of them for me to believe I was really pregnant." She paused. "There's one in my purse if you want me to go get it."

Nyla stared at her. "You have a pregnancy test in your purse?"

"Why did you think I insisted on hitting the Dollar Store after dinner?"

"Cough drops." Nyla shook her head. "You said you needed cough drops."

"Do I sound like I have a cough?"

Nyla sighed and sat down on the toilet lid. She put her head in her hands, then shook it slowly. "I'm a nurse. I teach safe sex workshops to teenagers. We've used a condom every time we've had sex." She looked up to see her sister watching her. "*Every single time.*"

"I don't doubt it." Mandi bit her lip. "Any chance they're expired?"

Maybe. Probably.

God, why hadn't she thought of that?

"I'm such an idiot."

"You are *not* an idiot." Mandi stood up and reached for the door. "Be right back."

Nyla sighed, hating how much she was leaning on Mandi. Dammit, Nyla was an independent, confident, grown-ass woman.

But she didn't feel confident at the moment. She felt like someone who needed her sister.

The same big sister who'd taught her to ride a razor scooter in the driveway.

The one who'd pulled back her covers and invited Nyla to snuggle when she had a bad dream.

The sister who fearlessly stepped up and said "she can have mine" when it turned out Nyla needed bone marrow. Like somehow, she'd just known they'd be a match.

And now she was giving her a pregnancy test. A test to determine if Nyla had gone and gotten herself knocked up by Mandi's ex-husband.

God.

She stood up again, praying Leo took his time on that walk. That Seth and Helen and everyone else believed the story about food poisoning.

"Here we go." Mandi came back through the door holding a purple-and-white box. "I trust you've done this before?"

"Yeah." She sighed and tore open the box. "Twice with Greg. I was a couple days late and thought maybe that would end up being the thing to make him want to get married."

"Thank God that didn't happen."

"True." Leave it to Mandi to find the bright side.

As her sister checked the door lock and pretended to fuss with her hair in the mirror, Nyla did her business with gravel churning in her gut.

This time around, she knew what she'd see on that little pee-soaked window. This time, it wouldn't come up negative. Call it intuition, but somehow, she knew.

"Need help?" Mandi asked without looking over.

"Nope." She flushed and set the stick on the counter, washing her hands carefully. "Five minutes, right?"

"Something like that." Mandi picked up the box and skimmed the back of it. "It says two to five minutes, but it could take ten. It also says it's better to do it first thing in the morning. More accurate."

Nyla nodded. "First-morning urine contains higher concentrations of human chorionic gonadotropin, but typically hCG levels double every two days in early pregnancy."

She was soothing herself with clinical facts, while inside her chest felt like she'd swallowed a bucket of thumbtacks. Sitting down hard on the toilet lid, she studied her nails. Wondered how long they had until the family returned.

"They'll be gone a while," Mandi said, reading her thoughts. "Bob got all excited when Leo told him how they built that pavilion using only hand tools and wood. No nails or screws or anything. You know those guys; they'll spend years studying the workmanship."

Nyla closed her eyes and wondered if Leo knew. If he suspected. Probably not. That was just Leo, good, kind, thoughtful Leo who'd instinctively known she'd prefer to have an empty house when emptying her stomach.

"Is it time?"

Mandi glanced at her watch. "I think so."

Nyla took a deep breath. Then she leaned up and peered at the test window. The line appeared faint at first, pink and solid. She held her breath.

A second line appeared.

Her heart plunged into her stomach and sank to the very bottom. "Positive."

"You're sure?" Mandi leaned in and peered at the window. "Yep. Seems pretty clear."

Nyla checked again to be sure. There was no mistaking it.

And no mistaking this was the worst timing imaginable. The family was in chaos. They'd just dropped two bombshells on Seth. The kid was leaving in just a few days for two months in Haiti.

And Leo, Leo was leaving for the trip he'd dreamed of for years. The trip he'd yearned for, deserved more than anything.

And Nyla's news would ruin everything.

Mandi stood watching her, studying her face. "How do you feel?"

Scared. Embarrassed. Angry.

Those were all the words she should say, right? She felt them, at least a little bit.

This was not good news. Not even a little.

But—

"Happy." Nyla closed her eyes. "I know that's horrible and I swear to God I didn't mean for this to happen. All that stuff Leo's mom said about trapping a man—"

"Duckie, no." Mandi dropped to the floor in front of her and grabbed Nyla's hands. "Listen to me, okay? He's a good man. He'll do right by you."

"That's exactly the problem." Nyla shot up, stomach rolling again. She gripped the counter and looked at her sister. "He's spent his whole adult life taking care of everyone else. His mother, you, Seth."

Mandi flinched but stayed sitting on the floor. "Okay. I see what you mean."

"Sorry. I didn't mean that to sound harsh. I just—"

"No you're right." Mandi got to her feet and leaned against the counter. "He's a goddamn saint. A martyr for every cause, and I don't mean that in a shitty way. He'd literally die for his family."

Nyla swallowed and started pacing, thoughts whirling like a drunk teen on a Ferris wheel. "You can't tell him, okay? He's days away from leaving on his test run of Leo's Selfish Dream. I can't ruin that for him."

Can't ruin the rest of his life, either. His plans, his dreams, the freedom he'd worked so hard to earn. She grabbed her sister's hand again.

"Promise me, okay? Promise you won't breathe a word to him."

"Nyla—"

"Promise!"

"Okay." Mandi nodded and yanked her hand back, which is when Nyla realized she'd been squeezing it. "But promise *me* you won't do anything impulsive."

"Like using expired condoms?"

Mandi's expression softened. "Not what I meant."

Nyla studied her for a long time. "I don't know what I'm going to do, okay? I can't be more than six weeks along, so lots of things can happen."

False positives. Plenty of things could cause it, from fibroids to ectopic pregnancy. Or miscarriage, that was common in early months. These were all things Nyla knew about firsthand but didn't want to think about.

But one thing she absolutely, positively wouldn't think about?

"If this is true," she said slowly, "I want this baby."

Mandi nodded. "I understand."

"And no matter what, this can't ruin Leo's life."

Mandi hesitated, then nodded again. "I get that, too."

"So, this information doesn't leave this bathroom. Okay?"

Again, the hesitation. "I've got your back, Duckie. No matter what. You know that."

Closing her eyes, Nyla sank into a sea of sadness and joy and fear and elation and a million emotions she couldn't name.

But floating on top, like a big, bright bubble? She wanted this baby. She wanted it more than anything, no matter how selfish that might be.

• • •

Four hours later, she sat curled against Leo on the sofa. Her plan had been to avoid him, to call it a night and head home so she wouldn't risk blurting her pregnancy secret.

But that changed the instant she saw tears in her nephew's eyes. "You're coming back after you drop Mom off, right?"

Nyla swallowed back her own angst, which paled in comparison to his. "Do you need me to?"

He'd blinked hard, fighting to man up, to hold back tears. "If you want. I mean—I kinda want to talk to you."

Her heart broke for him. "Of course. Want me to bring ice cream?"

He'd nodded and given her a wobbly smile. "Yeah.

I'd like that. And maybe I could ask some stuff?"

"Anything."

Just like Leo predicted, Seth's stoic response had crumbled into tears and turmoil once the shock wore off. For hours, they'd struggled to answer his questions.

Why didn't you tell me right away?

Does this mean I'm a bastard?

Is there a chance it's wrong?

Why would Mom do this?

Nyla offered to leave and give them privacy, but Seth had clutched her arm so tight she'd winced. "I know you won't lie to me, Aunt Nyla," he'd sniffled as he wiped his nose on his sleeve. "You don't even know how to lie."

The words sat heavy in her heart long after Seth had gone to bed. To bed, though not to sleep, since she could hear his music pounding at the other end of the hall. She knew she should make her escape. Just get in the car and drive like hell so she wouldn't spill her pregnancy secret to the man she knew could see right through her.

But Leo needed her. She could see it in his eyes.

"I guess we'll have more of that ahead of us." Leo sighed and dropped heavily onto the couch.

She hesitated, then settled on the sofa's edge beside him. "That was...hard."

Hard didn't even begin to describe it. She saw the ache in Leo's eyes and longed to reach for him.

But she couldn't stay. Couldn't risk blurting something so big. Not now, with everything so raw.

Leo looked at her, and Nyla held her breath. "He

asked me a bunch of questions about his biological father," Leo said. "Stuff I couldn't answer, but Jesus, hearing him call someone else his *father*—"

"I know." Nyla bit her lip. "You sure you don't want to try again? See if he still wants to talk?"

"He needs time," Leo said. "I'm trying to respect his boundaries. He asked for space, and I'm giving it to him."

Nyla nodded and forced a smile. "You're such a good dad." It took everything she could muster not to touch a hand to her abdomen. What kind of messed up instinct was that? "I'm not saying Mandi wouldn't give him space, but—"

"Yeah, I know." Leo's fingers found one of her loose curls and stroked it absently, like a boy rubbing the silk edge of his blanket. "If he were with Mandi tonight, she'd already have the bedroom door off the hinges so she could go in and demand he talk things through."

Nyla winced, though it was probably true. "Different parenting styles," she managed, feeling loyal to her sister. "But you're right. I'm glad he's with you tonight."

"Me, too." His voice sounded a million miles away, but when his gaze slid to hers, she could see he was completely present. "You're sure you're okay? Food poisoning's nothing to mess around with. I saw this special on botulism and how some strains produce this toxin that'll stay in your system for weeks."

"I'm fine." The lie slipped easily from her lips, but she didn't make eye contact. So much for Seth's theory she couldn't lie. "I really should go."

"So soon?" Leo glanced at his watch. "It's not even

eight yet."

"I have to work early tomorrow."

"I understand." Leo stood up and helped her to her feet. "Can I get you anything before you go? Crackers? Cream puff? Some of that hard cider you like?"

Nyla gulped as her stomach lurched. "I'm fine, thanks."

She made her way to the door on shaky legs, praying he didn't notice. When she felt his big palm on the small of her back, she nearly melted against him. How could she not tell him? This secret, it felt too big for her to hold inside.

But she had to do it. Had to make sure he got on that motorcycle in a few days and chased the dream he'd held for so long.

"Can I take you to dinner tomorrow?" he asked. "Seth's back with Mandi, so we could spend some time alone."

Nyla turned, forcing herself to fib. "I actually have to work a double shift." Not a lie, but also not the truth. Even with two shifts, she'd be out of the hospital by five. "What about later this week?"

If she kept it vague, maybe he'd get busy with trip prep and let things slide. She couldn't bear the thought of him leaving for the entire summer without spending one more night together, but what was the alternative? She couldn't burden him with this now. Not when he was so close to tasting freedom for the first time.

"You're off Wednesday, right?" He frowned a little. "God, that seems so far away. I was hoping to see more of you before I go."

She wanted that, too. But the more she saw him, the bigger the risk she'd let the secret slip. That Leo would find a way to let his own dreams slip through his fingers. "Sorry," she said. "It's just a really busy week. I'm covering for a nurse who's out on maternity leave."

Instantly, she wanted to smack herself on the forehead. Now that she'd introduced maternity to the conversation, she couldn't stop thinking about it. Could he read it on her face? See right through her, to the cluster of cells growing inside her. She hoped not. She held her breath, praying she could keep the secret inside just a little longer.

"I understand." Leo smiled and leaned in to kiss her. "I'll miss you. And I don't even want to think about how much I'm going to miss you this summer."

Another wave of ache hit her as she fought to hold it together. "This summer." She forced a bright smile she didn't feel. "That's going to be so great for you. I'm so happy you finally get to do your trip."

A smile tugged at the edges of his mouth as he leaned back against the wall. "Yeah. I know it's a dick move to take off so quick after dropping a bomb like this on Seth, but he'll be gone anyway, and maybe it's good for us both to take this time to get our heads on straight." He reached up to touch Nyla's face. "I'll miss you, though."

"I'll miss you, too." At last, something with no trace of untruth. "But you're right about getting your head on straight. The open road, the fresh air, sleeping under the stars—Leo, you've dreamed of that for years."

"I know." Still, the longing look he gave her shot right to Nyla's heart. "I'm glad, I really am. And I know it'll be great once I get out there."

"It'll be amazing." How peppy she sounded, how carefree and confident.

He leaned against the doorframe, looking wistful. "I know it's the running joke—Leo's Selfish Dream—but the truth is that it feels so fucking good to try that on. I've been a son, a husband, a father, but never just Leo."

She touched his arm, ignoring the ache in her chest. "You're right, you're absolutely right." She swallowed hard, grateful for the reminder of why she was doing this. Why she had to keep her secret for now. "You're so good at taking care of everyone, but it's important to take care of *you*."

He laughed, but his eyes held something much heavier than humor. "That's weird to even think about. I can't remember what it's like not to be shouldering all these other burdens—my dad's illness, my mom's emotional support, Mandi's school, raising Seth. My whole life, it's never been just me. I know that's selfish and awful and horrible and—"

"Leo, no." She touched his arm. "It's not horrible at all. It's called taking care of yourself."

Relief washed over his features. "I knew you'd understand."

She swallowed hard, forcing herself to smile. "I do understand." Which is exactly why she had to do it. Why she needed to let him go, to let him work things through in his mind without the weight of this burden.

She couldn't tell. No matter what, she couldn't tell. She could give him the summer at least. Longer if he needed it.

"I'd better go." She hugged him tight, tighter than she usually did.

As he squeezed her back and nuzzled her hair, she melted against him. She could stay like this forever. Cling to him like a life raft, like her beacon in the sea.

But that was a selfish thing to want. She knew that in her heart.

So she drew back and gave him the brightest smile she could muster. "I love you, Leo."

"I love you, too." He frowned. "You're sure you're okay?"

"Positive." God, she hated lying. "I'll see you Wednesday."

"Or sooner, if your schedule opens up."

"Okay. Good night."

"Good night, Nyla."

He kissed her then, soft and slow and achingly sweet. When she drew back, she felt needles of regret in her chest.

They speared deeper as she drew away, as she walked down the path to his driveway, knowing this wouldn't be the last time she'd let him go.

Not even close.

CHAPTER TWENTY

Nyla being tied up 'til Wednesday turned out to be a good thing. It gave Leo time to pack and make sure the bike was ready to roll.

Not to mention he found himself flying more than usual. Three different wildfires across the Pacific Northwest, each of them desperately needing air attacks to snuff the flames.

One took him to Oregon and an aerial glimpse of a town he hoped to see from the ground in just a few days. For years he'd dreamed of visiting, enjoying epic hiking trails and a craft beer scene he couldn't indulge in with Seth in tow. He'd even booked a tiny cabin, giving himself a two-night reprieve from dusty campsites and his stuffy little tent. It felt selfish to want this so badly, but wasn't that the point of Leo's Selfish Dream? Just one chance—one small opportunity—to do this thing for himself.

God, it would feel good to be out on the open road. No work calls, no family emergencies, no responsibilities except feeding himself and maybe showering once or twice a week.

It sounded like heaven.

It also sounded a little lonely, if he was being honest. That had never bothered him before, the idea of being on his own. For years he'd been excited by the idea of freedom and quiet and solitude.

When had it all changed?

Nyla.

He knew she was the answer even before the question fully formed in his brain. He hated the thought of leaving her for that long, but they'd survive it. Their friendship had lasted this long. This next stage of it would last a helluva lot longer. He hoped so, anyway.

Leo had just jumped out of the shower when his doorbell chimed. Glancing at his watch, he saw it was ten past six. Twenty minutes before Nyla was due to arrive.

As he wrapped a towel around his waist, he felt a surge of hope it might be her. He knew she'd be here soon, regardless, but that's how eager he was to see her. Maybe she felt the same eagerness, the same hunger to be with him.

Hell, maybe they wouldn't even make it to the restaurant. He was half naked anyway, and it wouldn't take much to get her there.

By the time he reached the door, he was already half hard.

"Nyla." One look at her face had him willing his dick to go down. "What is it? Honey, what's wrong?"

His brain blipped on the "honey"—too soon?—but Nyla blanched and pushed past him.

"Excuse me."

She bolted for the bathroom, slamming the door behind her.

What the hell?

He tried not to listen, but Christ, he could hear her over the hum of the bathroom fan. Was it still the food poisoning? Seemed like a long time to still be sick, but some strains could last a long time.

"You okay?"

The sounds from the bathroom suggested she definitely wasn't. Weird, since she hadn't mentioned feeling sick on the phone the other night. And the night before that, when he'd called to wish her a good night and they ended up talking sexy 'til well past ten.

What are you wearing?

Where's your hand?

Maybe I should come over…

They hadn't, of course—he had Seth all week—but God, he'd wanted to. He was getting turned on just thinking about it, which he knew made him an asshole.

Do something. Go help her.

His conscience kicked him into action, so he hurried to the bedroom to pull on pants and a shirt. Then he beelined for the fridge to search for ginger ale. Odd, he was positive he still had a can left, but it wasn't behind the milk. How many times had he told Seth not to help himself to the soda without asking?

A fresh pang of guilt hit him. He had a whole summer without Seth, and the thought bummed him out. When the kid came back from Haiti—when Leo finished his trip—they'd sit down together and drink all the ginger ale they could handle. That should fill the kid's quota for belch-inspired entertainment.

Giving up on the ginger ale, Leo grabbed a root beer

instead. He popped the top and grabbed a few Triscuits from the box in the cupboard. It wasn't exactly the soda crackers his mother used to give him, but close enough, plus he knew Nyla loved the little wicker basket crackers.

"Nyla?" He tapped lightly on the bathroom door. "Need any help?"

Ridiculous question. She was a nurse, and it's not like she needed assistance puking. But if she'd gotten dizzy and fallen and hit her head—

"I'm good!" Her voice was a little too bright. "I'll be out in just a sec." A pause while she ran water in the sink, followed by the hiss of his air freshener can.

He was stepping back from the door when her voice rang out again. "Want to stay in tonight and order take-out?"

"Absolutely." Would she really feel like eating? "I've got some crackers and soda for you."

Should he leave them out here, or retreat to the living room?

Best not to lurk in the hall like a creeper, so he headed back to the living room and set the refreshments on the table. Should he get a glass for the soda? Ice, or was it better to be a bit warmer? His mom used to say that, but nurse Nyla would know best.

He was still deciding when she walked out of the bathroom looking slightly less green. "Sorry about that." She offered a feeble smile and moved past him into the living room. "I can't seem to shake this tummy thing, I guess."

He studied her face, Spidey senses tingling. "I hope it's not serious."

"I'm sure it's fine." She tucked some stray curls behind her ears. "I'll be good as new in no time!"

Leo kept looking at her, the tingle getting stronger. Something about her looked different. He couldn't put his finger on it, but it seemed…familiar.

"Hey!" She forced a too-bright smile and lunged for the TV remote. "I've got a great idea. Let's binge-watch *Schitt's Creek.*"

"Okay." He watched her settle onto the couch, moving gingerly against the cushions. That, too, seemed odd. "You want me to rub your shoulders or something? Or I could grab some Ibuprofen or Pepto or—"

"I'm good, I swear." She grabbed one of the Triscuits and chewed. "Mmmm. These are good." Another Triscuit and another, like she was eating just to keep her mouth full.

Maybe he was imagining it.

Cautiously, he settled onto the couch beside her. "So, binge-watching a show, huh? You don't want something a little more interactive?"

She stopped chugging soda long enough to look at him. "What do you mean?"

"Just that we don't have much more time together before I go." He smiled and rested a hand on her knee. "I don't know, I thought it might be cool to visit a little."

"Visit?" Her voice cracked as she grabbed another cracker. "Sure, yeah, we can talk. Um, maybe we can take turns reading to each other? I've got this great book in my car, 'A Nurse's Guide to Pandemic Protocol.' It's really fascinating."

"Uh, sure." What the hell was going on here? "Maybe later."

"Cool." The crackers were gone, and she'd taken to drumming her hands on her thigh. Fending off another wave of nausea?

"You know, if you're not feeling well, we could do a rain check for morning," he said. "Do brunch or something."

"Morning?" Nyla shook her head as her face went a few shades paler. "No, I'm good. This is good. Great, actually!"

"Okay." What on earth was happening? "Want me to grab the takeout menus on the fridge? I've got Mexican, Indian, Chinese—"

"Um, let's wait." Her smile wobbled. "Soon, okay?"

"Sure, yeah, whenever you're ready." Jesus, this was strange. Where was normal Nyla? The one who laughed and joked and didn't act like a swarm of bees might be humming beneath her skin. It was almost like....like that morning at her parents' house?

"Is there something you want to tell me?" he asked. "Something...on your mind?"

"What? No! Of course not." She pressed her lips together. That lasted about six seconds. "I know. Want to have sex?"

"Uh, now?" God knows he didn't object, but—

"It'll be fun, I read this article about silent sex." She was grabbing for his fly, tugging at the zipper like his pants were on fire. "It's supposed to really intensify sensations if both people just agree not to talk or moan or make any noise at all. Just silence, pure, simple—"

"Whoa, slow down." He reached down and caught her wrist just as his boxers caught in the zipper. Probably because his over-eager dick stretched the fabric tight, which really wasn't helpful. "Let's just…uh, take it a little slower?"

She looked up, hurt flashing in her eyes. The faint shimmer of tears had him feeling like an asshole. He wanted her, he did. Desperately, hungrily.

But seriously. What was going on?

Blinking hard, Nyla sat back on her heels. "You're not in the mood?"

"It's not that. It's just—"

"Because look, we can cool things down if you want." She tried a casual hair flip and ended up poking herself in the cheek. "Maybe take a break for the summer."

His skin prickled, then went cold. "What are you talking about?"

She forced a laugh that was probably supposed to sound bright and easy, but came out more maniacal than anything. "Sure, it makes sense, doesn't it? You're heading off into the great blue yonder, and I don't want you to feel like you have to check in all the time or worry about things or even—"

"Nyla."

"—because really, the long-distance thing is sort of a trap and the last thing I'd want is for you to you feel stuck or tied down when you're out there tasting freedom for the first time in—"

"Nyla!"

She blinked. "What?"

He looked into her eyes, searching for answers. Searching for the sane woman he knew was in there. Searching for...

"Oh my God."

It hit him like a two-by-four between the eyes. The vomiting. The mood swings. The faint pigmentation around her eyes that he remembered from thirteen years ago...

"Nyla." He breathed her name like a prayer, too stunned to form more words. "Oh my God, Nyla."

She closed her eyes, chin dropping to her chest. "Dammit."

Leo couldn't stop staring, couldn't wrap his brain around what he'd just pieced together. "You're pregnant."

Slowly, she nodded. Her eyes were still closed, like she couldn't bear to look at him. "I wanted to make sure," she said softly. "I did three drugstore tests and then a blood test this morning and *oh God*." Opening her eyes, she blinked hard at him as tears glittered again. "I'm so sorry, Leo."

"Sorry?" He frowned. "What, like you got pregnant on purpose?"

"No! Of course not, absolutely not." Her throat moved as she swallowed. "And I definitely haven't been with anyone else. In case you were worried, I mean. Not that you'd think that but given what happened with—I'm shutting up now."

She clamped her lips together and looked at him. The silence lasted six seconds. "I'm so sorry."

"Pregnant." He had to say the word out loud again to be sure he hadn't missed anything. "Pregnant with my— *my child*."

She nodded, eyes searching his. "I didn't mean to tell you yet. I didn't want this to screw up your trip or your plans or your *life*, Leo. You have to believe I'd never want that."

"I know." He leaned back against the couch, too stunned to know what to ask. There were a million questions reeling through his mind, but she didn't need that from him. She needed support. A partner. A man to step up and be responsible.

And of course, that was him. He raked his fingers through his hair, already making plans. "I'll cancel the trip," he said. "I can stay here and go to all your appointments with you and make sure you have everything you need. You can move in here if you want, if that's easier, and when the time comes—"

"Leo, no." A tear slid down her cheek. She dashed it away fast and shook her head. "This is exactly what I *don't* want."

"What do you mean?"

Was she saying she didn't want him? That she wasn't interested in a future together? The thought made his chest ache.

"Don't you see?" Her voice was almost a whisper. "You've spent your whole life taking care of other people.

Looking after your mom, putting Mandi through school, raising Seth—you've never taken time to be just Leo."

"What if I don't want to be just Leo?"

The memory of his own words bounced back at him, the echo of their conversation just the other day in his doorway.

"I've been a son, a husband, a father, but never just Leo. I want to find out what that feels like, you know?"

Nyla was shaking her head, and he knew she remembered, too.

But everything had changed now, hadn't it?

He put a hand on her knee again, since she'd somehow shaken it off. Or maybe he'd dropped it, since it seemed he'd lost control of his limbs. His arms felt heavy, his legs leaden blocks.

"This is different," he insisted. "Nyla, I want to be there for you. I want to help you through this. I want to do the right thing."

"Leo." The ache in her voice sounded just like the one squeezing his chest tight. "Do you hear yourself? Those are all responsibilities. Urges to help someone else or be a standup guy, and yes, those are noble things. But I don't want nobility. I want you to be happy."

"I *am* happy." He grabbed her hands, surprised to feel them shaking. "This is going to be great. It will, you'll see."

She shook her head sadly, extracting one hand from his. Gently, she touched his cheek. "I want you to *want* to be a father, and that's selfish of me. I can acknowledge that, and I also can't force that. What I *can* do is let you go."

"Nyla, no—"

"For two months or the summer or however long it takes to give you the freedom you've wanted. And in the end, if that's the life you love, then I'm not going to be the one to steal that from you."

"But—" He stopped himself, no longer sure what he wanted to say. He'd been ready to insist he'd support her. That no matter what, he'd do his duty to take care of her, of his child—

His child.

The tightness in his throat squeezed so hard he couldn't breathe. Couldn't get the words out. He was scared and stunned and completely unsure what to say, what to do.

"Leo, I love you." She put her hand on his chest, and he closed his eyes, willing her to feel his heart pounding. To understand how lost he felt. "I love you, but I won't be your ball and chain."

He opened his eyes and looked at her. "I love you, too. And you could never be my ball and chain."

A tear slipped down her cheek and she gave him a sad little smile. "The fact that you love me, Leo—that's exactly why I could. How it could end up happening before you even realize it."

She unfolded herself from the sofa and got up, folding her arms over her chest. With another sad smile, she backed her way toward the door. "Please, Leo— take this time for you. And at the end of it, if you've gotten your taste of freedom and you want more, I promise there won't be any hard feelings."

"Nyla, wait—"

But she was already out the door. And for the life of him, he couldn't come up with any argument to make her stay.

Because the truth? The cold, hard, awful truth he hated? He did want that freedom, to taste it just once, just to know.

And he truly *hated* himself for wanting that.

For not chasing her down the sidewalk and out to her car. Out into the street, where he watched her taillights fade until the tears in his eyes forced him to look away.

CHAPTER TWENTY-ONE

"How about this one next?" Mandi pulled a VHS tape out of the box and showed it to Nyla. "It's Dad's handwriting, so I can't really read it, but I think it says Seychelles—that trip we took my senior year?"

Nyla squinted at the label. "No, that says 'sexytimes.'"

Mandi frowned and put the tape back in the box. "Let's pretend we didn't see that."

Their parents had taken Seth to Fred Meyer to grab some last-minute supplies for his trip to Haiti, while Mandi and Nyla dug through boxes their father swore contained the fancy passport holders he'd bought and then misplaced.

It was June 16. The day before Seth and Mandi left for Haiti, and the first day of the Leo's Selfish Dream test run. Not that Nyla was watching the clock, but odds were good he'd made it to the state line by now. Maybe farther, if he'd gotten an early start.

They'd talked last night, details about what he was packing and where he'd stay the first few nights. Twice, he'd tried to bring up the pregnancy.

"Don't, okay?" She'd taken a shaky breath and forced herself to sound cheerful. "Just focus on your trip. It's not safe to start a motorcycle ride in the wrong headspace."

After a few long, silent beats, he'd complied.

"You okay?"

Mandi's question jerked her back to this sunny spot at their parents' dining room table. "Yeah, of course. You?"

"Nervous." Mandi took a sip from her water. "The Haiti project is a big one. I hope Seth doesn't hate me for dragging him away from his friends for the summer."

"Are you kidding?" Nyla shook her head. "The memories you're giving him—the experiences he'll have—those are the kind of things he'll carry with him his whole life. He's got plenty of time for sitting around with friends watching TikTok videos."

Mandi's response was an uneasy laugh. "I hope you're right."

"I'm always right."

She hoped so, anyway. In the days since she'd pushed Leo away, she'd had bouts of wondering if she'd made the right choice.

But all she had to do was remind herself of those words he'd said.

"I've been a son, a husband, a father, but never just Leo. I want to find out what that feels like, you know?"

She did know. So she had to let him go.

Nyla rummaged in the box of tapes, not giving up on the passport holders. Or maybe she just needed the distraction. "You don't have to stay here and keep searching," she said. "If I find them, I can just bring them back to your place, along with Seth. Go pack if you need to."

"We're in good shape with the packing." Mandi frowned and studied her face. "I'm worried about leaving you, Duckie. The first trimester can be rocky.

The morning sickness, the afternoon sickness, the evening sickness—"

"Ugh, don't get me started." She made a face. "I'll be fine. I really will. My doctor says I'm healthy and everything looks good."

It was too soon to tell much, but she'd stocked up on prenatal vitamins and had already started eyeing her guest room for nursery potential. She might be determined not to let this derail Leo's life, but she was equally determined to set this baby up for a bright future. She didn't know what that might look like, but she was braced for whatever might come.

Even if Leo didn't end up being in the picture.

Mandi studied her face, worry lines etched between her brows. "You sure you're making the right choice? That you don't want Leo to stick around and be with you for—"

"No." She shook her head and dropped the battered map she'd been holding. "I don't want to be the reason he gives up something that means this much to him. I don't want to add to his list of regrets."

Her sister frowned. "But what if one of his regrets could be missing out on this?" She swept a hand over Nyla's form, her expression growing more earnest. "On feeling the baby kick for the first time or watching you get big and round and grouchy?"

Nyla shook her head and pushed away the box. "He's been through that before with you." Saying the words out loud sent an ache rattling through her limbs, but she pressed on. "These first few months, they're nothing.

Not compared to a lifetime spent wondering *what-if*. You've seen how sad his mom gets when she talks about all the things Leo's dad never got to experience. How could I ask Leo to do the same thing?"

Mandi's brow furrowed. "There's a difference between asking him and letting him do what he wants."

"You think I'm pushing him out of town with a cattle prod?"

Her sister didn't answer, probably because she couldn't. It was true, Leo had had plenty of opportunities to put his foot down. To insist he wanted to stay.

The fact that he hadn't just underscored Nyla's point. He needed to do this. The Leo she loved, the man she respected more than anyone, he'd never had a chance to stretch his legs. To explore horizons and see what else was out there.

And in the end, if he discovered something beyond this small town and family life? She'd be okay with that.

She had to be, right?

A knock at the door jerked her from the glum thoughts. "Probably UPS bringing more luggage for Mom and Dad's trip." She got to her feet, her movements already less nimble than they'd been two months ago. "I still can't believe they postponed it."

"Well someone should be here with you." Mandi didn't bother hiding her exasperation. "You won't let Leo stay and I'll be gone, so at least Mom and Dad can be here for you."

Nyla sighed as she reached the door. "You guys act like getting pregnant is like terminal cancer. I'll be fine."

She twisted the knob, only half paying attention to whether the delivery driver was standing there waiting for a signature. "I've got nine months to incubate this little spawn. I promise no one's going to miss anyth—"

The words died in her throat as she saw who stood on her parents' front steps. "Leo."

His deep brown eyes swept her face from beneath a curtain of helmet-rumpled hair. "Hi, Nyla."

She stared at him, blinking to be sure she wasn't imagining this. "You're supposed to be on the road. You're supposed to be halfway to—"

"I'm supposed to be with the woman I love." His eyes held hers, clear and bright and brimming with emotion. "With you, Nyla. That's where I'm supposed to be."

She shook her head, knowing she needed to argue. "Leo, I—"

"No, I need to say this." He adjusted his grip on the motorcycle helmet pinned under one arm as he glanced over her shoulder into the living room. "Can I come in?"

Nyla looked behind her to see Mandi scrambling up from the dining room table. "I'll just go check my… uh…cuticles."

"Where's Seth?" Leo asked as Mandi vanished up the stairs.

"With my parents," she managed. "They went out to the store to grab some things."

"Good. I need to *say* some things."

She stared in disbelief, struggling to wrap her head around the fact that he stood here in her parents' doorway when he was supposed to be on the road.

Hesitating, she stepped aside to let him in. "How did you know I was here?"

"I texted Seth from the gas station at the edge of town." He shouldered past her, surveying the room like he hadn't seen it for years instead of just a few days. "I needed to see you right away."

As he turned to face her, Nyla shivered under the weight of his gaze. His face was flushed, his eyes a little wild. He was the best thing she'd ever seen, and she couldn't stop staring. She needed to say something but wasn't sure what.

"You're here," she breathed. "I asked you not to be. I said you should—"

"I know what you said, Nyla." His voice was low, his body big and imposing and *here*. He was really here. "Here's the thing, though: I get a vote in my own life. For too long I didn't. I won't make that mistake again."

She swallowed hard, digesting his words as he set his helmet down on her mother's side table. "But your trip." She blinked back tears, not wanting to burden him with them. "You won't have an opportunity like this again."

"You're right, I won't." He stepped forward, eyes locking with hers as he touched a hand to her still-flat belly. "I won't have the chance to watch you grow and change and rest a hand on the baby bump when you don't even know you're doing it. I won't have the chance to hold your hand when you're sick or run out in the middle of the night because you're craving Ben and Jerry's. Nyla, I want to do those things. Not for you, and not even for the baby—for *me*. This is what I want."

"But—" She stopped herself, letting the argument die in the back of her throat. "Your freedom," she managed weakly.

"Isn't as important as my autonomy," he said. "The chance to make my own choices." His hand slid from her belly to the small of her back as he pulled her closer. "I choose us, Nyla. You and me and this baby. This is what I choose."

She blinked back tears, wishing she could argue. It's what she should do, right? But everything felt so right, being here in Leo's arms, so she let herself dissolve in his embrace. "I don't want to hold you back."

"You're not." He pulled her tighter against him, like he couldn't bear the thought of letting her go. "You're propelling me forward, into a future that's brighter than anything I ever could have imagined."

She choked on a sob, feeling warm and safe and treasured in his arms. Drawing back to look up at him, she studied his brown eyes. "I don't want you to miss out."

"Neither do I." He grinned. "That's exactly why I'm here."

The tears were falling in earnest now, big, fat drops that fell on her boobs, which were already outgrowing this flimsy pink bra they'd left hanging on the lampshade just weeks ago. How had so much happened in such a short span of time?

This is why. Why you don't want to miss a moment together.

She tightened her hold around his waist. "Are you sure?"

"Positive. All morning, riding through small towns and freeways and diners, you're all I could think of." He drew back again, touching her belly like he couldn't stop himself from doing it. "You and the bun in the oven."

Choking back a mix of laughter and tears, she buried her face against his chest. "So you made it." She tipped her head back to look up at him. "You at least got a day on the bike?"

"Uh-huh." He grinned. "Worst day ever."

"How far did you make it?"

"Out of town?" He flashed a sheepish look. "Not quite to the state line. I couldn't stop thinking about you. Thinking about all the experiences I'd have on my trip and how much they suck compared to the ones I want to have with you."

"Oh, Leo." She squeezed him tighter as she breathed in the smell of his motorcycle jacket. "I missed you."

He laughed and held her close. "Same," he murmured against her hair. "Let's try to keep that from happening again, 'kay?"

"Deal." She burrowed against him, sinking into the feeling of having everything she'd ever wanted. Of knowing it's what he wanted, too.

As she drew back to look at him, she saw her future in his eyes. *Their* future, together, all three of them. "I love you, Leo."

"I love you, too." He grinned. "Ready to start this journey together?"

She nodded and burrowed into him again, more ready than she'd been for anything in her life before.

EPILOGUE

Leo gazed out over the crowd, his chest nearly bursting with pride. He zeroed in on Seth—third row back, fifth from the end—and felt a surge of joy that nearly knocked him flat.

"Ladies and gentlemen, I present to you this year's graduating class!"

The crowd let up a *whoop* and Nyla clicked the shutter as Seth tossed his cap into the air. Beside her, JoJo tugged her mother's sleeve.

"Mom," the little girl whispered. "Can I throw things at my graduation?"

"Not unless your teacher says so, sweetie." Nyla clicked off another shot and waved to Seth from the bleachers. "Throwing caps is usually just for high school graduation."

Leo grinned and rumpled his daughter's hair. "If it makes you feel better, only kindergarten graduates get cupcakes."

His daughter beamed, satisfied with this explanation. "Can we go hug him now?"

"Definitely." Leo scooped JoJo into his arms, shifting her to his hip as he reached down to help Nyla to her feet. His two girls, the most amazing females he'd ever known in his life, and they were getting ready to accompany him on the trip of a lifetime.

But first, congratulating the high school graduate.

He set JoJo down and watched her scamper to Nyla's side. As they made their way down the bleachers, Leo caught Nyla's father's eye and smiled. "Kind of amazing how fast they grow up."

Ted smiled at his own baby girl and slipped an arm around Laurel's shoulder as they watched Nyla lead JoJo carefully down the steps. "Ain't that the truth."

Leo hurried to catch up to his wife and daughter as Seth broke away from the pack and headed toward them. He made a beeline for Leo, his blue robe swishing around his ankles. "Dad, did you see? I got my cap stuck on the sprinkler."

He gazed up, and sure enough, one tasseled cap dangled cheerfully above them. Leo grinned and pulled his kid in for a hug.

"Proud of you, son," he said. "You worked damn hard for this."

"You know it." Seth drew back and reached for Nyla next. "Thanks for being here."

"Are you kidding?" Nyla sniffed, swiping at her eyes. "I wouldn't miss it for anything."

Seth moved on and hugged his little sister, sweeping JoJo up into his arms. Mandi hustled up beside him, clicking off a quick photo before tucking her phone into her pocket as Seth set his sister down.

"Okay, my turn." Mandi pulled Seth in for a hug. "Sorry it took me a second to get to you. Major traffic jam at the edge of the stage."

Seth groaned as she squeezed him. "Tell me you got

video of the part where I tripped grabbing my diploma."

"Absolutely." Mandi laughed as she drew back to look up at the son who'd grown to be nearly a foot taller than her. "I'll show it to your future wife someday."

"Or husband." Bob stepped in behind her with Leo's mom right beside him, each of them clamoring for hugs. Nyla's parents joined the fray, lining up for their turn hugging the graduate.

Ted and Laurel looked happy and well-rested, Leo noticed. Cruise life agreed with them, or maybe the fact that both of their daughters looked so happy. They'd accepted the fact that Mandi and Leo were never getting back together. The fact that he and Nyla had been married five years likely had something to do with that.

"Dad." Seth turned to face him. "Can we show Grandma and Grandpa the bike?"

"They've already seen it, bud."

"Yeah, but not since we added the new exhaust system to mine."

Leo seriously doubted Ted and Laurel had any desire to admire the pipes on a vintage Triumph Bonneville that looked almost exactly like the one Leo himself had been tinkering with for the better part of a decade.

But Seth was excited, so Leo, by default, was excited. "Lead the way," he told his kid.

Seth grinned at his grandparents. "Come on. I know a side door where I used to sneak out during gym class to—"

"Seth." Mandi shot him a stern-mom look.

"What? I was going to say *study*. Isn't that better than

running around playing badminton?"

He didn't give her a chance to answer. Just turned and headed for the edge of the gym as the rest of the family fell in line behind him.

The space was sweaty and crowded, filled with parents congratulating their kids, sniffling as they adjusted the caps on their teenagers' heads and clicked photos with their phones. Leo put his hand on Nyla's shoulder, smiling down at her and their daughter as Seth led them out into the bright June sun.

Nyla caught his hand and grinned. "Feeling proud, Dad?"

Proud enough that he couldn't find his voice, so he just nodded and squeezed her hand.

"Daddy," JoJo said. "You're smiling like when mommy brings home ice cream."

Nyla laughed and squeezed Leo's hand. "Good observation, sweet pea."

Leo's chest tightened with joy as they strode across the blacktop of the parking lot. The weather couldn't be nicer, bright blue and sunny with tiny wisps of clouds on the horizon. Perfect for a motorcycle trip, which was exactly the plan.

As they approached the bikes, he let Seth take over explaining things to the grandparents. JoJo got in on the action, stretching up on tiptoe to admire the new seat he and Seth had installed just yesterday.

Nyla rested her head against Leo's bicep. "Can you believe we made it to this day? Two graduates in one year."

"I can, actually." He might not have envisioned it quite like this, but it was the future he'd always wanted for himself.

For himself and his family.

Seth was still talking, but JoJo broke away and tugged Grandma Helen's hand. "Daddy and Seth have to go on bikes, but Mommy and me get to ride in the trailer. We're bigger, so that's better."

"Can't argue with that logic," Leo mused. "When do we break it to her that she can't actually ride in the Airsteam?"

"Never," Nyla said. "I'll just distract her with road trip games and she won't notice. Plus she gets to sleep in it, so that's something to look forward to."

Leo grinned and pulled her close. He knew all about the thrill of looking forward to something, dreaming and planning and hoping for the future. Exciting, to be sure, but nothing compared to the reality of now. His life, exactly how it was meant to be.

"Check out this new nav system." Seth was pulling up the little computer to show his grandparents, who gazed at it like he'd just introduced them to a spaceship. "Here's where Dad and I are staying that first night. Then on Friday, Nyla and JoJo catch up with the trailer and we're all going fishing on the Rogue."

"Sounds like great fun." Leo's mom caught his eye and smiled, her own eyes twinkling with the same sort of pride Leo felt now. "Such a unique family vacation."

"Isn't it?" Leo put a hand on his daughter's shoulder as Nyla cozied against him.

This looked nothing like Leo's Selfish Dream, nothing like the family he'd imagined all those years ago when he was young and naive and had visions of the perfect family in his mind.

This right here, his reality, his family—this was better than perfect. Better than anything he'd dreamed of when he was young and still learning how the world worked.

"I love you." He said the words to Nyla, but he meant them for everyone here—his children, his in-laws, even his ex-wife.

As Mandi fired off another photo, Nyla looked up and smiled. "Love you, too. Congratulations to us, huh?"

"Congratulations to us," he said as he pulled her into his arms.

ACKNOWLEDGMENTS

Endless thanks to Karen for the germ of an idea that latched on to my brain with its fierce little puppy teeth and wouldn't let go. I owe you a glass of wine or twelve.

I am so grateful to the esteemed Susan Mallery for the full-day plotting workshop back in June 2018. Without you, this story could not have come together in quite the same way, and I'm in awe of your wisdom (not to mention that gorgeous cover quote!) Thank you also to Christy Carlyle and the late KariLynn Dell for lending ideas and enthusiasm, and to Katherine Kayne for all of the above, plus your hard work organizing it all. I'm honored to count you as colleagues and friends.

Thank you to Dr. Miriam Aschkenasy for lending your medical expertise to flesh out Seth's genetic backstory. Any scientific errors are mine alone.

While this book doesn't have as many smokejumper details as others in the Where There's Smoke series, I'm grateful to the crews at the Redmond Air Center in Redmond, Oregon for educating me about the air attack realm of wildland firefighting. Thank you to Bill Selby, Sam Johnson, and Tony Selznick for sharing your time and your stories. Any creative liberties taken with the details are totally on me.

While we're on the subject, huge thanks to the Central Oregon emergency response team (especially the badass air tanker pilot) who swiftly knocked out the blaze threatening my neighborhood last summer. I've lived in wildfire country for most of my adult life, but speed-packing pets and household goods brought the danger home in a new way. I'm positive my fears pale in comparison to what you experience each time you risk life and limb to fight wildfires, and I thank you for your service.

Huge thanks to Fenske's Frisky Posse for your ideas, support, and constant help with character names. You're the best street team in the world, and I love the snot out of you! Thank you also to Wonder Assistant Meah for keeping my shit together and enabling me to pose as a human most days.

For my readers: I am so damn glad to have you in my corner. Whether this is your first Tawna Fenske rom-com or your 40th, I appreciate you taking the time to read one of my books. You are the reason I do this. Well, you and the voices in my head.

Big hugs and gratitude to agent Michelle Wolfson of Wolfson Literary. We've had a zillion ups and downs since December of 2007, and I can't believe we've been together this long. Thank you for everything you do to keep my career on track and my head on straight.

So much love and gratitude to the entire Entangled Publishing Team, especially Liz Pelletier and Lydia Sharp for your editing genius and for loving this story like I do. I can't thank you enough for all you've done. Thanks also to the entire Entangled team for your tireless work on my books. Kudos and awkward butt-pats to Jessica Turner, Melanie Smith, Heather Riccio, Heather Howland, Curtis Svehlak, Hannah Lindsey, Riki Cleveland, Meredith Johnson, Katie Clapsadl, Kelly Enman, Kristin Curry, and anyone else I might have inadvertently forgotten here. Love you guys!

Huge, sloppy hugs and thank-yous to my family for all your support and laughter. Dixie and David; Russ and Carlie and Paxton; Cedar and Violet—I appreciate every single one of you, and I'm glad you're in my corner.

And Craig: What can I say about the guy who makes my toes curl and my heart flop around like a dying fish (er, that sounded romantic in my head). You're the best thing that ever happened to me, and I'm so freakin' glad you're mine. Also, you have a great butt.

The Best Kept Secret is a sexy, laugh-out-loud romantic comedy with a happy ending, however, the story contains elements that might not be suitable for some readers. Talk of death, divorce, and infidelity are included in the characters' backstories, but there is no cheating in the romance and there is no death shown on the page. Alcohol consumption, drunkenness, and nausea and vomiting are depicted in the story. Readers who may be sensitive to any of these things, please take note.

*Three sisters + a small town where
everyone knows everyone else's business...
what could possibly go wrong?*

the
SWEETHEART
DEAL

MIRANDA
LIASSON

Pastry chef Tessa Montgomery knows what everyone in the
teeny town of Blossom Glen says about her. *Spinster. Ice
Queen. Such a shame.* It's enough to make a woman bake her
troubles away, dreaming of Parisian delicacies while she
makes bread at her mother's struggling boulangerie. That is
until Tessa's mortal enemy—deliciously handsome (if arro-
gant) chef Leo Castorini, who owns the restaurant next
door—proposes a business plan...to get married.

Leo knows that the Castorinis and the Montgomerys hate
each other, but a marriage might just force these stubborn
families to work together and blend their businesses for success. The deal is simple: Tessa and Leo marry, live together for
six months, and then go their separate ways. Easy peasy.

It's a sweetheart deal where everyone gets what they want—
until feelings between the faux newlyweds start seriously
complicating the mix. Have they discovered the perfect recipe
for success...or is disaster on the way?

What happens when a city girl crashes a small-town wedding and crashes right into her nemesis?

The
WEDDING
CRASHER
and the
COWBOY

ROBIN
USA TODAY BESTSELLING AUTHOR
BIELMAN

Kennedy Martin is shocked when her ex calls days before his wedding, expressing serious second thoughts. Doesn't he see his fiancée's actually the glaze to his doughnut? Now Kennedy has no choice but to crash his wedding and convince the man he's with the right woman.

Instead, she crashes into the absolute last man she ever wanted to see: Maverick Owens, her old college nemesis. Maverick is still as awful, infuriating, and just The Worst as ever—even if he looks way too sexy in his cowboy hat. And of *course* he's convinced she's actually at the seaside ranch to ruin the wedding.

Now the only way to get some face time with the groom and save this marriage is to participate in all sorts of pre-wedding events…with Maverick. Stuck on a canoe, making small-talk at cocktail hour, and even a hoedown with her worst enemy? This just might be the longest week of her life…

*Falling in love wasn't part of the fake marriage ruse
in this new small-town romantic comedy.*

accidentally
PERFECT

MARISSA CLARKE

Workaholic Lillian Mahoney has given *everything* to her job.
The hugely popular lifestyle show she helped create monopo-
lizes her time, energy, creativity, and anything remotely resem-
bling a life. But all it takes is the show's womanizing, egoma-
niac star throwing a massive hissy on live TV to utterly im-
plode Lillian's career in a New York minute.

Now Lillian's hiding out in the gorgeous and completely
unknown seaside village of Blink, Maine. Out of gas. A stolen
wallet. A broken heel. And worse, she's somehow managed to
completely piss off the town's resident hunk, Caleb Wright.
She'll show that hot, grumpy single father *exactly* what she's
made of.

But Blink isn't quite what Lillian expects—and neither is
Caleb...or his feisty teen daughter she can't help but love. And
while her entire life and career are in shreds, Lillian might just
discover what happens when she gives her bad first impres-
sion a second chance...

AMARA

an imprint of Entangled Publishing LLC